Victor Victor Victory

Myrna Combellack

First published in 2025 by:

Cornish Fiction

© Copyright 2025

Myrna Combellack

The right of Myrna Combellack to be identified as the author of this work has been asserted by her in accordance with the Copyright, Designs and Patents Act 1988.

Cover design: Shark Fin Media

Cover photograph: Roland Woods: Over 100 Seals at Godrevy

All Rights Reserved

No reproduction, copy or transmission of this publication may be made without written permission. No paragraph of this publication may be reproduced, copied or transmitted save with the written permission or in accordance with the provisions of the Copyright Act 1956 (as amended).

[ISBN 13: 978-0-9541918-6-3]

Printed and bound in Great Britain by:

Book Printing UK Remus House, Coltsfoot Drive, Woodston,

Peterborough PE2 9BF

For Max Frisch and his fire raisers

Just call me Peter

'Well, I be darned. Look at that. Blowed clean out.'

On the television, a huge explosion which had taken out a terraced house in a small town somewhere up north. A black hole where a house should be. Up and down the road, cars moved, paint seared to bare metal, destruction everywhere. Police erecting yellow tape. A reporter gasping into a furry microphone, looking over her shoulder.

'Poor beggars. Couldn't happen here. No mains gas.'

Victor and Jane Everley forgot the news broadcast as soon as the screen was switched off. They were just sitting down to supper at the table in the kitchen when the doorbell rang. They raised their eyebrows, looked at each other, looked at their hot pork chops, which were already cooling, and they were on the point of ignoring the buzzer. 'I must change the doorbell. Sounds like a bluebottle in a jam-jar.'

'Could be Sandra from the choir.'

'Who?' Victor knew very well who.

'Choir committee.'

'Better answer it, then, but don't let her keep you long.'

'No, Victor.'

Jane got up and went to the front door. She was not yet sixty. In her frilled apron tied at the waist with a little bow, she looked like one of those little professional housewives from a fifties advert. She opened the door of the bungalow and looked out into the soft, sideways rain that the locals call mizzle. There was no car outside. She could see as far as the white low fence and gate. Soggy brown leaves were blowing about, that was all.

She closed the door. 'Nobody there.'

'It's that bell. Another crank thing I'll have to alter here. At least it's not that Sandra woman. Eat your food.'

'It's never sounded for nothing before, Victor. Perhaps it's the wind. Or the rain. There's something wrong with the electrics here. Didn't I tell you so?'

They were three quarters of the way through eating their pork chop, potato and beans when the buzzer went again.

'Leave it.'

They ate a mouthful.

'It's a horrible evening. All this rain and wind.'

'When is it not?'

'It'll be lovely in the summer, though, with all this global warming.'

He made no reply. It was Jane's idea to sell up in Chingford, cash in the pensions and live in bliss here, in a sprawling bungalow with a view of the sea from one dormer window in the attic and a road outside.

'Retirement bliss.' Victor could give the impression of being a dour man, but really he was proud of himself for sticking at the work in the City all his life, commuting on the bus and tube, raking in a pension and a lump sum, keeping himself to himself as usual at his leaving party and quietly moving out of London on the proceeds of the sale of the house on the main road at the earliest possible moment. He still favoured Surrey, somewhere around Loxley, but inland Surrey was punishingly expensive and had no proper ocean. Jane wanted to live by the sea. So, they came here, to a nineteen-thirties bungalow that was cheap and only needed upgrading. This was their first winter. Next year, he would have the windows triple glazed and the boiler changed, and the attic insulated. Then it might be bearable. If not, there was always cavity wall insulation. A thirties mundic-block house made a terrible investment, but Victor had done some research online. Provided you kept the roof on and let no water in, mundic would last as long as good concrete block. He'd read all about it. It was water that turned this sort of material into sludge. Mundic may have rendered the place un-mortgageable, but as far as he could see, mine-waste was as safe as houses. Some owners swore by it. There were even on-line clubs for mundic dwellers. These houses were cheap, they looked like any other house, and anyway, Victor and Jane had no children to leave it to. Jane thought it was pretty. And she said the people in the choir were friendly. At least it was pebble-dashed, matching Plombe's, the next bungalow along Sandy Road.

It was not until they were having a coffee in the living room with its nice new beige wool mix carpet, sitting in their Ercol chairs, that the doorbell sounded once more.

Dinner was over, there was no more to do but watch the evening news and weather again, load the dishwasher and go to bed. Nothing on. More sensation about that explosion up north. Therefore, without consulting Victor, Jane left the warmth of the sitting room, went down the little hall with its white-framed pictures and brolly stand and opened the front door.

There was no outside light. Only this afternoon, Victor was saying that he really must fix that light. She was unable to see anybody at first. Oh yes, but there was someone there: a figure in a black wool coat, clutching a long, thin bag, the sort of bag students tote around to carry art work.

'Hello dear,' she said.

He was a young man, quite tall, though bent over a little against the wind. Rain was dripping from his short brown hair. He stepped forward into what light there was.

'Good evening,' he said. 'I sincerely hope I am not disturbing you. Only, I saw your light.'

He thrust forward a scruffy card, pinned to an inside jacket. The card was misted up inside the polythene covering.

'I am an art student.'

There was a pause, while he seemed to be trying to remember his lines for his pitch.

Jane smiled with encouragement. She was a primary school teacher by training. People said she had a gift for bringing out the best in people, children and adults alike.

At last, he said, in an accent that she could not quite identify, though she was always hearing foreign accents in the primary school in Chingford, 'Sorry, I am no good at this.'

'Yes? How can I help?'

'I am an art student. I have some art.'

There was a pause.

'Well, I don't think we. . .'

'Please. . .'

'. . . need anything at the moment. There are only the two of us. . .'

He set down his wet bag on the red quarry tiles in the porch. Water was dripping from the cuffs of his coat and his hair.

'At our age, we've collected all the paintings we're going to, you see.'

He held back a sneeze. She judged he was seventeen to nineteen years old. Behind her, in the light and the warmth, Maxine Croxall was intoning the evening news. Something about twenty million people displaced due to climate change and forty million people displaced due to war. In front of her was the boy and the rain and the night.

'You'd better come in and warm up. I'm sure my husband won't mind.'

He blinked and took a step forward. 'Is there somewhere I could show you?'

She stepped back, opened the door of the dining room. There was a small blast of cold air. It was chilly in there. The central heating system must have become redundant years ago and she was not yet confident with the mobile gas heater and its bottle.

He moved to place his bag on the teak table.

'Wait. Let me put down the oilcloth.'

He drew back.

'It's teak, you see. Nothing special, but. . . we've kept it oiled and unstained this long…'

'You call it an oilcloth?'

'Yes.'

'My mother had an oilcloth.'

She waited for him to go on. Something had gone very wrong in his life.

'What colour was it?' That was a stupid thing to say.

A spell was broken. A shutter came down. He placed his portfolio bag on the orange and blue coloured oil cloth and drew out some soggy pencil drawings.

'This is my art,' he said, 'which I am selling.'

Cheap, Chinese art, she thought. Unsellable, wet, or dry.

'Of course,' he said, 'I cannot sell it now. It is all wet at the edges.'

He looked into her face. She saw that there was a deep scar on his forehead and that the scar sprawled across the eyebrow and ended at the bridge of his nose. 'And anyway, these drawings are not very good. I would never draw like this. These are just Chinese drawings for sale.'

She did not know what to say, so she said, 'What would you draw, if you could draw?'

He looked towards the dark window. 'Perhaps a mountain, with a stream at the bottom. People in orange and blue colours. Men in pyjama. Perhaps a donkey or two.'

Jane thought, you're in trouble. You're lost. Displaced. You've been displaced a long time.

Victor came down the hall, shaking his newspaper. 'There's a draught.' He looked through the dining room door. 'Who is this?'

'Peter.' The young man stepped forward and held out his hand. In the chill of the dining room, soaked through by the rain, he trembled slightly. 'I am Peter, you know.'

Peter, you know. Odd. Not quite. Something not quite.

Victor went into polite mode, muttering, 'Welcome, welcome,' looking down at his carpet slippers. 'Welcome to our humble abode. We have plenty of pictures already, as you see here in the dining room. Canvas paintings, unframed. Mainly nineteen seventies, but this is not the best of it. I keep the investment paintings under the bed. Japanese prints.'

Jane frowned slightly. Victor had only yesterday been instructing her to say nothing about the treasures under the bed. Victor's nest-egg.

'How interesting. Art is worth collecting, but not this.' Peter looked down at the inferior work he was spreading on the table. But I have to try, you see.'

Under the forty-watt bulb and the green glass retractable lamp, Victor and Jane were peering up at him.

'Are you unemployed, then?'

'I have to earn some cash. I am living on the camp on Bodmin Moor. Camp for the stateless people. You understand. In the evenings, we try to sell some things. Some people try household things, brushes, sweeping things, but I am trying paintings because I am an artist. I like art.'

Victor sighed and looked down at his slippers again. 'Well, put his coat in the living room by the fire, Jane. I'm afraid this is a holiday bungalow. In the winter, it's beginning to be uncomfortable, the heating is inadequate. It's on the list to do something about.'

Jane busied herself with the coat and with a mug of instant coffee.

In the dining room, Victor found himself wrangling over the price of a painting. He got it down to a reasonable sixty pounds, and then went to get his chequebook.

'I'd better have cash. Sorry, but people try to cheat, because we come to the door.'

Victor and Jane exchanged a glance. He hesitated, then went off to the bedroom for some cash.

Victor held out two twenties and a ten. 'I've only got fifty. You'll have to come back another day if you want more money. That's all I keep here.'

Jane's neck began to redden. 'I think I have some more in the John Bull Toby jug.' She reached into the jug perched on the picture rail shelf above the sideboard.

'Jane will get your coat, as well. It must be dry by now.' Victor looked at the clock. Two hours had passed. Where had the time gone?

Peter packed up his paintings. 'I will leave this one as well, Victor, as a bonus. It's too wet. I can't sell it.' He left a soggy watercolour on the table and went into the living room for his coat. Jane was holding it closer to the electric fire, where it was still steaming.

'Oh,' Peter said. 'I could not help noticing. Glass ornaments.' He walked across to a display cabinet with little glass animals, popular in the sixties and seventies, when Jane was at Teacher Training College.

'My glass menagerie. Victor bought me my first one, that pig within a pig within a pig. I've been collecting them ever since.'

'Do they break?'

'Yes, they do. They break in little shards. Quite dangerous, like needles. But I try not to let them break. You can still pick them up in charity shops, for next to nothing.'

Peter looked around. 'A painting on the wall, a John Bull toby jug and a collection of glass ornaments in a glass and metal cabinet,' he said, and he smiled broadly at Victor and Jane. 'Thank you, thank you both, for letting me show you the paintings. And thank you for buying one. I know you didn't want to. You have enough pictures on your walls and… well, thank you. This little bit of money will…'

Peter stepped into the hall. Jane handed him his coat, still damp but drier than two hours ago, when he first stepped into the porch. Victor began putting on his own overcoat.

'Well, do knock on the door if you're down this way again, Peter.'

'We don't promise to buy another painting. Victor will see you to the bus. Just a minute…' Jane brought out a woollen scarf from the charity box under the hallstand. She held it up.

Peter wound the poorly knitted scarf around his neck.

He looks like a lost little child in that blue, white and red scarf, Jane thought, as she automatically pushed down the switch for the outside light, but the outside remained in darkness.

'Sorry, the light doesn't work.'

Peter looked down at her. 'I know someone who could fix that.'

Victor said, 'Another thing I have to get around to. So many jobs to do when you move in. We had everything just right in Chingford.'

The rain was still sweeping across the road, the first real storm of winter. Sand was blowing up from the beach, blasting at their hands and faces as Victor escorted Peter to the carpark, where the minibus should have been waiting.

'We're cutting it a bit fine. Nine o'clock. You said it was leaving at nine?' What on earth was Victor going to do with him if the minibus wasn't there? He realised he hadn't taken his little pill. Angina aside, he began striding out towards the beach. He heard the café flagpole clanking in the wind.

In the carpark that overlooks the beach, there was darkness. No cars, not even a courting-couple on a night like this. No minibus. Somehow, Victor had always known that there would be no bus.

'They've gone without me,' Peter said.

'Yes, they have.'

Victor walked over to the boarded-up ice-cream hut, which at least gave some relief from the gusts of wind and rain that were blasting up from the open sea. 'Do you have a mobile?'

'A mobile? No.'

'Is there a phone number for the camp, Peter?'

'I don't know it.'

There was a pause when Victor began to chew his lower lip.

Peter looked around. 'What's in the bus shelter? I could stay there.'

That's a good one, Victor thought. 'Have you seen it?'

'No?'

'The bus shelter has nothing more than a pole to sit on. The parish council put it there to prevent the youths from drinking and camping there all night.' The last wooden bus shelter went up in shooting flames and sparks at the end of the summer.

'There must be a shed. What about that huge hut on the beach?'

'That's the surfing and life-saving hut. It's got equipment in it. It's alarmed.'

Peter seemed calm and accepting. It was Victor who felt panicked. The wind had brought on the pain in his chest.

'There will be a shed in somebody's garden. Is there an allotment near here?'

'I can't let you break into somebody's shed. This is Portmarrow.'

Peter moved out into the wind. He held out his hand. 'Thank you again, Victor. Good night.'

Grasping the hand held out to him, Victor weighed the price of a taxi against the wrath of Jane. Would she be angrier about the forty-mile taxi fare or angrier about letting the boy go off into the night, or about bringing him back home? For a moment, he wondered what he would want a stranger to do about a lost son of his, if this was his son, if he had ever had a son of his own.

Victor made up his mind. He felt his cheeks puffing in and out. 'I think you'd better come back to the bungalow. You can sleep in the dormer bedroom. There's a mattress up there, no bedstead, but there's a blow-up mattress we used before our furniture came, when we moved down from Chingford. It's a bit makeshift, but you'd be surprised how comfortable.'

Peter shook his head. 'I don't want to put you to any trouble. You've both been very kind.'

'No trouble.' Victor just wanted to get indoors. The tightening grip in his chest was making him gasp. 'You can get the bus to the railway station in the morning. Or you can take a bus the whole way. Cheaper. In fact, I'll take you into town in the morning.'

Was it the effect of the wind and the blown sand, or were there tears in the boy's eyes?

He pumped Victor's hand. 'By the way, I am Pieter Davidovich. Just call me Peter.'

On the right coast

Morning. Victor stood for a moment in the doorway between the hall and the porch, staring out at the road to the beach. Overnight, the wind had blown itself out. Sand was piled up against the telegraph pole opposite, an annoyed-looking black-back gull was sifting through some rubbish from a bin-bag that had split open.

Victor had on his city coat. His attaché case was standing upright, waiting for him to step out to the car. The club minutes and accounts of the right yacht club were neatly stowed in an ocean blue document box. Victor was waiting for Jane to join him at the door for the morning send-off.

He looked back to the narrow stairs that led directly from the hall to the dormer bedroom. He'd not had a good night. While Jane lay dreaming, Victor lay awake listening to the wind in the telegraph wires and the gobbing noise in the guttering on the roof which the locals call launders. It was a horrible night. He couldn't let the boy stay out of doors or break into a neighbour's shed. He wouldn't be responsible for that. He'd done the right thing in bringing him back home to sleep in the dormer bedroom. But he did wonder. All night, he wondered about the boy. Where was he from? What was he doing in Portmarrow, selling Chinese sentimental paintings? What was all that nonsense about a camp for the stateless on Bodmin Moor that had no telephone number?

What was the boy's accent? Faintly foreign, but nothing you could pin down. What colour were the eyes? Blue. Tall, slightly bent against all that wind, with the tiredness of the long-term homeless. Shiftless, but a nice, polite little chap. Nothing you could point a finger to.

At one point, about three in the morning, at the height of the storm, he'd got out of bed and turned the brass key in the lock of the bedroom door. Ten minutes later, he'd got up again and turned the key the other way. Jane would get up for a few minutes at about four.

She would be upset to find the door locked and would start a rattling with the doorknob.

He wondered whether any water had come down the chimney. You had to watch for that. He would ask Jane. She would clean up the soot. Or that boy. He could do it.

'Give him some breakfast and send him on his way,' he whispered to Jane as she handed him his coat.

'He's expecting you to take him to the bus.'

'No, I forgot about the accounts committee. Tell him goodbye from me and wish him luck.'

Victor buttoned up his coat, tucked in his navy-blue lambs-wool scarf and hurried to the car.

Marvellous, he thought, as he backed out into the traffic. Where do all these vehicles come from, so late in the season? They should have gone back up country by now, these idling tourists, back to their factories. Not that there are many factories left in Coventry, the Midlands, wherever the hoards come from. Back to their offices. If I'd known, it was going to be like this in the autumn. I was expecting some peace and quiet.

He waved to Roy's postman with his red bags and trolley, wearing his long shorts, still exposing the summer tan on his skinny legs. Nice chap. Always cheerful. You'd have to be, I suppose, faced with all that wind and weather. Still, the sun is shining now.

An offshore wind, as the Commodore will tell me when I get into the office. He'll be waiting at the door. Always says the same things in the same order. Coffee, Victor? From the dratted new machine, if you can work it. You're welcome to it: I'll stick to one of these. Swigging a Lamb's Navy before the clubroom clock has a chance to strike eleven. That's the Commodore, but genial. Genial and amusing. Used to be something in the Royal Navy. Well, we all used to be something. Do I miss it? The commute? The fumes? My desk? My desk. They never tell you who will get your desk. I wonder who occupies it now. Somebody from Surbiton. Ronnie Goodman? Probably. That little ape was always out to get my desk by the window, with his wife always at the Pilates and his daughter at the stables. We have nobody, Jane and me. Nobody. No cousins, uncles, aunts. Nobody. I'm not always fair to Jane. I should give way more often. That's what all that clutter is about. Those glass animals in the cabinet. Always fiddling about with them. A substitute for children, that's what it is.

Nobody's fault. My fault? Her fault? Nature's fault. The fault of nature. Anyway, there are enough people in the world. Seven billion of them, a good proportion of them on the south-coast road this morning. I hope she's managed to get rid of that boy. Foreigners. Swarming over here and occupying our... Cornwall's not infested with them, not yet, except in the care industry and on the farms. You can't say anything, of course. Look at Chingford. Ours used to be a nice little road, one of the larger ones on the Mount. In the end, you couldn't open the bedroom windows for the noise and the stench of diesel. Glad to be out of it. Got a good price out of those Poles, have to say that. Never the same place when they put that mosque down the road, people in white sheets pushing you off the pavement. Not allowed to say it, not even to yourself. A bloody police state, in the end. Overcrowding.

 Victor turned down the heater and opened the passenger-side window. A blast of fresh salt air, seaweed, ozone. Wonderful. This is the life, Victor. This is the life.

The Commodore was waiting at the door, empty-handed. Waiting with two others, dark-suited, committee members. Something was up. Victor re-gripped the handle of the attaché case which held the club's accounts as he walked the length of the ropewalk, past the empty yard, down towards the race office.

He tried a quip. 'Somebody's funeral?'

The Commodore looked down. The other two, the Events Secretary and an old soak who was normally at this bar this time of day, looked to the Commodore.

Here we go, Victor thought. Victor's been a naughty boy. What has Victor done now? A hundred hours of checking, checking, checking, free and gratis, and still the books aren't right and never will be, not while that Steward is overseeing the cellar and that Monica is in charge of the bar.

Victor was ready for them.

'Committee Room,' the Commodore said. He led the way, followed by the funereal ones.

Meanwhile, Victor's mind raced around the accounts, in and out, up and down the columns of figures. About sums, Victor might not always be right, but he was never wrong.

There were glasses and a jug of tap water on the mahogany round table. The committee room doubled as the library, the Founder and first Commodore looking on benignly from a Hogarth frame. Three leather-edged blotters were out, three new pencils. The Commodore would sit facing the room, the other two in profile to Victor, who would face the oily river from the far end of the long table.

He was right. This was to be an inquisition, then.

Passing a Georgian desk, Victor took up a blotter and plonked it squarely on the end of the table.

Victor, a Company Secretary, had, over the course of thirty years, survived three take-overs, numerous rounds of redundancies and reorganisations in that plate-glass London Bridge office, all far away in his memory now, but still very much at the spark-point of his instincts. Before he sat down, he surveyed the retired dentist and the bar-prop. He locked eyes with the Commodore, who finally gave way and sat in his seat, a milli-second before Victor pulled out his own chair.

Whatever this meeting was about, half the room would certainly need a drink before Victor did.

Victor did not open the attaché case. He was not going scuttle around, pretending that all was well. He linked his fingers and cracked his knuckles.

The Dentist, Kipling, flinched. The soak, Arman, failed to notice. Victor looked past the Commodore's left ear to the riverbank, the little cottages and primitive warehouses, white, Cornish cream, and Suffolk pink-painted cottages beyond. May's clanging boatyard. Out there, in the grey river something surfaced, creating ripples that were soon obliterated by the water taxi.

Here we go, he thought. Think I'm a stooge? Think I'm a poodle?

Down the hallway, the founder's French clock chimed the quarter-hour.

'The point is,' Victor started, as though they had all been in a fierce little debate for hours, 'the columns of figures, yes, they add up now. I've seen to that. But the fact is, the Club is losing money, when it should be making money hand over fist. You have a healthy membership, especially since you let in women...'

The Commodore leaned heavily on the table, and it groaned.

'Had to. Legislation. Couldn't argue in this day and age for continuing as a gentlemen's club. And the cost of women…'

Without referring to his papers, Victor said, 'The cost of women has been less than a thousand pounds. You gave them the boatmen's cloakroom and lavatory. You obtained a new shower second-hand and installed a closed sanitary bucket. There ought to be a properly enclosed one that gets emptied every week by a professional company on a contract.'

'Well, they're just yachtsmen girl-chaps, used to roughing it. We've had a lot of expense, one way and another… the disabled facilities, which was more legislation.'

'You cemented up some steps and made a ramp.'

There were sighs, then grunts, then silence.

'Point is,' Victor said, 'the bar. There needs to be an urgent stock-take. I understand, I need permission from you to make frequent, unannounced stock-takes.' He watched the water taxi plough back across a tide which was picking up in speed and he waited for the gasp, which came on cue from all three sides.

'But we can't. The steward would think we did not trust…'

Victor opened his attaché case. He lowered his voice. This was the part he always enjoyed: the irrefutable facts of waste. 'Figures don't lie, people do. People are forgetful, people favour their friends. People order steak and chips: not all of the chips go out. Next thing is, there is a plate or two of chips on the bar for favoured friends. It happens. I've seen it happen here. All of these things, lack of portion control, a little free drink now and then, it doesn't take an accountant to show you that a bar, which should be making money, becomes the club drain. There is your problem, finance officers, the bar, the steward and the waitress.'

'Oh, but now…'

'But dear Monica has been with us for years. Monica was here when…'

The dentist stepped in. 'We couldn't just start checking up on people. That wouldn't be right. Monica arranged the entire French evening. She spends hours here after she finishes, not being paid.'

Sucking up to you, Commodore, the wrong side of the bar, in the desperate hope of finding comfort beyond the minimum wage and the backstreet flat overlooking the bins, if only you could see it. Victor sat still, waiting for the implications to sink in. They themselves were the group of insiders responsible for the bar losing money. Were they really so unaware?

As if on cue, the oak door swung open. A wooden hostess trolley on the larger side precipitated through, propelled by Monica. There was a silence while coffee cups and saucers, sugar and milk jugs were handed around. Plates, paper napkins and doilies, a plate of biscuits from the Spar shop were plonked in front of the Chair. Monica retreated to nods, smiles and even a wink. The door closed on her again.

One by one, they stood up to pour hot coffee from the jug. Victor remained in his seat. He never liked to compromise a meeting's concentration between food and naked sums. Food introduced social intercourse. Anything could happen when people began talking trivia in a boardroom. In his own small sphere, you could say, Victor was a master. As the dentist began sucking on a small pink wafer biscuit and the Commodore began his rapid stirring-in of a spoonful of white granulated sugar, Victor cleared his throat.

'To recap, in order to be satisfied, I need to do an urgent stock-take before the staff are able to get wind of what is happening. And I need to set up a calendar of spot checks. I need to see the butcher's delivery notes. I need to see everything relevant to the bar and restaurant.'

The others shuffled. Arman opened his mouth to speak, but it was full of coffee and biscuit, so he kept silent.

'Well, I'm not sure we should go so far. Awkward. The membership would notice, think something was up.'

'Something is up, Chairman, and I mean to get to the bottom of it before I am willing to present any accounts for approval.' Victor allowed for a dramatic pause. 'If you want a Treasurer, that is. When I agreed to look at the accounts, you let me know that Mr Jones, a good yachtsman but hopeless with book-keeping, failed to keep on top of it and got into a fine pickle. He resigned his membership. I told you that I can sort it out… and I can. But only with the proviso that you let me scrutinise anything I want. You need an accounting till, by the way.'

'The expense…'

'Will pay for itself, probably within weeks, the way this bar is leaking small change. Your Monica can't count, you know. She's dipped me successfully on two occasions -- and I used to shop in the Polish shop in Chingford before I came to Cornwall.'

The others looked mystified.

'The Polish grocer in Chingford was able to dip anybody except me.'

There was a pause. It seemed to Victor that the other three were drawing in together, white heads perceptibly growing closer, some slow-motion scrum forming. He was disappointed, but he told himself he didn't mind. Figures were figures and facts were facts, take it or leave it. When he was invited, he liked the idea of being the Treasurer of the best yacht club on the right coast. Loved it. He, without a racing yacht or any craft at all, and living on the wrong coast, as well. But he wasn't going to be taken for a fool. He held to professional standards. Anybody who ever had anything to do with club books would see the problem immediately. Where would they find another Treasurer who would put in a couple of hours a day sniffing out the irregularities, taking the Steward himself to task?

The Commodore got up from his chair, peeling back his blazer and white cuffs to look down squarely at his solid Seamaster watch. 'We'll reconvene tomorrow. I have a dentist's appointment, as it happens, for what's left of the old gnashers. Thank you, all. I'll give you a lift as far as the crossroads, Charlie.'

It crossed Victor's mind to leave the folder on the table, but he picked it up and put it back inside his attaché case. He put his blotter away in the desk and looked up at the founder's clock, with its broken mechanically driven phases of the moon, still ticking steadily and persistently. Almost noon already. He thought about pausing for a drink at the bar so that he could monitor Monica's behaviour, before returning to Portmarrow for a ham sandwich with Jane in the kitchen. He might ask Jane if she would like to accompany him to the Club tomorrow, read the newspapers and wait for him to finish his meeting with the Finance Committee.

He wondered whether she'd got rid of that foreign boy, Peter, what was he called? Pieter Davidovich, that was it.

Peter and Jane

Jane stood at the bus-stop with Peter, feeling self-conscious. What would people think? Well, they wouldn't think anything, of course. People aren't narrow-minded like they used to be in a seaside village. I wouldn't be feeling so strange in Chingford, on the Mountfield Road bus-stop, she thought, standing here with a young man a third my age.

'It's taking a long time,' she said. 'The bus. Normally, in the summer, it comes every hour, but it's off-season now, so anything can happen. We've never been here, off-season, before.'

Peter looked down at her. He looked thoughtful. 'The bus, yes. I must take the bus to town, then get the train to Bodmin Road, then find my way back to the camp. Somehow. I've trekked so many thousands of miles before, over rough ground, down railway lines, I can do it.'

Jane's hand left her raincoat pocket and touched the back of her neck. 'I should have looked it up. I should have gone to Victor's computer. There is bound to be a phone number. They would come out for you and pick you up, I'm sure. After all, you do all that work for them, selling their paintings.'

'The paintings.' He gripped his portfolio tighter under his arm. 'I should be out selling this evening.'

'Where? Here in Portmarrow?'

'Could be anywhere. Depends where they take us. Always a new place. No freedom, Jane.'

'Goodness. You will have been missed. We kept you overnight. It's our fault for keeping you talking. I'm sure I should try to contact the camp myself for you. It's alarming, this statelessness, when I think of it. You poor soul. I don't know what to do for the best.'

Peter took hold of a lapel of her raincoat and guided her further into the bus-shelter. 'You have done all you could do, much more than anyone would do, you and Victor. I am grateful. You don't know how much. That full English was wonderful, it reminded me of my mother's goodness, and now I must go back to the camp, Jane, as soon as I can. Otherwise, I might be excluded and lose my place.'

'What happens then?'

'I don't know. A lot of people just disappear. I don't think they really look for them. Nobody knows what to do with us, you see, Jane.'

A pair of teenage girls went by, leered into the bus-shelter and sneered. One, a canary blonde with a pigtail, hissed.

'I don't know what to say, Peter. We were only trying to help, but the problems you face seem so huge.'

He lowered his voice. 'Every day, Jane. Huge.'

'Daily.'

There was a long pause. Jane wanted to say, perhaps you could come home with us again, I don't know whether Victor would mind, but best not to say anything at this point. Not now, until I could have a word with Victor, at the right time. How would Peter earn a living? We couldn't keep him indefinitely. And would the authorities send him back?

Back where?

'Nobody else is waiting at the bus-stop. I wonder whether we've missed it or whether the timetable has changed or whether there is any bus at all at this time of the year, except the school bus, of course.' She gasped a little, a quick drawing in of the breath, as though what she was about to propose was somehow inappropriate. 'We both have a pensioner's bus pass, but we use the car, the buses are so unreliable. I wonder whether we ought to go home for a cup of coffee and wait for Victor to come back from the Yacht Club. He shouldn't be long. He's gone to present their accounts. He's a volunteer. He would give you a lift into town.'

Peter stood back. 'Oh well, I don't know. I may be in trouble already. If I am not back at the camp, I may not be allowed back. There are always new children arriving. They call us children, but sometimes some of us are a little bit older. We go out and earn some money for the camp.'

Jane dug her hands into her pockets and stared up the road, to the run-down Victorian seaside villas, their gates swinging or missing, their old wooden window-frames and their new plastic window-frames and doors. This half done-up village, she thought. What have we done, moving here?

'It will all be better come summer, Peter,' she said. 'Victor won't be long. I've been standing on my feet far too long. I need a coffee. Just an instant.'

She went out into the sunlight and began to walk towards the bungalow, Peter following behind.

When they got there, Victor was just pulling into the waste-ground where he kept the car.

'Hello. Missed the bus again? This is getting to be a habit.'

'The bus didn't come. We came back for a coffee. My legs are killing me. I thought you'd give Peter a lift to the railway.'

'Yes, of course I will. It's lunch time, anyway. See what we have in the fridge, Jane.'

He led Peter into the dining room and began a one-sided discussion on the shockingly low price of nineteenth-century Japanese prints. By the time the table was laid, Jane was hearing laughter and animated voices from her position at the work-top in the kitchen. Well there, it was good to have someone else around, she thought, young company. Good for Victor. When the telephone rang in the hall, she answered it cheerfully.

It was the Commodore. 'This is difficult, Jane. Before Victor goes into the bar tomorrow, would you ask him to look into the Club office?'

'That sounds ominous,' Jane said. 'Anything wrong? He's just arrived back. You can speak to him…'

'Not now, Jane. That wouldn't be appropriate. Just ask him to call into the office before going into the bar and restaurant.'

'Whatever is it? You can tell me.'

The Commodore appeared to hesitate. He lowered his voice. 'Victor called our barmaid and waitress, Monica, a wog.'

'What?' Jane laughed. 'That's not my Victor.'

'I have it on good authority, there are witnesses, your husband said to Monica, "You speak very good English for a wog." There's been a complaint.'

'Who complained? That sounds ridiculous.' Jane caught sight of herself in the hall mirror. The look of amusement had not quite left her face.

'As to the complainant, I'm not at liberty to say.'

Jane felt herself bristling. 'Well, why are you so sure it happened, then? What does Monica have to say?'

'It wouldn't be appropriate to discuss it with you over the telephone. Just ask Victor not to go into the bar until he has seen me in the office.'

'I'll tell him.' Jane heard her voice change to a tone more brittle.

She fetched the greengage jelly and can of Ideal milk on a tray.

Victor looked up. 'Who was that?'

'It was the Commodore. He said, don't go into the bar until you've been in the office tomorrow.'

'Oh? I've just left there. Did he say what it was all about? Changed their minds about a stocktake, I suppose. About time they heeded the advice of a professional.'

'It was something you said. Apparently.'

Peter looked out of the window at two passers-by pulling along a small dog with a large collar.

'What? What did I say? Don't be silly, Jane.'

Jane glanced at Peter, then at Victor. She lowered her voice. 'That Commodore, he said, not to come into the restaurant or bar until you have been in the office and seen him. It was something you said to Monica.'

'To Monica?' Victor stood up and began to glower at Jane. 'What did I say to Monica? I've certainly implied plenty about her to the Finance Committee this morning.'

Jane looked down to the floor. 'Something about her speaking good English for a wog, and before you say anything more, Victor, you do have a tendency to speak before you think, you know you do. There are things we just can't say these days.'

Peter stood up and looked around for his coat and portfolio.

'Sit down, Peter. I never said such a thing. She does speak good English for a Portuguese, anyway. A wog is a wily oriental gentleman or a worker in government service. That's Indian. Everybody knows that. Nothing to do with Portuguese people.'

Peter hesitated by the dining room door, while Victor and Jane contemplated the accusation. 'I'd better go now. Thankyou for the…'

'No no, sit down, dear boy. I'll take you to the railway station later. This is a bit of a blow. I've never been accused of anything like this. Bring in some fresh coffee, Jane. Take this Ideal milk back and bring in the double cream. Never mind the old heart. And never let it be said I am unkind to a foreigner. My home is your home, Peter. Indeed, it is. And as for Monica, well…'

'And you say your friend can re-wire the entire house, in exchange for bed and board for a few days, for as long as it takes to do the job, which will not be longer than a fortnight?'

It was well past the time of the last bus and the last train. They were all in the living-room, Victor and Jane in their Ercol chairs, Peter on a spindly dining-room chair called The Windsor between them.

'Let me understand the plan,' Jane said. 'You and your friend leave the Camp and stay here for a few weeks to get the job done; we get a local qualified electrician to 'sign off' your work, then you go on your way. But where will you go? You'll be out of the system. Where will you stay after that? Where will you get any money? Aren't you better off at the Camp? We shouldn't interfere with the system.'

Peter handed Victor his coffee and spoon. He handed across the sugar-lumps in their blue glass bowl. 'We will have your reference,' he said. 'We need a reference. We don't have anything at the moment. Paul is a good electrician with plenty experience. He used to climb the big pylons. We just need a start. At the Camp, we are going nowhere. I came as a child, they keep you as a child, doesn't matter how long your beard is. All you need is one chance, but you don't get one.'

Victor laughed and tucked his recliner into the upright position. 'Sounds perfect to me,' he said. 'Perfect. You don't mind the attic? Can be quite warm in the summer, I expect. No proper insulation.'

'They'll be gone before summer,' Jane said.

'Long gone, as you say,' Peter said. 'But we can fix extra new insulation while we are doing the electrics, you know.'

So Long to Jane's Little Bit of Freedom

'Are you going to the yacht club now?'

The boiled eggs and toast were finished. There was silence from the attic. Peter must still be asleep. All night, there had been no sound at all. Well, just a very faint sound of scraping at about three in the morning. Victor may have imagined it.

'No.' Victor paused, took a sip of lukewarm tea, and sat back in his spindly little tubular yellow chair in the kitchen. 'I don't think I shall.'

Jane knew when to say nothing and to wait.

Victor glared out of the window at the barely acceptable fence and the streaked west side of the bungalow next door. Goodness, these small buildings received a battering over the autumn months, and it wasn't really winter yet. A good time to get properly insulated. Get some new Dimplex dual-purpose heaters. They were called Quantum, or something like that. Highly recommended. Time to say goodbye to the ungrateful yacht club, and invest the money spent on driving to and fro to the other coast in looking after his own immediate interests, for once.

Victor sighed heavily and sat upright. 'The Yacht Club can go hang. They're going broke and serve them right. They've been told. No, I'm going to send their accounts back, all of the incomplete records that the previous Treasurer made a mess of, but they're not going to receive the work I've already done for them free and gratis. Oh no. This morning, I'm going to the post office with their bundle of papers for second-class delivery. Racist language, indeed. That will put them in their place. Let them find a Treasurer as well qualified as Victor Everley for their yacht club.'

Oh well, Jane thought. That's my little bit of freedom up the spout again.

Victor went out in his shirt sleeves, slamming the door behind him. She knew he was hurt and upset by the Yacht Club accusing him of racist talk. He needed to be valued, she thought. Well, all of us feel the need to be valued, now and then, but with him, it was a flaw. A great big flaw. There was all that business over the redundancy payments and all that hoo-ha about early retirement at London Bridge. Victor wouldn't have any of it, not for himself. Oh, he was happy to send other people down the road, but not himself. He was determined to go on working up to the age of sixty-five. Nothing would persuade him to go early. He'd made himself so useful, even the Vice-Chair respected his wishes. Once his mind was set on something, he couldn't be shifted from it, she knew that. His father was the same: made sure he was the only man who knew where the drains were in Gravesham. They didn't dare fire that one. Yes, she thought. Even a Stalin would have hesitated to shift her father-in-law, not that Victor cared. Hadn't visited him for years. She wondered how the old devil was or whether he was still alive, even. There wouldn't be anything left for Victor when he was gone. Victor was never the favoured one. The old man let it be known that nothing was coming his way, no inheritance for him: Victor was always out there on his own. Victor was the brainy one, hard-working, assiduous, always resented. Well, that was all right. They had two private pensions coming in between them. They were hardly deprived.

She chose a new J-cloth and wiped down the kitchen surfaces. Eleven o'clock. Coffee time. Where was Victor? He'd only gone out for a minute to post those papers. Where was the boy, Peter? He hadn't come down yet. No point in boiling up the coffee if nobody was around. He ought to be up by now. He had a train to catch, back to Bodmin, back to the camp, out of their lives. She'd miss him.

She went to the foot of the stairs and called his name.

No sound.

Perhaps he was tired, dead tired. All that selling for pennies.

She climbed the long, straight stairs, a few paces, her hand on the stair rail.

'Peter? Coffee time. Are you there?'

She went almost as far as the attic door. She raised a hand to knock gently.

'Here I am.'

Jane looked around quickly. Peter was in the doorway to the porch, his short shadow pooling on the orange patterned carpet of the narrow hall. He had pulled up a hood over his hair, so that she barely recognised him.

'Peter, sorry, I thought you were still upstairs. I was calling you down for a coffee. It's coffee time. Victor should be back soon. I don't know where he's gone. He only went out for a minute.'

Jane turned and began to descend the stairs. Her sandals felt large on her feet. She felt her nails push against the leather straps and peep-toes.

Peter continued to stand in the hall, looking up towards her. Behind him, inside the porch, she saw a black bicycle, old-fashioned, with a lamp. It was leaning against the brickwork.

'Oh that.' Peter grinned and came forward a few steps. 'I paid five pounds for it. Do you like it?

She said nothing, thinking, you were going on the train home, back to Bodmin. You were going this morning. That business about re-wiring the house with your friend, you didn't mean it.

'It's not worth any more than that. What do you think?'

She reached the bottom step. 'Well, I don't know. I don't know. Let me think. Aren't you going to Bodmin today?'

Peter reached out to steady her arm, though it was the bottom step, and she needed no help. 'I could, yes. I could go and look for my friend. Now I have my bicycle, I could cycle there. Nonetheless.'

She laughed, a nervous laugh. 'No, you couldn't, Peter. Far too far.'

'Far too far. Far too far.' He savoured the expression a little and grinned. 'Come on, let's make coffee now.'

He led her gently into the kitchen, explaining, there was a gentleman outside the shop who wanted to sell his bicycle. It only needed a puncture repair, but he had no puncture kit.

They had coffee and then lunch. Peter laid the table, buttered the bread on the loaf, then cut the slice. Jane was greatly amused. She had never thought of doing that before. Peter said that when you were always camping in the open air, you had to do things that way.

Victor joined them as they were tucking into ham and eggs, with fresh mushrooms from the field behind the bungalow. Victor was in good spirits, now that he had lifted the weight of the prejudiced Yacht Club from his shoulders. The post-master was on form, he said. Old Roy was taking his skiff out this afternoon if the weather held. He might do some fishing for bass. Marvellous chap. With global warming, even the pilchards were coming back, Roy told him. Pilchards were the same as sardines. There used to be a canning factory on the south coast, years ago. At Newlyn, he thought. Victor wondered whether the factory was still there. They might take a trip down and see. Something to do. Possibilities were endless now that he'd got rid of the snob-ridden Yacht Club.

Jane opened the kitchen window a notch. Warm, salty air swept through the room, sweeping away the odours of the day's fry-up.

Victor leaned back on two legs of the spindly yellow kitchen chair. 'Oh, and by the way, Peter, when are you getting in touch with your friend, so that we can get the new wiring done? We must get it all done before winter comes. Might not seem like it today, but autumn steals on apace, eh?'

'A pace, yes.' Peter stood up and slapped Victor on the back. 'Yes. I will go today, this afternoon. I will take my bicycle to town and go on the train, and I will bring him back. His name is Paul. Paul Rabinovich. He is a nice… chap.' He grinned. 'A nice chap. Together we will get the new wiring of this bungalow done.'

Victor seemed puzzled. 'I didn't know you had a bike.' His tubular chair swung back on its four legs.

'He bought one this morning,' Jane said. 'From a man in the village. There's nothing wrong with it, it just has a puncture.'

'I've got a repair kit somewhere,' Victor said, springing the chair back onto two legs again. 'I'll repair it if you will bring back your friend. Leave your bike here. I'll take you to the railway station. I did promise, after all.'

Peter collected his coat, his bag, the charity box scarf which Jane had given him two nights ago and went around to the passenger side of Victor's car.

From the red-tiled doorstep, Jane waved to them both, under the round arch of the porch. Idly, she picked up a beige pebble which had fallen off the pebble-dash surface of the outer wall and put it in her pocket. Lots of the pebbles had fallen, leaving little pockmarks in the plaster.

She went upstairs again to Peter's attic, picked up the sheet and duvet from the blow-up mattress to wash in the machine. She checked the shower and thought that she would give it a clean later. She wondered whether Victor had thought about the expense of buying two beds for the young men, that was, if they were coming back.

An Excursion

It was such a lovely day, one of those autumn days on the north coast when the air is so clear that you could almost touch Shag Rock.

'It's called Shag Rock because there are so many cormorants on it. It's just too far to swim to, so it's an ideal nesting site. Very few people ever get there.'

Paul laughed. 'So why is it called Shag Rock?'

Jane stopped walking and looked serious for a moment. She was a little out of breath. She cleared her throat. 'I don't know. The local people's sense of humour, I suppose. The two birds look much alike, but shags are solitary. Cormorants live in colonies, just as on the Shag Rock. There are no shags there.'

'Oh, you're talking about two birds.' Paul laughed again.

Peter and Paul stopped walking and looked out to sea. They had been striding up the cliff path, three abreast; now they were in a line, Jane leading the way.

At Hevva Point, they all sat down in the heather. The pilchard hut was the half-way point. It crossed Jane's mind to explain that it was called Hevva Point because of the cry the heuer made when a shoal of pilchards was spotted, but there had been such awkwardness and confusion over Shag Rock, she decided they didn't really want history lessons.

It was a little early to break out the sandwiches. Jane wanted to go further up the path to the top, to show them the circular remains of the reinforced concrete war defences, the gun emplacements, where there was at least some shelter from the wind.

'A bird's a bird, just a bird,' Paul said. There was now a bitter tone in his voice. 'What does it matter?'

'Well, there are differences between the…'

Paul got to his feet and walked away.

There was silence between the two of them for a while. Jane kept looking around to try and see where Paul had gone.

Peter chose a stalk of grass to chew, lay back for a moment, shading his eyes from the sun.

'Take no notice,' he said. 'Paul is moody. He wants to get on with the job. Always restless.' His voice had already taken on the laziness of repose.

'Yes, but what did I...?'

'Paul had a bad childhood. No childhood at all. He has trouble adjusting to this safe place. He has trouble sleeping.'

Jane, still sitting bolt upright, looked down at her trousers and the laces of her walking boots. There were grasses and the fine roots of heather between the welts and the soles. They would get a good clean and buffing up after this outing. She focused on a white speck on the horizon.

'Yes, I notice he is often up at night.'

Peter shifted, crossed his legs, and leaned on an elbow. 'I hope I don't disturb you, Jane.'

Jane jumped to her feet. 'No. Goodness, no.' She turned and looked down at him. 'We're so lucky to have you. I wonder where Paul has gone. I wish he would come back now. It's only another few hundred yards to the top.'

'I'd rather stay here, out of the wind. I feel lazy. We've walked far enough. The sun is warm here.'

Peter got to his feet anyway, while Jane fiddled with the straps of her rucksack. She drew out a headscarf she had bought at a charity shop in Llandudno, years and years ago. It was a silly thing, with foxes and horses with riders in spurs in the design, but it was a large Liberty scarf, and she'd kept it all these years to ward off the wind on her walks with Victor, though with his heart condition now, those walks were fewer and fewer. She wondered whether Victor had enough puff to get up to the top nowadays.

At the high point, Jane looked back. Peter, yards behind, had lit a cigarette and was struggling with the wind to keep it alight. Filthy habit, she thought. She and Victor had given up years ago. He used to smoke full-strength Players, and she smoked Embassy, with the brown tip. She'd read somewhere recently that the tips were worse for you than the tobacco. One generation never learned from the previous one. Still no sign of Paul. He must have gone home.

The white spot on the horizon had a funnel. There was a trail of black smoke. She could not tell whether the ship was turning and steaming away up the Bristol Channel. She thought not. It seemed to be following the coast a little further.

'What have you seen?'

Peter was behind her. In her headscarf, she had not heard him approach. She stepped back a pace from the edge.

'What? Oh. There's a coaster or something. I've been watching it. It will turn soon.'

'So, we have arrived, and this is the concrete defence.'

'The defences. You're not interested, are you? I suppose you've seen defences, real defences, modern-day ones.'

'Yes, plenty, lots.'

'Anyway, the pillbox will keep us out of the wind. Victor and I always sit outside by the wall. It's muddy inside and full of disgusting litter.'

Peter looked all around. The place was strewn with shale. He put his hands over his ears for a moment. 'You look very nice in your headscarf,' he said. 'It suits you. Should wear it more.'

'Thank you. Would you like the cheese or the beef to begin with?'

'I would like a surprise.'

'Beef it is.'

Jane sat on a mound of flat stones, took out a Thermos flask and a pack of sandwiches. Peter stood at the edge of the cliff, where Jane had been standing a few minutes before. The wind was steady, flapping in a lively stream at his trouser legs. It could veer at any moment, of course, and suck him over the edge. She could not see his face and could not guess at what he was thinking. It crossed her mind that he would not be surprised or sorry to be sucked over the edge, but surely that could not be.

He turned quickly. 'I don't like the edge.' He raised his voice above the noise of the wind and the sea.

'Come back over here, then, and eat your sandwich. You make me nervous, Peter.'

Jane handed him a paper-covered sandwich.

He came back and sat on an earth mound. 'I don't like the edge,' he said again. 'I saw a man throw his dog over the edge. He had to leave. He could not take his dog.'

Jane was at a loss. She looked at his face in silence.

He looked down at his hands. 'Not on a cliff, with sea. On a hill. There was no time. No gun. The dog could not survive.' He gazed out over the crinkling, shining sea.

'It's all right,' Jane told him. 'When Feathersone-Dilke's sailors took the settlers off Tristan da Cunha, they shot the dogs. It was better that way.'

'Where?'

Jane continued to look at Peter steadily. 'Tristan da Cunha, a remote British island, somewhere in the South Atlantic, I think. The island blew up. It was a volcano. The Royal Navy steamed over there and took the islanders off just in time. They thought nobody was ever going back. Ask Victor to show you his stamp collection. 2013 was the fiftieth anniversary of the re-settlement. He has four first day covers. They'll be worth a lot one day.'

'First day covers. There is a lot I don't understand, need to learn.'

Nibbling at the edges of her sandwich, throwing a piece of crust to a young gull which was hovering close by, stamping up and down, watching her every move, Jane said, 'So, what are you going to do when you leave us, Peter? Do you want to go to university? College first? What is your position in this country? There's provision for young people like you, surely...'

'I can't think about it, not now,' he said. 'Not now.'

He looked irritated. His mood had changed. He seemed restless, ready to move on, back down the cliff path.

Jane sighed heavily. She would like to have questioned him, pursued this business of where he was from, where he intended to go. An old sensation close to anxiety, held back for two weeks, began to creep into the shades of her mind. She wasn't sure of Peter, certainly wasn't sure of Paul. She'd wanted to talk about it with Victor, lots of times these two weeks that the boys had been sleeping in the attic, but Victor seemed so newly animated, so happy, it didn't seem right to place any doubt in his mind that Paul was anything but capable of re-wiring the house. It was just that, well, the fact was, these young men, they hadn't actually done any wiring yet.

There had been the trips to the beach, the daytrip down the coast to see the seals in their caves, the expedition to the quay to see whether there were any freshly landed fish – and there were. They came home with a bucket full of assorted fish. Victor celebrated by buying a small chest-freezer for the garage that was full of packing cases from the old house and never used for the car. There was the cookery lesson, when she showed them all how to cook bass *en croute*, with puff pastry she made herself. She hadn't done that for years and years. She let Peter draw the fish's head in the pastry and score in the scales with her chef's knives. It had been all so, so joyful, somehow.

As he got up to go, Jane touched Peter's arm. He seemed to flinch. The pleasant features of his face turned into a scowl, just for an instant, quickly righted. 'Peter, when,' she said, 'when is Paul going to start on the electrics, or is he not up to it?'

The young man looked down and began to brush at the legs of his trousers.

'It doesn't matter, it really doesn't matter if we have to get a qualified electrician to get the job done. Only it needs to be done. I don't mind paying for the job to be done properly. We love having you both here with us, but we don't want to lose the plot, do we? Winter is coming on. The electrics in the bungalow are old and quite dodgy, as Victor says, and we really do need the work to be started. We don't want to find ourselves in a pickle with winter coming on. We'll need to use electric heaters, and we'll need to have a meter for Economy Seven, so that we don't pay over the odds for electricity. It all has to be done and approved before we can use it.'

Peter had become rigid, as though he had been thoroughly told off. He looked up at the horizon, far off, where there were now no white dots, no funnels, no ships. 'I was having such a good time: I didn't want the work to begin. The sooner that begins, the sooner that will all be over, and we will have to go. I was hoping for a few more days, but it was silly of me. Forgive me. Paul and I will begin immediately, tomorrow. We have to just get our wire and other things.'

'Victor will take you into town to get what you need.'

'It's OK, we can do it. We can go on the bus. One thing, when we start, there will be lots of drilling, a lot of dust. Why don't you leave for a few days, go somewhere nice? Victor needs a holiday. He worries. You could take him away for a few days.'

'Oh, a bit of dust, what's that? Somebody needs to clean it up. You boys are not very good with the Dyson.'

'We will be when we are working. We will be clean then.'

'Well, let's hope so.'

Jane tidied their picnic area, re-packed her rucksack, and started down the hill.

There was a chill in the air now. Only the late surfers in wetsuits were still in the water. The last of the beachgoers had left the place to the evening dog-walkers. She hoped she had not been too direct with Peter. It was just that somebody needed to say something and by the looks of it, Victor was never going to. He was too trusting. Time was slipping gently by, and these boys had done nothing yet.

To Business

That evening, before they all turned in for the night, the four of them had the conversation they should perhaps have had several weeks before.

Around the dining room table, Paul, the qualified electrician, qualified but not qualified in this country, explained that a 'Part P Compliant' person would have to issue the necessary certificate when the job was complete, and they were finished. All of the present wiring would have to be stripped out before they started on the new. This meant putting in a temporary supply, which would provide lights and power for tools to work by, but not much else. Cooking would be out of the question. The old fuse-boxes were no good, new consumer units would have to be installed.

'No cooking? For how long?' Jane looked alarmed.

'We have to do a first fix, then a second fix, when we can connect up the appliances. It takes time, and it means you will be living on a building-site. This is why,' Peter said, 'I suggested this afternoon that you both go away for a few days and leave us to it. If you trust us, of course.'

'Of course we do. It's just that, well it's just come home to me what all of this new wiring involves.'

Victor spoke up. 'It has to be done, of course it has to be done. It's so old, it's quite hazardous. I thought I'd explained that before we came here, Jane. Some of this wiring goes back to the seventies, for God's sake.'

Jane got up and went to the kitchen to tackle the washing-up. Four people put a strain on the kitchen, the budget and everything else. The men never seemed to think of helping her. She imagined herself trying to cook on the Gaz camping stove. Never a good idea at the best of times. Peter was probably right; it was best to move out for a few days. But that in itself was an extra expense. That was never going to be cheap, either. You couldn't hire a holiday bungalow just for a few days. There was a big deposit to be found, and what of all the valuables lying around? What about the glass ornaments? What about Victor's Japanese prints? What if the young men just walked off with them? Peter was an artist: he must know what they were worth. And then there was the stamp collection. Why did she open her mouth about that, this afternoon?

Jane tackled the saucepans first, rinsed off the plates and stacked the dishwasher. She set it going and strode back to the dining-room.

She stood in the doorway.

'I don't think we can just walk out of here and leave the place for the wiring to be done, Victor. You can't hire a holiday cottage just like that. Have you seen the prices, even off-season? No, I'd rather stay here and put up with the mess. That's what Peter and Paul will be doing, after all. They'll be sleeping in the attic with all the dust, won't you?'

All three men looked taken aback.

Peter, then Paul stood up slowly. 'It's late. We'll say goodnight.'

'Thank you for another lovely meal.' Paul rubbed his belly.

'Top notch. Thank you.'

The young men smiled brightly and went upstairs to bed.

Jane closed the dining-room door. She sat down in front of Victor. 'I don't trust them,' she whispered. 'There's something not right. We never got to the bottom of this Homeless Camp of theirs on Bodmin Moor. We should ring up County Hall and ask about it. These places have to be licenced. Somebody must know.'

Victor sighed and without looking at her, held up some careful and comprehensive drawings, done with a fine drawing-pen. He looked flushed.

'Something not right as per this? This is the plan, and it is quite brilliant. Full of things I'd never have thought of in a million years. Paul knows what he is doing, all right. Don't go and spoil it all now, Jane. Look at this, all the costings. Eight double sockets, twelve ceiling lights, four switches, twelve light fittings, two for a TV and phone, one smoke detector and one fan: and that's just for the kitchen. He's brilliant, Jane. And you're quite right, we don't have to leave. We can stay here with them, and we can even help. It'll be an education. So, let's put all these drawings away for the minute and get to bed. I'll take them to town tomorrow to get what they need for the First Fix. First Fix, eh? It's all happening now.'

He got up, came around to Jane's side of the table, where she was staring at the wiring diagrams. He ruffled her hair. 'Yes,' he said. 'You won't understand all the drawings. I understand the diagrams a little bit now, now that they've been explained to me.'

At bedtime, before he put out the light, Victor said, 'Paul already went and saw Roy at the post office today. He asked about his holiday cabin on the towans, where Roy's brother and their family stay in the summer holidays. He said, yes, we could stay there for a few nights, on a nightly rate, no deposit necessary, because he knows us.'

Jane put the bookmark back into the novel she was reading. 'There you go,' she said, 'why is Paul so darned keen to get us out of the way? How did he know about Roy's holiday cabin?'

'Roy advertises it in the window of his post office. Why are you so prickly about this all of a sudden, Jane? I thought you wanted a new kitchen as much as I do.'

'Oh, a new kitchen now, is it? How much will that cost? What's wrong with the kitchen we've got? It goes with the age of the house.'

'We'll get a cheap one. The cheapest one we can find. In fact, we can get one second-hand. Will that do you? They can't put new wiring behind existing built-in kitchen cabinets, Jane. It can't be done.'

Jane settled her pillows, lay on her back and stared up at the woodchip painted ceiling.

'Victor, we're not rich. We only have one little home. Winter is coming on. We are trusting our home to people we don't know, with dubious origins, from a foreign country, we don't even know which foreign country.'

'Oh, I see. Who's the racially prejudiced one now?' Victor snapped out his bedside light.

'I've said it before, and I'll say it again. I don't trust it. I don't trust them. How competent are they? They're nice enough boys, I'll say that, but we need a second opinion about this re-wiring from a professional, somebody we know, a local man who is accountable, somebody who is insured if something goes wrong.'

'And which local electricians do we know?'

'There are yellow pages for that, and reviews on the internet.'

Victor switched on his lamp again.

'We've been over this,' he said. 'They'll strip out the old wiring: that can't do any harm, can it. They'll put in the new wiring where the old wiring was, except that they will use new fittings, new double sockets, only more of them than we have now, a new cooker switch, new shaver points, new kitchen fan, new bathroom fans, residual circuit devices, smoke detectors, fire alarms for the first time, and a new Big Ben bloody doorbell. What more can you want? Then, when they have done all of that, with the up-lights and the downlights and the spotlights and whatever else you want, they will call in your qualified local electrician to connect it all up and sign it all off, as they call it. Give us a certificate. Are you happy now? Can I get some sleep now?'

Jane said yes, and meant no, she was not happy. She spent much of the night trying to think what Peter had said about his origins. In the ochre glow of the streetlamp, the dark bedroom furniture seemed to crowd around, accusing, and complaining. She could remember very little of what Peter had said. Had he ever said anything thing much about his past? There were snatches and fragments. Something about pyjamas and headscarves. Paul, on the other hand, was a complete mystery.

She drifted off to sleep, dreaming of donkeys with packs on their backs, climbing through steep hillsides, wandering along uncertain trails, dusty in summer, snow-covered in winter, people in bright clothing, rivers, and streams with muddy, slippery banks.

'I want none of it.' She shook herself awake. 'I don't want a new kitchen. I want my life back. They'll have to go.'

No-one was listening.

In That Chalet By The Sea

Now that October had come and wet, stormy weather was the norm, Jane was bored in a way that she had never been in her adult life. In Chingford and even in Portmarrow, there was always cleaning and baking to fill a spare moment, but here, in The Cabin, a sort of shed in the towans, there was nothing to do at all, nothing to be done except stare at the ocean, and there was only so much of that you could do in a day.

She had started a sort of crochet project which was both challenging and boring at the same time. She had started a Fairisle jersey for Victor, which involved a lot of coloured strands and a lot of counting. All was well until it came to the armpits, the problem of the welts that should have been easy to overcome and was not. Both of those projects lay damply on the sofa.

She'd gone into Hayle and bought felt to make some toy, a pink pig. It sat in its bag.

'When the water falls out of the sky, it stinks of Creosote in here. Are you listening?'

No-one was listening. The planks in the walls absorbed her voice. Victor had cleared off, as he always did, every morning, leaving her with washing-up in a Belfast sink mounted on concrete blocks that emptied into a bucket. That was the kitchen: that, a table and a camping stove. The house on blocks swayed in the wind, its galvanised iron roof straining against its fixings. The marram grass whirled and swirled around it. The gutters and the downpipe made noises, half musical, half other-worldly.

She peered down the sandy bank to the Rogers' shack. They'd gone to Thailand, where they went every winter. What a strange, idle life they must lead. Who were they? How did they earn a living? How did they collect their pensions? She supposed, anything could be done in this shiftless world. Did they live in a shack in Thailand as well? All they said was that they lived on the beach, or near the beach. Perhaps they had a smart apartment. She thought not, from the little they'd told her. Now, their bicycles were locked away in the shed behind their chalet. Everything was battened down for the winter. There were even barriers erected against blown sand. They'd said that one Spring they'd arrived back and had to dig their chalet out, there was so much sand. How could one live like that, permanently, at their age? What would become of them when they got very old? Presumably, Nanny State, as Victor called it, would provide.

'All I want to do is to get back to my bungalow,' Jane told the sand dunes and the view from the window. 'That's all.'

Victor returned in high spirits with the day's groceries. She watched him rush up the sand bank like a boy, the stiff breeze tussling his silver hair. It's lengthening by the day, she thought. Before we came to Portmarrow, he used to have his hair clipped in town. Then he had his hair clipped lopsidedly in the village. He didn't like the atmosphere in the hairdresser's, too Cornish, too local. He felt excluded. Jeered at, was his phrase. Then, he'd bought some clippers so that she could have a go at it, herself, since she'd complained about it so much. That was a disaster. He'd been good about it: the difference between a good and a bad haircut is two days, he'd said.

He burst in the door through the wooden porch. The whole cabin shook. He sat down heavily, his face reddening. 'That's yours,' he said, handing over a Tesco bag with food for the day. 'This gas fridge is no good. It's so small. I'll be glad not to have to shop every day.'

Amen to that, she thought.

He handed over her change, fished out his newspaper and settled down. Now was the time for a coffee. He looked at the back, the front, and the middle of the paper, then threw it down.

He doesn't even check what the stock market is doing any more, she thought.

'Well,' he said. He spread his knees, leaned forward and raised his voice. 'We soon won't have to worry about the size of the fridge anymore. I'll find out who owns that piece of waste ground where I park the car, build a big garage, and have an American fridge in there, alongside the other chest freezer, eh? Then we won't have to go shopping for months. For months, Jane.'

'Oh?'

'Yes, oh. The first fix is finished. It only took two days. And now, they are on to the kitchen, the thingies for the appliances. They want us to be able to move back in with at least the kitchen and bathrooms ready. I can do the decorating myself. By the way, they want you to choose the kitchen and bathroom taps. I've brought the catalogue home. It's in the car.'

She should have been sharing his enthusiasm, she knew that. She also knew that this was the point where she should be up and over to the kitchen area to boil a kettle for fresh coffee, but the listlessness, brought on by the smell of creosote, or the smell of rotting seaweed brought by the breeze, or the unsettling high winds, or the grains of yellow sand that caught in the corners and in the spaces between the floorboards, or something more undefined, left her semi-sprawled in her upright chair, one elbow crooked behind the back of it.

'I'm going to take you to see it. After lunch. You'll be really surprised then, and really really pleased.'

'Oh good.'

The words should have conveyed pleasure, but they conveyed both weariness and anxiety. Even

Victor, in his enthusiasm, looked up and seemed puzzled.

'I don't know what to do with you sometimes,' he said, quite quietly. 'It doesn't matter what we all do for you, nothing is good enough.' He returned to his newspaper.

Jane really did not feel like preparing anything for lunch. She couldn't think of anything to make. Potato cakes from last evening's left-over mash, perhaps? She had some onions, flour and eggs but no chives, so she felt unable to begin. A feeling of emptiness and the lack of a proper kitchen in the shack had put her off her appetite. She felt around her ribs, aware that she was still losing weight. She went on sitting in the upright chair, thinking I must do something about making Victor's lunch.

Victor was hungry. At nearly one, he threw down his newspaper again and said, 'Hey Jane, I know: I have an idea. Let's go to The Cornishman. It's a nice, quiet pub. If the sun comes out, we could sit in the garden and have a ploughman's. How about that?'

'That's a good idea,' she said. 'Anything to get away from this stench of wood preservative and rotting seaweed.'

Victor grinned encouragement. 'Oh, it's not as bad as all that here. A lot of people pay a lot of money for the privilege of roughing it here.'

'Yes, in the height of summer, and then only for a fortnight.'

She fished out a change of clothing from the soggy wardrobe. Because of the sloping floor, she wasn't able to shut its door again, so let it swing. God, but this place was damp. One of Victor's yacht club blazers had mildew on the shoulders.

She picked up her handbag and wandered into what passed for a kitchen. The plastic drainer did not match with the bowl, which did not match with the bin, which did not match with the tea towel or oven cloth. What a dump of a place.

'Time to go,' she said to herself. 'Time to get out and go.' She wondered how the Rogers were braving it out in Thailand. Or was it all just wonderful there?

A plate full of cheese and bread, pickle, salad and a lager and lime cheered them up. The seasonally laid-off locals in the poorly lit bar turned around and scrutinised them for an instant but they were able to escape to the conservatory to watch the garden birds, the low cloud and the rain as it ran down the mud splashed windows into the deserted carpark.

By the time they arrived at the waste ground by the bungalow, a little after three, the sun was out, and Jane was in a positive mood. It was so nice, so uplifting to see her little pebbled-dash home again. And there was Paul by the door, smoking a cigarette outside as he'd been asked to do, taking a break from all that work. She waved enthusiastically as he turned back indoors. There were the masses of cardboard and polystyrene wrappings from the kitchen unit carcases, awaiting collection by the re-cycling people. There was the mound of old, tangled wiring, waiting for collection by the scrap metal merchant. There were the remains of the old kitchen units, which she really wouldn't miss at all. Before she entered the house, she waved to Sandra from the choir, nodding emphatically yes, she would definitely be at the church hall for choir practice on Thursday. Definitely.

Jane sniffed as she entered the hallway: dusty but dry. No sign of damp.

Victor was ahead of her, picking up tools and putting them down, looking at dust-coated packets and reading instructions.

She turned into the dining room. Everything was almost as she had left it, undisturbed under her old bed sheets. The dining room wiring had been stripped out and the room had yet to be re-wired. The old-fashioned up-lighters on the walls had been removed. It would all have to be re-plastered, she thought. In the living-room, a space had been kept clear, where the boys could sit in the evenings, if they wanted, but they appeared not to be using the room at all. The vacuum cleaner was half full in the centre of the room. They'd clearly been keeping the place as clean as they could. Yes, they were quite right, Victor and Jane would have found it far too hard to stay in the house while the ground floor was being done.

And now she looked at her new kitchen. 'Oh, it's French Grey. Oh, how lovely. I didn't think it could look so... lovely.' She gulped air.

Victor was behind her. 'And it's only a cheap one, too. People don't keep their old kitchens nowadays. It's amazing what you can do when you have a good fitter, eh Paul? See? I told you so.'

'Yes, you did,' she said. 'I was wrong, and I apologise. I thought you could keep the old kitchen, which obviously you couldn't. It's wonderful. I love all those spotlights. They will make cooking such a pleasure.'

'And it's all been re-designed. Peter hasn't started on the tiling yet. He learnt tiling back at the base, didn't you, Peter? He says he's really good at it. Here. Take the catalogue. He wants you to choose the tiles. He says he can make ten-pence chip-shop tiles look like a million dollars. So, you've got nothing to worry about. All that worry. For nothing, Jane. Wait 'til you see the bathroom. The shower's big enough to get in with me and the dog, not that we have a dog yet, but we might, you never know. The bath shop had it on a special. I love that square showerhead.'

She stood in the doorway to the bathroom. Some inexplicable fear surfaced. 'No bath? I do like my soak in the bath, Victor. You know that.'

'Oh phooey, Jane. Nobody has a bath nowadays. Baths use far too much water. It's a Roman shower, really smart, with different shower fittings and we got it for a third of the price. I love that colander shower head and look at all that grey-tinted glass. And look at this smashing bathroom cabinet. Wave your hand under it and it lights up like a doxy's dressing-table.'

Paul was behind them. 'I too love glass,' he murmured, 'shatter-proof glass. Quite safe if you fall against it, you know.'

Jane stepped back into the hallway quickly. She looked up the stairs. The attic door was shut, the swirly patterned orange stair carpet was as clean as it could be on a building-site. That would have to be replaced. The colours in the house were all wrong now. The stairs would look nice in light grey.

She passed her cool hand across her flushed cheek. 'When do you think it will all be finished? When can we come home again? It's getting quite hard living in the shack on the towans, quite dreary in this weather. The kitchen is terrible, it's indescribable. I can't cook properly there.'

'Well, you will be able to cook properly soon, eh, men? All over the world, there are people with no oven, just one gas burner and a charcoal fire in a pit. These boys know all about that, don't you, chaps?'

Peter nodded, then looked at the floor. Paul scowled and nodded at the doorway to the porch. The pair stood shoulder to shoulder and said no more. It was the signal for Victor and Jane to go. The visit was over already.

'I'd like us to have a date when we could move in again, though,' Jane said. 'Something to work towards. So, Roy knows when he will be getting his key back. It's only fair to Roy. He may have other lettings for the chalet.'

Paul looked thoughtful. He seemed to be calculating. 'I think, probably, the end of the month. I can finish off the kitchen and bathroom, then you can move into your bedroom. The dining room and our dormer bedroom will take a little more time. They are only small things to be done, like the alarms. We can hurry it up and get the certificate first.' He smiled, a quick smile which wiped itself clear in an instant. 'I know people. I will arrange it.'

A Splendid First Day Cover

Victor paid over his £12.50 and Roy slid the long-awaited packet of double-dated First Day Covers celebrating Brexit under the bullet-proof glass shield and through the coin tray.

Victor snatched it up. 'Look at this little beauty,' he said to Roy. 'Great artwork. Should be worth a fortune in a very few years' time. A historical landmark. I don't know why you won't collect these yourself. You're in the best position never to miss one of them. Better than money in a post-office savings account, I can tell you.'

Roy laughed. 'I think I see enough books of stamps from Monday to Friday. I'm glad they come up to expectation, though,' he said. 'Me, no, I can't see anything in it myself.'

'What, collecting?'

Victor was still taking in the beauty of the little treasure when Roy strolled around to the parcels hatch and opened the stable door. There were no customers in the post office and card shop. It was mid-week. Pensions had all been collected and apart from the odd Amazon parcel to weigh and put in the bag, there was little to do. They were in a lull before the mad Christmas rush.

'Put those things away safely, come over here and have a chat,' Roy said. 'I've barely seen you since your wife handed back the keys to the chalet. I wanted to ask how you are doing with your Israelis.'

'Who?'

Victor looked up sharply.

'Your Israeli guests. The boys who are fixing up your bungalow.'

A stab of pain flashed through Victor's chest and was gone as soon as it came. It left him puzzled.

'They're not Israelis, Roy.'

'No?'

'No.' Victor paused. A cold wave started to flow from his feet to his chest. With his elbows, he leaned on the counter. 'Why do you think so? They're asylum seekers, like I told you. We don't know quite where they're from. We don't ask. It's not protocol to ask. They destroy their passports, you see. Terrible business. They don't want to be sent back to wherever they came from, back to wars and retributions. Always living in fear. We don't know the half of it, in this safe country.'

Victor looked down to his purchase, the patriotic flag, the large photo-portrait of the Prime Minster, with his name in large upper-case lettering running vertically down the envelope. This issue would sit very well with the 'You Made Britain Great Again' collector's piece with Margaret Thatcher's portrait, now costing £45 to buy. Strangely, my collection comforts me, he thought. It confirms who I am. I never thought of it that way before.

Roy said, 'Oh well. Only, they were in here the other day, speaking Modern Hebrew.' Roy thought about it. 'It could have been Romanian, but no, it was Hebrew, definitely.'

This was like a hammer-blow to Victor.

'What makes you so certain? It must have been Romanian. Or Arabic.'

'No, it couldn't have been Arabic. I can't speak it, but I'd recognise it.'

What had begun as a casual enquiry now had the overtones of a quarrel.

'Victor, they were speaking Hebrew.'

'Well go on then, how do you know?' Victor found himself digging his fingers and thumbs in, clinging on to the counter.

Roy tried conciliation. He didn't really want to go on with this. 'Look, Victor, the origins of your guests are not my business. They were speaking Hebrew, not as foreigners to the language, but as second or third generation native speakers, OK? That's all I can tell you.'

'Yes, but how do you know, Roy? You're not Jewish, are you?'

Roy hesitated. He looked into the distance. 'All right. Since you ask, as it seems important to you, when I was a lad, my father left the Royal Navy. He'd been passed over for promotion and he felt he'd had enough. He retired to Suffolk, where property was cheaper, and we lived there. It was very different from Havant, it was unbearably quiet. I was only a teenager, and I felt I was missing out. I wanted adventure, but I didn't want to go to sea like my father. In those days, you used to be able to go and work on a kibbutz. I already had some experience with haymaking and fruit picking on the farms close to home. The Israelis were building their country, and they didn't mind that you weren't Jewish. They just wanted to get their settlements, and their agriculture established. They needed hands. I had a great time for a few years, and then I came home, that's all.'

'So, you'd recognise the lingo.'

'Yes, I would, and I did. As surely as somebody living in England would recognise English.'

This felt like betrayal, but Victor had to say it: 'All right, Roy, so do you remember what they were saying? Were they talking about us?'

'As I remember it, they were having a bit of an argument. They were all but whispering, but my microphone was on. I couldn't hear everything they were saying, though by the time I realised what language it was, it was all over. It was something about a primer. They used the English word primer, like they do.'

A cool wave of relief. Victor let go of the counter. 'A primer? Oh, that's all right. That will be about my painting the house after they've finished. Oh, that's fine, but they don't have to buy my primer or undercoat, I can do that. You had me worried for a minute. I thought… I don't know what I thought.' He shook his head and checked his watch. 'Lunchtime. Jane and the boys will be waiting. It's a hottie today. They never start without me. I'll be off.'

'Yes, and I must close up for an hour.' Roy came into the shop and followed Victor to the door. He put up his hand to slide the heavy bolts to. 'Can't be too careful, sub post offices get robbed these days,' he said. 'Sawn-off shotguns and that sort of thing. We must go fishing on the rocks, one night, Victor: catch some bass. Bass is a very expensive fish nowadays. Time was, you could just lean down and pick one up out of the sea. Not anymore.' He paused. 'Look, it wasn't Romanian. They do speak it there in Israel, but I don't know why I said it could have been. I must have been dreaming. It wasn't.'

'Well, makes no odds,' Victor said. 'Who cares? Mystery solved.'

Roy watched Victor cross the road and scurry home.

Lunch was fish and chips, straight from the chip-shop, served on a new oilcloth and tablemats on the dining-room table, because Jane remembered that Peter's mother had an oilcloth.

Peter looked around the room. 'Still plenty left to do in here,' he said. 'Paul can do the plastering. He's good at that, aren't you, Paul? Paul was best at plastering. You and I can do the scratch coat, Victor, and Paul can do the skimming.'

Victor let Peter go on about plastering to Jane, then he said, as casually as he could make it sound, 'So, where did you learn to do the plastering, Paul? It takes a lot of practice, I understand.'

'We could just go over it with Artex, or we could do it properly, first tank the wall, plasterboard and plaster. It's up to you,' Paul said.

'A plastered wall would look the best,' Jane said. 'Artex, no. No no no. Not in my lovely new house. Not now we've got this far with it, with the beautiful kitchen and bathroom and all. I hate this old Anaglypta wallpaper.'

'Oh, I'm not so sure about covering up the walls, not in a mundic house,' Victor said. 'You have to keep watching for damp in a mundic house. You don't want to hide the damp and then find out that a problem manifests itself suddenly, perhaps years down the road.'

'Damp? Oh yes, you and your mundic again. It has to be tanking, plasterboard and plaster.' Paul screwed up the newspaper with the remains of his fish batter, chips and mushy peas and hurled it all high up against the chimneybreast. The parcel of food burst and scattered across the room. He made no move to get up.

Peter got to his feet and began to collect the rubbish. 'Where are your manners, you lout? He has no manners. It's his childhood. He lived in a warehouse. Say you're sorry to these people. He has no manners, Jane, Victor. Sometimes, he flips, he goes a little mad. He's a bit crazy, after all he's been through. Go for a walk, Paul. You will feel better after you go for a walk.'

Victor looked down at his own hands, his broad gold wedding-ring, his once neatly trimmed nails now rough with neglect and attempts at DIY. Cowed into silence, Victor said to himself. Cowed into silence and the big, big question avoided.

Paul fished out a last cigarette and a lighter from his pocket. He lit up casually, stretching out his legs, flipping the packet across the table and on to the floor. He'd never smoked in the house before, never in front of the Everleys.

Victor and Jane continued to sit at the table, stunned, not exchanging a glance, while Peter got a dustpan and brush and busied himself with the noisy vacuum cleaner.

'Would you get an ashtray, dear?' She said to Peter quietly, when at last he turned off the machine. 'You'll find one in the glass cabinet.'

Her voice was trembling.

Paul Is Dangerous

'He's dangerous,' Jane said. 'He's unpredictable. I don't like it.'

Victor eased his grip on the steering wheel for a moment. Not knowing what her feelings were, he was not going to mention the violent incident with Paul and was relieved when she did.

'I'm more interested in who they are and where they're from. Something Roy said to me the other day. And Paul only flipped his lid when I asked him where he learned his trade. He may not be who he says he is.'

Jane turned down the blower on the dashboard. 'Who does he say he is, Victor? Has he ever said where he comes from? I don't mind Peter, but I don't like that Paul. I don't think there's anything wrong with Peter. But we can't get rid of Paul without Peter, just because of what Paul has turned out to be like. No, that wouldn't be fair. I don't think Peter would stay without him, and Paul's the electrician, anyway.'

The car was swishing down the road in the rain. They only had a few minutes to have this urgent conversation before they arrived at the church hall and Jane's choir practice.

'I'd get rid of the pair of them for two pins, tonight, and get a proper builder to finish off.'

Jane visibly relaxed. She sat back in her seat, watching the wipers sweep to and fro. 'Not in this weather, Victor. They've done the wiring; we're only waiting for the electrician to sign it all off. We're nearly there. Let's give it a few more days, then they're done. Then let's just get rid of them as soon as we can, when they've finished the dining room. Doesn't matter about the dormer bedroom. We never used it, anyway.'

'That reminds me. I must have a look at the dormer, if they'll let me. They never seem to want me up there.' He was speaking almost to himself.

Victor brought the car to a halt outside the church. He kissed her cheek. 'I'll pick you up at nine. I'd best get back and see what Paul's up to. I don't trust them in the house these days. I'll check the Japanese prints when I get back, make sure they're all there.

Have a good singsong with the ladies. Blow out the cobwebs. I'll make a mug of cocoa later.'

'I'll have a dark chockie bickie. Two.' She laughed and waved.

The old spark has returned, Victor thought. A refurbished house done practically free of charge and new decorations to come. Nothing can stop us now.

Awkward. Monica, the barmaid at the Yacht Club had come to choir practice. That nonsense with Victor and the accusation that he'd called her a wog still seemed raw and unresolved to Jane. She could not help but notice that Monica waved quickly and just looked down to her music case, avoiding Jane's eye.

Monica was one of the few who always chatted with her at choir practice. She'd discovered quite quickly that the women in the choir were a dreadfully insular group. During tea-break, they regularly looked straight through her.

Their choice of songs was very peculiar as well. They'd had to learn *Myfanwy* in Welsh, by rote, because only the choir mistress spoke Welsh. She wondered what Portuguese Monica made of it. She quite liked *Trelawny*: they always began with that.

Then there was the chorus, *Kernow, Kernow y keryn Kernow*, something about the darkness of mines and waves of the sea and Arthur, of course. Very nationalist. Now, because it was nearly Christmas, it was Thomas Merritt Carols. She wondered at times whether she'd joined the wrong choir. This old parish organist's carols were supposed to be sung all over the world, but she'd never heard of them.

It was all up-hill work, and she would have given it up if it wasn't for the fact that she had so little to do in Portmarrow, and it gave her a break from Victor for a regular couple of hours a week. The trouble with Victor was, he thought life was all for him and all about him, and it really wasn't. It really wasn't.

As Jane struggled through the soprano lines, she thought, at break, I'm going to cross over to the altos and I'm going to be decent to Monica, let her know that I'm by no means a racist like my husband.

Break-time came, and before allowing herself to hesitate, Jane made a beeline for Monica, who was also left alone by the locals. She thought Monica looked relieved that someone had come over to talk to her.

'Hello, Monica,' Jane said. 'And before I say anything else, I just want to say how sorry I am that my husband made a stupid racist remark to you. I can't excuse him but if I know Victor, he would have said it without thinking. He really doesn't understand much about people's feelings sometimes.'

Monica laughed. 'Oh that. I was really surprised and embarrassed about it. I only just happened to say to somebody that Victor Everley told me I speak English well for a wog. I didn't know what a wog was. I didn't know you can't say that. The Commodore made such a fuss about it. I'm sure Victor isn't a racist.'

'And now he's resigned, not only from being Treasurer but he's handed in his membership altogether. Just when I'd got used to going over there for lunch.'

'Really? Oh, I feel really bad now. I shouldn't have said anything. It wasn't I who complained.'

'I'm sure it wasn't you, Monica. These men. So, how are things at the Yacht Club?'

Monica shook her head slightly and looked into the distance. 'Oh, you know, the same. I should think about moving on, really. Nothing much going on. Such a little town.'

With such little people in it, Jane thought. 'You know what?' She said, 'We're having our bungalow refurbished, I'm having a new kitchen and dining room and when everything is done, we're going to invite you to dinner. I'm sure Victor would be glad to see you. We haven't made many friends here.' She looked around at the Cornish women chatting. 'They're so… they're so insular. They all went to school together, you know, and we're from up-country as they call it.'

Jane fished out her coffee flask from her music-case. Jane noticed the short, dark hairs on Monica's arms, the brown moles and olive skin.

'I'm not just a waitress and bar staff,' Monica said suddenly. 'I am from an old family. My ancestors were adventurers and then we were in India, and they were all nobles because of their strong loyalty to the king. We all speak fluent English very well, all of my family. My great-grandmother was a Braganza. I just wanted an adventure abroad, but I've stayed here a long time.' Monica looked as though she was about to cry.

'Is that so?' said Jane. 'Well, I never. I'm sure Victor will be very sorry for what he said, when he knows who your great-grandmother was.'

Victor Fishing

'No, not like that. Look, if you just stick a prawn on the hook, as soon as you cast it will fly off. Come here. Your weight is too light, Victor. This float will just lie flat on the surface. Let me set you up.'

In the twilight, the jumping, pulsing prawn slipped from Victor's grasp. He looked on in despair while Roy set the depth for Victor's float with beads and weights and what looked like elastic knotted several times over and tied off in Roy's front teeth.

'We want to be three feet under the surface.'

Victor was shivering already. On a thirty-foot ledge, trussed up in a lifejacket, he was out of his environment. It was dark. There were strange lights in the sky and over the sea. Shag Rock was a great looming, bird-muttering presence. He wished he was home having a cup of cocoa. If he wanted a bass, he could always buy one from the fish monger. Those live prawns in Roy's plastic pot were all a sickly grey, not pink. Everything was stinking of seaweed. He'd had no idea they had to collect live bait from under the pontoon first, before they set out for the rocks. He'd got his sleeves soaking wet, doing that. They were dripping cold. One thing I've learnt about myself tonight, he thought, I'm a city boy, the little man in the bowler hat. Through and through.

'This is the best time, after a storm.' From the cliff ledge, the surf was growling, huge, rough and luminous. Roy consulted his tide tables in the light of his phone again. 'We're on an incoming tide, two hours after low tide, Victor, right? Up here like this, we won't have to move the gear back. This is the best time, I tell you, only we're a bit late. Pity we've had to set up in the near-dark, but that's OK, we're nearly done now.' Roy laughed. 'This time of the year, we'll get you a really big bass to take home, eh, Vic? Jane and those Israeli boys will be pleased. Anything under 50cms we throw back, all right? All right, agreed. Now listen, if it's a bass, you'll get a thump on the line. If the line runs out fast, you reel in fast. Sometimes they start swimming towards you.'

'What do I do now?'

'Now? Settle down and wait.'

Settle down and wait. That was retirement. He wished Roy wouldn't call them Israelis. They couldn't be Israelis. Couldn't be Palestinians, not with Peter's blue eyes. Mid-Europeans. What did it matter? The boys had certainly livened up the winter for himself and Jane, that's for sure, but Victor would be glad when it was all over, the work done, and they could settle back down into their old routine, sausages and beans and fried bread in the kitchen. Never again, he thought. No more moving, no more painting and decorating. No more blinking wiring. Never.

'How long will we be out here, Roy?'

'Oh, four hours, maybe, unless we get really really lucky.'

Really really lucky. Mother always said I was lucky. Lucky to get into the grammar school, lucky to get into the accountant's office, lucky to pass the accountancy exams, just lucky to pass the CSI exams. Unbelievably lucky to be a Chartered Secretary at London Bridge. Not hardworking, no, no acknowledgement for that, nor for my choosing a good wife to pay the bills while I studied at night and kept working my way up. Not hardworking nor even clever, no, God forbid that, but lucky, just lucky, lucky like a Bingo player. Lucky.

Mother had been dead some twenty years, but still the old rage haunted him, even here, when he was supposed to be enjoying himself out fishing for bass with Roy at night.

Roy turned on his headlamp to give Victor a lesson in fishing from the rocks. 'All right, so we'll have a look at the bait while we're waiting. Nice, long piece of squid here. Making sure the hooks are well clear. Prawn on the end to wriggle about.'

Victor looked away as Roy pushed the line up the prawn's tail end and cast expertly.

That was it, Victor thought. That was what life was. A line up your rear end, all set up, wriggling around as somebody's bait, cast off into the dark, three feet below the surf. A sprat to catch a mackerel, a prawn and a bit of squid to catch a bass. That was what it was all about. But he'd survived it all. Survived to wriggle away, all the way down to Portmarrow, his little backwater, his little rockpool to hide from the treacherous world of pike and things.

There was sheet lightening, far out to sea. Once, Victor thought it lit up a cargo vessel steaming away on the horizon in the dark. Or was he dreaming? On the next flicker of light, he saw only empty, moving and shifting water.

'Tide's coming up nicely. There's a little bit of wash. Let's hope we'll get some fishing soon. So, this live bait will go on this smaller hook. It will be swimming around there like this, then your bass will come along like that, eat the bait and get hooked on the bigger hook. See?'

Victor saw. He seemed to see it all now, with perfect vision, the live bait, the little fish and the big fish. But that was not the whole story, because now he was here at Portmarrow and he was in the moment and he was retired, yes retired. He felt a momentary surge of joy. Retired from that London life of little fish and big fish.

'… and we might have trouble keeping the bait out at that distance. What we've got at the moment is a big pull… might have to shorten the cast…there now, what fish could resist that?'

The live bait, the little hook and the big hook, Victor thought. What fish could resist that? He thought of the homeless men in his bungalow, stateless, forced to do a complete re-wire for just a place to stay for a week or two. Just a matter of luck. Homelessness, statelessness could happen to anybody. Nothing was what you might call fair. He felt pride, yes pride, that he was able to do something for them, send them on their way having done a small something for them, let them stay for a while, in exchange for a complete re-wire of the house. Britain had taken them in, and he had housed them, just for a while. He must have a look at the dormer room, see what they were up to there, only they always seemed so reluctant. Perhaps they were untidy. Without a woman to tidy up after them, they would be. Could you ever expect the homeless to be tidy people? What sort of homes would they have come from?

Victor guessed they'd been there hours and hours. The sheet lightening had long ceased. He hadn't worn his watch in case it got soaked or got lost. Roy was out there in the gloom, fiddling about with his rods. The float had gone down again suddenly. Roy was up on his feet and reeling in. Now he came striding back to Victor. 'Another dogfish. I'll throw it back. You can increase the bait size or increase the hook size, but if all we get is dogfish… we'll pack it in and go home. Four dogfish in the last four casts. That's all we'll get now. Forget it for tonight.'

'Really? Can't you eat dogfish?' The sizeable fish was curling up into a ball. This was all new to Victor.

'Dogfish? It's what they call rock salmon.' Roy laughed. 'You know, what you get in your fish and chips around here. I'm not staying out on the rocks half the night to catch that, Vic.' He began packing up to leave.

He wouldn't let anybody else call him Vic. Roy had done it twice. That was taking advantage. Once you let people do that, your dignity and respect were gone. Fled. He should have said something, but the moment was past. Now he feared he would forever be Vic.

So, Who Are They?

'No. Absolutely not, Jane.'

'Oh well, have it your own way. It's just, I thought, well, what with Monica having so few friends, and with our new French Grey kitchen, it would be nice to entertain her a bit, when the kitchen's up and running properly. Nothing fancy, you know, just bass *en croute*, especially if you'd caught it yourself. Nobody speaks to her at choir practice, you know.'

'I'm not surprised.'

'What?'

They were approaching Als an Marrow, looking down towards Fisherman's Cove, far below them. Victor wondered whether this place had a name. What was the rock formation? Dolomite and Devonian shale? How bereft of seabirds it was here, he thought, not like that place near Filey, where it was like a Hong

Kong for birds, with gulls and kittiwake and puffins and goodness knows what else.

'There ought to be more seabirds here, Jane.'

'Please don't change the subject, Victor.'

They stopped walking and faced each other. Perhaps it was because of the stinging wind in their faces and the sudden gusts that threatened to take them off the cliff if they got any closer to the edge, that they were both irritated. Having to walk on the tarmac road made the excursion irksome. In the summer, they'd seen an adder move off a rock and slide into the heather as they approached on the unmade track. It had all been so leisured, so full of wildlife. In early December, the seascape seemed leaden, the clouds too low, the clifftops empty.

Several yards behind them, Peter and Paul also stopped walking, sat down on the verge and lit cigarettes, putting their heads close together and cupping their hands so that the flame of the lighter didn't go out.

'All they need is a pair of AK-47s to look the part.' The words were out of Victor's mouth before he thought twice about it. He should not have said it and was immediately contrite.

'Oh Victor, don't be so daft.' Jane laughed and began to walk on. 'Shall we wait for them to catch up? Anyway, I want to know why you are so against having Monica to dinner. We don't know many people here either. It's not easy to make friends in a new place. Not easy at all. If I had known.'

Victor put up the hood and pulled the toggles on his royal blue Berghaus waterproof jacket. 'It might rain. I felt a few drops a minute ago. Look.' He gasped. 'Let's just pause a minute. I want to tell you something.'

Victor wanted to say, I think I have heart trouble. I just can't keep up like I used to. My knees want to buckle, and I want to sit down. Instead, he said, 'Look.' He swallowed hard to stop himself from gasping again. 'Cast your mind back to the London Bridge office. There was practically nothing I could tell you about it. All those times you said over dinner, "What sort of a day have you had?" I couldn't say anything, could I? Like every other Chartered Secretary, I was bound by a code and I still am. All of that still applies today, Jane.'

Jane took a tissue out of her pocket and wiped her eyes. 'I thought you loved the yacht club. You really enjoyed going there. And when you resigned, I could hardly believe it. You loved the place, Victor.'

'I can only say that I am bound by confidentiality, by a code of practice and I can't have that woman in my house for dinner.'

'But what has she done? God, you're so stuffy sometimes. It doesn't matter if you did call her a wog. She's forgotten all about it. She didn't know what the word meant anyway, and she wasn't at all upset. It looks worse if you won't have her over now. It looks like you really are a racist, like the Commodore said you were.'

'Oh, he did, did he? It's all coming out now.'

'Well, yes, he did, Victor. He told Monica what the word meant when she asked him. But she didn't mind. She knew you didn't mean anything by it.'

They stopped talking. Still a few yards behind them, Peter and Paul loitered on the verge of the road. Were they interested in the view? The cars passing? Victor thought not. Why were they always there, just out of earshot? Why was Peter wearing Jane's old Trespass waterproof? And weren't those Jane's deck shoes on his feet? Talk about taking over.

There was a lull in the wind. Victor said, 'Listen. There are good reasons why I resigned my membership of the club and gave up the treasurership. I must think about my own probity, and I cannot have that woman in my house. That's all I'm going to say on the matter.'

'Oh well. And why were you accused of racism? When you are so clearly not a racist. Peter and Paul can attest to that. She's a nice woman, quite lonely, and she comes from a good Portuguese family, she told me.'

Victor stared across the bay to the white line of St Ives.

'I still can't have her in the house. Sorry.'

Jane walked on, Victor behind her, struggling to keep up. And behind them both, Peter and Paul.

When they got to the top of the rise and around the bend in the road, Victor's pace picked up. The headland and the bay opened before them.

'I know,' he said. 'Let's give them the slip by going down onto the ledge.'

'That's mean, Victor.'

'I know it is. Come on. Be a sport.'

She followed him through the heather, down the tiny hidden pathway to a broad, grassy ledge. This was their secret little picnic spot. The road was above them, the sea far below. Out of the wind, it was a safe and secure nest for humans. Victor scanned the empty cliffs for seabirds. Nothing. He handed the binoculars to Jane.

'Her mother was a Braganza.'

'What?'

Victor had been thinking how elemental it all was here. Should have moved here years ago. All those years in that office overlooking the street, pieces of newspaper blowing up and down, blowing around in circles, stuck in the grille below the window. And yet. . .

'That's what she says. Monica. Her mother was a Braganza.'

'Really? Who's that when she's at home?'

Victor unhitched Jane's little haversack. She sat back against it, using it as a pillow. 'A little snackette, Jane? It must be lunchtime by now.'

'Oh, all right, but we've only just got here. Don't you want to keep them for later?'

'Bags I get the ham and mustard. You can have the egg and cress.'

'Thank you, Victor.'

They busied themselves with the sandwiches, re-folding greaseproof paper, settling down with coffee from the flask. Above them, a car went by, then they heard Peter and Paul sauntering past, chatting, their words snatched away by gusts of wind.

The day melted into seascape, with murmurings of surf on rocks far below. Undefined thoughts and memories drifted in and out of Victor's mind. A huge cloud-shadow drifted over a mercurial grey and silver ocean.

Only the suffering is real.

This thought came and went. Its voice was so clear, Victor wondered whether Jane had said it to him just then; but Jane, lulled by the sounds of the sea and the warmth of the sun, was drifting off into sleep.

Strange things, thoughts. They came and went in secrecy, leaving no trace.

Minutes later, Jane sat up straight to see Victor listening intently, both hands cupped to his ears. Above them, Peter and Paul were rushing up and down the road, shouting something in a language neither had heard before, clearly panicked.

'They're looking for us. They've lost us.' Jane moved to get up.

'No, stay where you are. They're frantic because they think we're missing. Why?' Whispering, Victor grasped and held on to her arm.

'Come on, Victor. This is stupid. We shouldn't be hiding from our guests, after all they've done for us. We'll look silly when they catch us. And we'll look selfish, eating and drinking while they're up there looking for us. They'll be thinking we've slipped and fallen over the edge.'

Victor continued to listen intently.

'You're hurting my arm, Victor.'

Victor let her go. She left the ledge, walked rapidly up into the wind, up the pathway through the heather, waving and calling, leaving Victor to re-pack the rucksack with the remains of the sandwiches, the flask and the litter.

By the time he got back to the road, the three of them were well ahead of him, laughing, making their way back down towards Portmarrow, Peter's arm around Jane's shoulders.

Victor took his time to get back to the house. It seemed to him that Paul kept looking back to make sure that he had not slipped away again. And what language was that? The panicked language they used when they thought they had lost Victor and Jane? Was it Hebrew, as Roy said? Of all the languages, was it really Hebrew they had in common? All of it made less and less sense. What were they doing in the attic? He hadn't been up there for weeks. If only they went out at the same time, he could go and investigate properly.

He moved on down the hill at his own pace and arrived in time for tea. The three of them were arranged around the dining-room table, drinking the Earl Grey and eating the saffron buns that he'd picked up from the bakery yesterday for his wife. Peter's chair was jammed up against Jane's and the boy still had his arm around her shoulders. He'd formed a habit lately, uncorrected by her, of calling her, Mama.

Victor was handed the last, misshapen bun.

'So, what have you been up to? Did you stop off somewhere? Did you stop at the shop?' Paul seemed anxious to know.

'We were about to send a search party.' Jane seemed to be laughing at him. He poured his own tea into the cup with the chip.

'So,' Victor said, from his corner of the table. 'Are there a lot of people fleeing from Israel, then?'

The effect was electric. Paul did not move. He sat frozen for a few seconds, taking in the question. Peter removed his arm from Jane.

'Fleeing? What makes you say that, Victor?' Peter was speaking in a new, small voice.

Paul, the first to recover, leaned forward. 'Well, no, Victor. Why should they? Israel is a great country, I've heard. Everybody wants to live in Israel. I understand.'

'So, they don't want to leave, in order to avoid conscription or something like that?'

'Conscription? The army? Well, I think the Palestinians, they cause trouble all the time. They breed like rats and tunnel under the fences that they build to keep them out. Well, a lot of them come into Israel to work and go home again, you know.' Peter looked as though this was a preamble to a long explanation. He was shut down with a grimace by Paul.

'Why do you ask that question, Victor?' Paul leaned forward.

'As if we would know anything about it.' Peter leaned forward.

'Yes, why would you ask Peter and Paul that question, Victor?' Jane seemed concerned, more than puzzled.

'Oh, I don't know,' Victor said, with a pleasant smile. 'Look at the Irish, now. Where do they come from? You know, Birmingham, Guildford, the band stand, all the pretty horses.' He took his cup to the sink in the kitchen and threw the contents down the drain. He raised his voice, so that they could hear clearly. 'A continuous assault on England and the English, I understand.'

Victor heard Jane's chair scrape on the floor as she crossed the dining room and strode down the hall. She came up close to him, a snarl twisting her face. 'What do you mean by that? You embarrass me, you embarrass yourself all the time. Will you stop all this racism?'

Victor leaned against the sink. 'I don't know. I don't know what I mean by it.'

I just want this to be over, he thought. I don't want this to be what I think it is.

A shadow covered the doorway, obscuring all the light from the hall. It was Paul, standing there, four-square. 'We'll finish the dining room and go,' he said quietly. 'We'll go before Christmas.'

'No, no, stay. Victor is not well. He doesn't know what he is saying sometimes, do you, Victor? I'll make you another cup, Victor. It's his heart. Sit down in the chair.' Jane began fussing around him.

Peter looked over Paul's shoulder at Victor and Jane standing at the new stainless sink.

Victor to the attic

Victor said nothing to Jane, who was fiddling about with the breakfast dishes. As soon as he heard the front door close, he went up the stairs and pushed the attic door wide open.

Peter was kneeling on the bare floor, re-winding some cable. 'Yes?'

Victor stood on one foot in the doorway. 'Oh, Peter, I just came up to ask how you were doing. I heard the door go, you see.'

Peter got to his feet. Inside a packed duffel bag, a mobile phone rang once, then stopped.

'You have a phone. I didn't know you had a phone.'

'It's Paul's phone, to contact to his mother. What can I do for you?'

Victor thought hard. Why was he here? To spy on them. 'It's just about a few things. The noise.'

'It'll save a bomb, Victor.'

'What will?' It was hot and oppressive up here in the roof, with the heating full on.

'Oh, I know it will, but if I might say so, Peter, my wife worries about what you two are doing up here.'

'We're wiring, Victor.'

'Fact is, she lies awake at night thinking and worrying about what you might be up to.'

'Up to? We're rewiring, Victor, like we said we were. Rewiring the house for you, free of charge, because of your generosity to us, letting us stay.'

'Yes but, there's cable everywhere. Holes drilled in the walls. You need to be careful. Mundic block just crumbles away, when disturbed.'

'No crumbling away here, Victor. Sound as a bell. Safe as houses, as you keep saying.'

'Jane worries, you see. She has heart trouble. High blood pressure, enlarged heart, you know how it is with women. She thinks the world of you both. By the way, what is this?'

'Sorry, what is what?'

'This cake of beige stuff, Peter. Says, 'Semtex H.'

'Semtex H? Oh that. Says inert/faux. Replica. Says realistic training saves lives. It's soap, Victor. Soap on a rope. Novelty soap. Have a look in the en-suite. You'll see some hanging in the shower. Can you just move aside a minute, while I use the drill? Sorry, I didn't mean to push you aside. You all right? It might get a bit dusty. Take one of the paper masks. Dust is no good for the old lungs.'

'Thank you. That's another thing. A thin film of dust everywhere downstairs. Jane doesn't want to mention it, but it gets on her nerves, having to clean it up all the time. She's had to take all her glass animals out of the cabinet and wash them.'

'Well, you know what they say, Victor. If you want omelettes, you have to crack eggs. This job won't take long. We'll be finished and gone in no time at all. Tell her not to bother with dusting at this point.'

'What is all this orange putty?'

'Putty? Oh, that's Paul again. He loves his clay. He makes models and things with it, a bit childish. He's just a big kid, is Paul. You'll have to forgive. The man never had a childhood. He's got some in our little fridge here. Keeps him stable. If you don't mind, Victor, I'll have to crack on, before Paul comes back from the post office. We're stepping out later for a breath of air. Will Jane be wanting any shopping? We don't have much, but what we've got is yours. Where would we be without you? Shivering in an abandoned warehouse, that's where. Paul was only saying, a few hours ago…'

'You're welcome. You're very welcome here, Peter. Never let it be said we have any prejudice against foreigners or the stateless. Nonetheless, Jane will be glad when you've finished up. That's all I can say.'

'Won't be long now, Victor. Can you organise a cup of coffee? The Taylors is really smooth. I don't like that instant any more than you do. Any Taylors left over? Tricky, dusty work, this.'

Victor sat down on the neatly made bed. 'I notice, your English has come along very well,' he said, 'with a lot of idioms lately. I suppose you picked that up in the camp on Bodmin Moor.'

'Bodmin Moor, here and there. I have plenty time to learn. Jane teaches me.'

It seemed to Victor that Peter's accent was slipping again into something foreign, now that he had been reminded.

'Yes, my wife is very generous.'

There was a pause.

'Coffee, Victor?'

'Coffee. I'll have to ask you to come down if you want coffee. I'm not so steady on the stairs with trays. Where's Paul?'

'Gone to post office, as I told you.'

'Collecting benefits, I suppose.'

'Benefit? Your government doesn't give us any money. Your government gives money to you, not to us.'

'Ah, now that's where I have to differ with you, Peter. We go to work to pay for our pensions in this country. Nothing is free.'

'Except your wiring. Your new wiring is free.'

Victor got to his feet abruptly. 'Paul tells me that you will be finished on Christmas morning, and you intend to leave us in the afternoon. Well, Christmas is pretty special here in Britain, which is a country that is Christian. Everything will be shut up. No transport, no shops. I don't know where you're going, but you must stay and share our Christmas meal with us. You've done so much for us.'

'And you have done so much for us, Victor.'

Horrible little bastard, Victor thought. Creepy little foreign turd.

Another Explosion on the Tele

It was the first item on the news.

Jane was sitting in her chair under a reading lamp, manipulating four knitting needles, crafting a heel back into Victor's heavy hiking socks. It was some time since she had attempted any knitting, and she was uncertain about how to get the heel right.

Victor was listening very carefully.

'... a massive gas explosion which has completely blown out the whole front of the shop. The street has been cordoned off and we are asked to stay behind the police barriers in case there are any devices in the building. It is not yet known whether anyone was in the shop or upstairs at the time.'

Gas or devices? Devices or gas? The initial electric wave that travelled down Victor's spine now dissipated into blank, grey fear. An accident due to old gas pipes, faulty fittings or carelessness? There seemed to be a lot of explosions about, lately. Or devices? The reporter didn't know, or she wouldn't have put the two items together. Gas is gas. A device means...

'Seems to be a lot of it about lately?'

'What? Explosions?' Jane looked up.

So, she had been listening, after all. Lately, she'd been cloth-eared about anything and everything except cooking and knitting.

'There was an explosion the same night Peter first came to the door. Don't you remember, Victor? It seems such a long time ago now.'

'Was there? Oh yes. Right at the beginning of all this.'

Jane put down her knitting. 'I know you find them irksome, but they've done us proud, and I feel we owe them a nice few days before they have to go wherever they are going.'

'And where are they going, Jane?'

'I think they said, they have another job.'

'Oh? How did they achieve that?'

'Agency.' Unseen, Peter came up behind Jane's chair. 'Booked by agency. The heel is beautiful,

Mama. Like new. He bent down and kissed Jane's neck. Victor will be pleased to wear that, for hiking, won't he?' He looked up at Victor, the blue eyes blank.

Victor got up and switched off the television at the wall. 'I'd rather a new pair. Those old ones itch. You can have them, Peter. Or will they be too big for your boots?'

Jane laughed. 'Too big for your boots. Oh Victor.' She looked up at Peter, who was still behind her, leaning over her chair. 'He can be very funny. You see what I have to put up with?' She took off her reading glasses and rubbed her eyes. She handed her glasses to Peter, who wiped the lenses and put them into their case. 'Well, that's it. I'm off to bed.'

'Where's Paul? I want to bolt the doors and go to bed too.' Victor wondered whether Paul had gone out to make a discreet phone call, on a subject that he and Jane could not be party to.

'Paul? I don't know. He went out for a walk, I think?' To Victor's ears, Peter's voice had gone into squeaky mode, the tone that squeezed itself out when he was sounding cautious.

'What, at this time of night?'

'I'll wait up for him,' Jane said. 'I've plenty to do. I still have to soak the fruit overnight to make the Christmas cake tomorrow.'

'You will not. I'll wait up for him.' Victor sat down heavily in his chair again and folded his arms.

'I'll phone him, if I can get a signal.'

'Oh, you have a mobile as well, do you? You don't need a signal; you can use the land line in the hall.' That way, Victor thought, I will know the number, seeing they're not going to volunteer it. 'And by the way, I'm taking Jane up to Plymouth tomorrow. We're going to buy a few things for Christmas. My wife hasn't seen any proper shops since we moved down here.'

'Really? Tomorrow? Oh, that's lovely,' Jane said. 'We always buy each-other a surprise Christmas present, Peter. We'll have two more to buy this year, Victor. Oh, lovely. You didn't tell me we were going to Plymouth.'

'We can stop off at the Camp on Bodmin Moor on the way back,' Victor said.

'Why?' Peter's voice had recovered.

'Oh, I don't know. We can pick up the rest of your possessions. Have a look over the camp. You know.' Victor winked to Jane, who blushed and looked away.

Peter moved to the doorway. He took out his mobile and punched in a number. The phone was answered immediately. 'Paul,' he said, 'will you come home now. Victor wants to put the bolt on the doors.'

He did not wait for a reply. He snapped the phone cover shut, said goodnight and went upstairs.

Jane sat glumly staring at the wall.

'What?' Victor still had his arms folded, sitting bolt upright in his chair.

'I just wish you wouldn't be so unpleasant, Victor. They've made a lot of difference to our lives. We'll never be able to thank them enough. I find myself being piggy in the middle all the time, trying to keep the peace. You should be grateful to them. I know I am.'

Victor looked over his shoulder through the open door, glancing towards the stairs. He got up and shut the door, then spoke to her quietly. 'You just don't get it, do you? That camp for foreign nationals doesn't exist. I'd swear to it.'

Jane seemed to hold her breath. The colour drained from her face, leaving pink blotches on her neck. She spoke in a whisper. 'Yes, but. But if that should be so, and I don't believe it for a minute, that means, what else is a lie? What about our electrics, Victor? What about our wiring?'

He took hold of both her cold hands. She was ailing, he thought. How much more can she take of all this disturbance to our lives? 'Never mind the wiring. I can get a local chap to sort it all out. We could get it all re-done again if we had to. There's still enough in the bank to do it. I'm not worried about that. It's the fabric of the building that bothers me. It's only a little pebble-dashed structure made of mundic block. I don't want our bungalow to fall down. But even if it did, Jane, even if it did, we are insured. So, stop worrying. Don't worry yourself. We'll sort it out.'

She shook him off. 'I wasn't at all worried, Victor, until you said they might be telling lies about the Camp. Why should they do that? We'll have to find out, we'll have to do something about it. We can't just let them go on. You'd better be right, Victor, because this suspicion of yours is very troublesome. Very.'

Victor stood up. 'You go on to bed,' he said. 'I'll stand by the door and wait for Paul.'

To Bodmin Moor

'I hope they'll be alright.' Jane used the vanity mirror on the passenger side of the car to look back at the boys as they stood side by side in the road, Peter waving, Paul smiling his 'uptight' smile, as she had come to call it.

'They'll be alright. I've checked the Japanese prints and the cash boxes. They never touch anything. I don't know what they're interested in, but it's not our worldly goods.'

'Well, I think they just want a home, Victor, and we've certainly given that to them, for a few weeks. Home cooking, soft beds. Not bad for a pair of homeless people, talented but homeless. Still, I wish it had worked out better.'

'Meaning?'

'Meaning, I wish you could have got along better with Peter, all these weeks.'

'Yes, I wish a lot of things about them, Jane.' He switched up the windscreen wipers a notch as rain came pelting down on the already waterlogged land. 'Any rate, what am I getting for Christmas this year?'

'Not telling. You know the rule.' Jane laughed.

She loved this time of the year, Victor thought. From the time they realised they were alone in the world and no relative was going to help with anything, and they'd saved every penny, even sharing a cup of cocoa before bed, they'd let birthdays go by with some small token, but they'd honoured Christmas properly.

Even then, they'd agreed on a budget for presents. The wine she bought him to put away because it would surely mature in value, first studying the catalogues and the wine books: when would they ever say, enough, we'll drink it? What would happen to it if they just died, today, on the road, wiped out by some suicidal nutter on the by-pass? They'd both made a will, each for the other, but they'd never thought past each other's lives.

But then, wasn't that enough? The vultures would come circling soon enough. Chances were, when one died, the other would book into a nursing home, putting the little bungalow back into the auction, and nursing home fees would soon mop up any spare cash.

'Are we stopping off on the way to Plymouth or on the way back?' Jane seemed anxious about it all.

'Shopping first, cup of coffee, stop off at Jamaica Inn on the way back. How's that?'

'Won't it be too late for lunch by that time?'

'We'll get a sandwich somewhere. The main thing is, I want to stop and ask about how to get to that Camp. I can't just go blundering around the Moor without some directions.'

'You really intend to go there, then?'

'Yes, I really do. If it exists at all. And I don't think it does.'

Victor slowed down, to join the bottleneck at Three Barrows.

Jane sighed. 'I've been thinking about it half the night. I don't think they would lie to us about something which is so easily checked. I wish we'd done our homework before, though, because I feel foolish about it, especially as you've already told them you intend to go looking for the Camp. I'm rather surprised they didn't say they were coming with us today. They're normally stuck to us like barnacles.'

Victor pumped the horn at an over-taker in a flash Mercedes, who grinned and put up a pink finger. Victor dropped back a little.

'I don't know why you feel foolish, Jane. They're the ones who will be feeling foolish if their Camp can't be found. That's why they didn't want to come to Plymouth. In fact, I wondered whether they were going to say they were coming to Plymouth, and then give us the slip. You know, get on a bus and go, never to be seen again. Hooray.'

'You really can be unpleasant sometimes, can't you, Victor?' Jane slumped down and stared out of the passenger window at the rain.

The Christmas shopping ritual was more fraught than usual. Plymouth's streets were windy, cold and unfamiliar. It was difficult to find what they wanted. Then, they crossed the length of the Hoe with all their bags, only to find that their little café was closed for the winter. It was a long trek back to the carpark.

'Want to try the Barbican, Jane?'

'No, let's go on down the road to Bodmin Moor. I'm as curious as you are now, about this Camp, this Detention Centre.'

It took them an hour to get to Jamaica Inn. At Callington, Victor stopped for petrol and made enquiries. No, there was no detention centre, not on this side of the moor. Perhaps on the other side of the moor, Davidstow way, perhaps, but definitely not on this side.

At Slipperhill, two men at a farm gate said no, there's nothing around here, nothing like that, pard, and then went back to their incomprehensible conversation about a moorland pony.

At Jamaica Inn, Victor had the impression that they were being laughed at.

'Well now, let us see. Bodmin Jail used to carry out fifty public hangings in a day, but they don't do that no more now.'

Victor hated the leisurely way they talked to him, with the sly grin and the slow batting of the eyelids.

'No, they ebn done no 'angings since 1909. All that business moved to Exeter, more's the pity. We don't get none of that down 'ere now. Good for business. People used to come for miles around.'

'What do 'ee want to know for?'

'I was told a story,' Victor said, 'that there was, that is to say, is, a detention centre for young people on the moor. They go out to sell pictures and other things from there, in a minibus. They're all foreign youngsters, asylum seekers from war zones.'

'Foreigners? No, we don't want no more foreigners 'ere. We got enough foreigners already, what with all you emmets. I never 'eard of no detention centre around 'ere. Mind you, there's a lot a things go on on the Moor.'

'Ooo ess, a lot a things go on on the Moor.' They turned their backs and tried to look out of the mean little square-pane windows, misted up, spattered by blown grass and twigs.

Victor returned to the table with the orange juices. 'They're pulling my leg.'

'Who are? Those men at the bar?'

'All of them. Peter, Paul, now these village idiots.'

'Victor, stop it. Don't call people village idiots.'

'They don't know anything about a detention centre. I knew it all along. Well, I wonder what these Jew-boys will have to say for themselves now, assuming they have the brass neck to be there when we get home.'

'Jew-boys? What are you talking about, Victor?'

'Oh, something Roy said. He mentioned they were speaking Hebrew in the post-office.'

'But they couldn't be Israelis.'

'Why not? They could be bad-boy Mossad, running away.'

'Because nobody is running away from Israel. People are running to Israel.'

'Haven't I heard that somewhere before, Jane? Come on, let's go home, that's assuming we still have a home to go to.'

'Why do you say that?'

'I don't know. I don't know anything anymore, Jane.'

They said very little to each other in the car. Victor drove carefully. The road was full of traffic, people like them who had gone to bring home toys and other goods to wrap and present to others on Christmas Day. For Victor and Jane, anticipation of the Christmas rituals had now been replaced by anxiety. What was happening in the bungalow at home?

As they drove on to the waste ground beside the bungalow, unloaded their bags and stepped onto the path, the new security light snapped on. The front door opened. There was Peter, smiling with happiness to see them. Paul was behind him, grinning his grin.

'Let me carry your bags. They're heavy.'

The young men had been vacuuming and doing some feather duster work. The hall was spotless. In the dining room, two places had been set with silver from the best cutlery drawer. There was crystal, the second-best napkins and a horrible bottle of wine which had come from the Costcutters on Beach Road.

'Oh. I'm very, very touched. It's so kind of you.' There were tears in Jane's eyes. 'You've even dusted inside the glass cabinet.' The animals were twinkling and gleaming like diamonds under the new fairy lights.

'We didn't think you'd notice, but yes, there has been a lot of fine dust, as you reminded us the other day, Victor. And in the kitchen, we have a pork joint in the oven. It's been on a low setting for six hours, so it's thoroughly cooked. We thought you would like pork because everybody likes pork, eh, Victor?'

Paul was in the kitchen, wearing one of Jane's pinnies, fussing over some vegetables in a colander.

'Where did you get the joint of pork? From the freezer?'

'No, we bought it from the pork butcher down the road, Victor.'

'Where did you get the money for that?'

'I give them money,' Jane said. 'They must have some pocket-money for little personal things. Look now, they've been saving it all up to give us a lovely meal when we came home.'

She put her arms out. 'I am so grateful to you both,' she said. 'So very grateful. I never imagined you would go to so much trouble for us. I don't know what we would do without you.'

'Well, you'll certainly have to do without them after Christmas.' Victor went in search of his newspaper and found it pristine, still folded, untouched.

The front page was full of the gas explosion up north. The rest of the terrace of shops had fallen down and the fire brigade and local council were clearing up the mess. People were still not allowed back into their properties. Victor wondered why it took his imagination, why it bothered him so much, why the story filled him with dread. As he turned over the page, he realised Peter was behind him, looking over his shoulder.

'It happens,' Peter said, 'especially when weather is cold, especially up north. Old gas main pipes, you see. But there is no gas in Portmarrow. Paul is ready. Put away your paper. Dinner is served. Paul used to be a waiter in a grand hotel. He has done a lot of jobs.'

Is that right? Victor thought as he heaved himself out of his chair. I wonder how you are going to explain your way out of your non-existent Camp for young migrants on Bodmin Moor, Peter. That should be a lively piece of dinner conversation over your pork joint.

Jane allowed them to be waited on and fussed over for as long as it took to serve. Then she insisted that Peter and Paul at least sit at the table with them, and the young men were persuaded to drink a little glass of wine. More plates were warmed, and two more side-plates and knives were put out.

'And what did you have for supper?' Victor asked.

'Crackers,' Paul said.

'Crackers: that's not enough.' Jane insisted they tuck in and accept second helpings of everything.

'We stopped off on Bodmin Moor and nobody was able to enlighten us about that rather elusive Camp of yours, for young migrants,' Victor said, as soon as the first and only course was eaten. 'From Callington to Davidstow to Jamaica Inn, nobody had even heard of it.'

'Would anybody like an apple?' Jane got up and fetched the fruit bowl.

'That is because there is no static camp there. We were subject to a gang-master, but we are free now, thanks to you. He kept us in a caravan.' Peter looked sincere enough.

Victor looked at the ceiling. 'And your gang-master had a mini-bus.'

'We went out to sell the cheap paintings and other things. I sold paintings, as you know, because I like art.'

There was a pause.

Elbows planted on the table, Paul leaned forward. He shifted a little under the light. He pulled the dining room table's hanging lamp up a little. The beam cascaded over all of them, earnest players at cards. 'Myself, I like to tell the truth from the start,' he said. 'There are three ways to deceive people. The first is to joke all the time, make up some amusing stories, never to be serious. The second is to tell a sentimental story. Peter goes in for that sort of thing, you know, the pyjama and the donkeys. But I find that the best is the absolute truth. Nobody ever believes it.'

'And what, in this case, is the truth?' Victor took a cigarette from Paul's packet and lit it. He had difficulty inhaling the smoke.

Peter leaned forward and took the cigarette from him.

'Not good, Victor. Not good for the old lungs. Truth is, Victor, at least for myself, I will never be able to tell you who I am and where I am from. People like us, we destroy our papers. We don't want to, because it is our identity, sometimes all we have left of ourselves, and we panic about it. We grieve. But we must do it because we face being sent back to the violence that drove us away from our family and our home in the first place. If we have no papers, no passport, no identity, we cannot be sent back, only sent into detention.

'Do you know what happens to gays in Chechnya? The police beat them. Before they hand them back to their families, advising them to kill them, they have to name ten other gays. And so, it continues. A few lucky ones, they hide for months in a safe house, waiting for a country that will take them, Belgium or Canada. Out of the thousands, only a handful have been resettled in this way, maybe a hundred or so. But then, there are others.

'On the TV you see us arrive in England in some port, we don't know where. It could be Cornwall; it could be Kent. You don't like it. It makes you unhappy. You don't want to see suffering people here. Hordes of us. You haven't the room. We come in containers, we come in little boats, we used to come in the back of lorries, not so much now, because they have heat detection. And your government wants you to hate us.

'Some are lucky. They disappear and they go to work in this green country with the little houses and gardens with flowers. Except, one way or another, they find they are a slave. They have no more freedom than they had before. But at least they are not being shot at or set on fire. If they break a limb or have a toothache, they can't go to the hospital, in case they get detained, though detention can sometimes be better, especially for women and girls. Those who still have a mind or a memory of who they were, they wonder what will happen to them. Do you ever wonder what has happened to so many, Victor? The steady, daily trickle through all those ports like Lowestoft and Plymouth and Falmouth and little fishing ports like Newlyn, over all of the years? Even Portmarrow, perhaps, which has its little harbour, not much used now, except by little boats.

'Then, there are the few who come officially, the children. In such cases, everybody wants to be a child. But in such cases, they never leave Kent. Your government promised a thing called dispersal, but this dispersal does not happen. So, the only sort of dispersal is our sort of dispersal. We slip away. And then, one day, after many experiences you would not think possible, if we survive, you find us here.'

Jane, who had been hovering in the doorway, came forward with the bowl of fruit. There were red apples and green grapes and yellow bananas. Nobody reached out to take any of them.

Victor sighed heavily and sat back in his chair. 'I don't know,' he said. 'I don't know.'

'In any case,' Jane said brightly, 'you'll be dispersed again soon. Whatever you go, we'll never forget you, will we Victor?'

Jane began stacking up plates and cutlery. Peter moved the heavy pile to the new grey kitchen. Victor followed him out. He shut the new glass kitchen door.

'So, the other day, the soap on a rope, the Semtex, what you said, it was all a joke.'

'All a joke. I was joking with you, Victor.'

'And the plasticine?'

'All a joke. Paul does not make models with his hands. Never.'

He paused, as Victor caught his breath and put the flat of his hand on his chest. Victor breathed out carefully.

'Look. Come with me. I will show you something. Can you make it up the stair?'

'Yes, of course I can, Peter.'

At the top of the steep stairs, in the dormer bedroom, all was neat and tidy. There was no dust. On the walls, there was no exposed wire anywhere, just fresh gypsum plaster, drying in blotches to a paler pink in the overheated bedroom. Even the beds were turned down as though they were in a good hotel. Victor wondered whether Jane had been up here, tidying. But he and Jane had been out in Plymouth all day. The boys themselves must have tidied everything. Only a pile of cardboard boxes was stacked up in a corner, from floor to ceiling, waiting for rubbish day, he supposed.

Peter went to the en-suite shower. Victor followed, beginning to feel foolish, and hangdog.

'Look, I'll show you,' Peter said. He pulled down the Semtex soap-on-a-rope and broke off a piece. He ran the taps and rubbed it with his hands.

Victor flinched and turned away.

Peter lit a match and played the flame over the orange soap, then he held it there. The soap began to burn a little. 'Joke soap-on-a-rope, you know, Victor. Harmless.'

Peter threw the match into the washbasin as it burnt down towards his fingers.

Victor thought, under the sulphurous stench of the smoke from the match, there was a faint smell of rose water.

He turned and looked at the big cardboard boxes, neatly stacked from floor to ceiling. 'What are these boxes, Peter? What does this BB18 mean?'

'BB18? They are fuse-holder boxes. They are some cardboard boxes for moving out. We are leaving.'

'You have rather a lot of them.'

'Yes. We didn't need so many.'

A Very Strange Choir Evening

'God, look at it out there.'

It was a cold, wet night. Rain was hammering down again. Jane did not feel much like attending the choir practice in the damp and barely heated church hall, but she thought it was essential to attend, just before Christmas. She was unsure about when the practices were due to stop for the holiday and when they were to start up again. Choir was Jane's only connection with the community, her only night out during the week. The other women were little short of hostile, but she was looking forward to seeing Monica from the yacht club, despite the awkwardness around the business of Victor refusing to have 'that woman' in the house. Still, Monica need never know about it, and she could put off having her over for dinner until Victor came to his senses.

'And what are you going to do with yourself this evening, Victor?'

'Me? I'm going to have a drink with Peter and Paul. Crack open the whisky. Relax, for once.'

'Really? Well, do be careful with alcohol and don't give it all away. There's Christmas to worry about yet.'

'Oh, worry, worry, worry. I'm glad I took you in the car. Your shoes would have been soaked through. Don't try to walk home. I'll fetch you shortly after nine. I'll be there, so don't for Pete's sake start walking in the wet. I might pick you up straight from the Cornish Arms.'

Jane slammed the car door shut and rushed through the puddles. She was a little early, but never mind.

Oh, but that was odd: the Church Hall was in darkness but the old Methodist Sunday School beside it was lit up. Perhaps people were in the middle of decorating the Church Hall and it wasn't available this evening. There was a looming Christmas tree with unlit fairy lights strung around it in the main entrance. The place looked deserted.

She'd never visited the Methodist Sunday School. In this village, Methodist and Church of England meant practically the same thing. They held joint services these days, now that Christian attendance to worship had fallen off everywhere. It had always been like that, the butcher told her. The Cornish tradespeople used to go to the Methodist Chapel in the morning for the singing and the Church in the evening to be seen. There used to be the Bryanites as well, but their chapel was pulled down to make way for some bungalows. According to the butcher, people used to go to one chapel or another, then there used to be a bust-up over something, and then half of the congregation would decamp to the other chapel.

There was some lively singing going on in the hall. As she opened the iron latch on the heavy door and peered in, she realised that everybody had turned around to look at her.

A band on the stage stopped singing and playing.

There must have been five or six men on the stage with banjos and guitars, a fiddle and drums and whistles and thirty or more people in the audience, most of them from the two choirs. The male-voice choir seemed to have joined the ladies this evening. Jane stood rooted, wondering what to do.

A familiar figure came forward rapidly. Sandra from the choir. 'Did you not get my message?'

'No, what message?'

'Choir is cancelled. This is a benefit concert. I did ring you. Victor answered.'

'When? Sorry, that must have been after he dropped me off. I was blundering around a bit in the rain, looking for the choir practice. Have you started?'

'Oh no. It's a private benefit concert.'

'Oh, well I'll just...'

The heavy door latch closed on her again. She was left in the dark. That was very rude. Now, what should she do? Ring Victor. But Victor had the mobile with him. She looked outside. The rain was still pelting down. In the orange glow of a streetlamp, Jane noticed a white light switch just inside the door of the vestibule. She switched it on.

There was a primitive wooden chair and table, with a stack of numbered hymn books. She sat down for a moment and thought. What to do? Brave the rain, or wait until it eases off?

Inside the hall, the band started up again. The sounds came tinny but clear and distinct, thumping and angry through a speaker in the vestibule.

You found you couldn't beat us after thirty years at war
In spite of your Choppers, foot patrols and armoured cars,
We never will surrender or get on our knees and beg,
So go crawling back to England with your tail between your legs.

This is horrible, Jane thought. I don't like this. I'd better go. After more of the din, there was a pounding of feet on the hall floor. It seemed like a stampede, but she realised it was appreciation for the band. She was standing up and ready to go when the lead singer announced, 'My Little Armalite.'

Her instinct was to flee when she heard lines of *The Rising of the Moon* and *The Patriot Game*. She'd been excluded from this, it was not choir practice, it was alien, she didn't understand, but she was conscious that she was not supposed to be there and not wanted.

I'll go, she thought. I'll walk home and wait for Victor, if he's gone out. When the men come to pick me up, they will realise I've left the hall and gone back home.

She waited a few moments longer for the rain battering the roof to abate, so that she could make a dash for it; but the door opened, and Monica came in, shaking her scarf. Jane had never been happier to see her.

'Oh Monica, they're not doing choir practice. It's some kind of benefit concert, they said. We're not invited. Did you not get the message either?'

'Message? No. I've just come on the bus. It took well over an hour. I wish I hadn't. I'm soaked through. Are they in there? I'll go and tell Sandra. They could have given us some notice.'

'No, don't go in, Monica. They're singing Irish songs. They... I think it's some sort of political, nationalist...'

Monica laughed. 'What on earth's wrong, Jane?'

'Listen, listen to them.' Jane pointed to the old Tannoy speaker high up on the wall.

All they could hear now was people milling around. The music had stopped.

'Irish? Oh, the Celts. We had quite enough of them in Portugal and Spain.'

The hall door burst open. A tall man with orange hair that stuck out all over his head stood against the light, shaking a collecting tin.

Monica looked him up and down, then turned her back on him. She got her phone out of her bag. 'I'm ringing for a taxi. Goodness knows if the bus will come back tonight. I'm not going to stand in the rain. The bus might never come, and I might be stranded here.'

Jane found herself smiling weakly at the man with the collecting tin.

'And will you be making a small contribution?' He spoke mellifluously. She recognised the voice from the Tannoy. 'For the widows and orphans.'

'Which widows and…'

He came forward into the vestibule. 'Have you been listening, ladies? Will you not join us in the hall, now? Now, what is all this about going home? The night is young and full of promise. This collecting tin,' he said, placing it on the table, 'is a lucky collecting tin. It has several hundred English pounds in it already.'

Jane could not help but laugh.

He drew up a chair. 'The name's Kenny Crabbe,' he said, 'born in Kerry. We sing all over, my friends and me. We're collecting money for the New Celtic Alliance. You may have heard of it. The Troubles are over, yes. But you know, when war ends, there is a trail of sorrow and tears. Men in prison, men with limbs missing, hundreds of women and children left weeping with no-one to bother a bit or care for them.' He gazed towards the still open door to the outside.

The orange glow of the streetlamp bathed his face, draining it of colour. 'So, we form a showband and sing. Mainly in the Celtic countries, where they understand the need.'

Jane felt confused. 'I don't understand. Troubles?'

He leaned forward and looked into her face. He lowered his voice. 'No, you really don't, do you? You're English, aren't you? I thought so. I could tell.'

'What else could we be? We're retired. We're from London. We've just moved here. We're not tourists, we not going back. We live here now.'

'But you're living in a Celtic country. Do you not know that now?'

Jane began to shake her head. 'Cornwall? A Celtic country? I don't really know what that means. This is an English county, or a Duchy, something to do with the Prince of Wales.'

Kenny Crabbe stared at the wall for a moment. 'Where do I start?' On the back of a buff-coloured envelope that he took from his pocket, he drew a rough map of Britain and France and Spain. With a carpenter's pencil, he shaded in Brittany, Cornwall and Wales. 'There.' He put a dot in mid-Cornwall. You're here. You're among the p-Celts', he said, 'the Cornish and the Breton and the Welsh. In their own languages, they can understand each other. The Manx and the Irish and the Gaels way up in the north, well they're a different Celt, but they're all Celts together. They understand each other too. They've got the English surrounded, if only they knew.'

Just as Jane began to think this is very confusing, a bit boring and can hardly be true, this is a bit fanatical, he winked heavily, a music-hall wink, and put the envelope away.

'So, do you sing in the choir? Will that be the male-voice choir or with the old girls? I saw you come in. I wonder why you weren't invited. You're a nice enough little woman.'

'Well, thank you very much, Kenny Crabbe.'

You look like an ancient, worn-out lion, Jane thought, with all that hair and that soft, battered face, in this pale light. Quite romantic.

'I'm waiting for my husband to pick me up, so I won't come in. But I'm listening to your songs, really, I am.' She pulled out her purse. 'I haven't much on me. I thought it was choir practice, and I didn't need any money. If I had known you were coming, I...' She put her change into the tin, coin by coin.

The man called Kenny Crabbe shook the tin again. Jane laughed and opened up the folded wallet in her purse. 'Here,' she said. 'Take what I've got, but I must keep twenty pounds back for shopping.'

In a lyrical voice, he began telling her about the Troubles, how they began and how they ended, though everybody knew they were never ended, not really, only the little pause button had been pressed for rest, because there was no denying the history, which draws everybody in and will never let anybody go, and in the end only the mothers and the children and the men and the boys suffer. It's an old tribal thing, of Lowland

Scots and English and the united Irish, together forever in a despairing cause, didn't you know. It started with the flight of the Earls, then the Lowland Scots moved in...

Jane was mesmerised.

He asked her whether she'd heard of Brendan Behan. He told her about Ciaran Bourke and Luke Kelly, 'with hair like mine, only not so tidy, ruined by fame and destroyed by hospitality.' Then, he threw back his head and in a powerful voice, he sang, 'There's a hungry feeling...' He told her what The Old Triangle and the Royal Canal meant to prisoners of war, and the sound of his voice struck a note somewhere in the back of her mind.

When Jane looked up, Monica was outside in the dark street, getting into her taxi.

Jane shook herself. She was beginning to ache under her wet clothing. 'I'd better go too. I really don't fit here.'

'Oh, for sure. Come on inside. I'll introduce you to the lads. You know, the Wheal Maid miners' choir is not just a group of silly old fellers. The knowledge lies with the Cornish. Just a few miles inland from here, Bickford Smith built his safety fuse factory. Nobel experimented with his nitro-glycerine and built his factory just up the coast. When the huge explosions went off in the car bombs, they used to laugh themselves silly. Hard rock miners. They could crack a mountain open with a spoonful of black powder and a poker. What did you say your name was?'

'Jane Everley, but I'm English.'

'Jane Everley. Come on in, lovely Jane, come inside to the real world.'

Jane got up and followed him.

In no time at all, she was eating a saffron bun and drinking tea from the metal teapot, warming up and feeling much better. The women were talking to her. She was enchanted when Kenny Crabbe stood in front of her on the stage, swaying slightly, singing in a soft, ancient voice, 'I gave her gifts of the mind/ I gave her the secret sign/ That's known to the artists who have known/ the true gods of sound and stone…'

Jane knew she was in love with this way of life, whatever it was.

Like the lighthouse beam in a fog, she saw Peter looking through the door, searching for her.

She knew instantly that something was very wrong at home. He had been running in the rain and his coat and shoes were wet through. His hair was plastered to his face. His breathing was wild. Sandra caught him and tried to lead him to a chair at the back of the hall. He ignored her and rushed up to Jane.

'Victor, ambulance.'

'What?'

'Victor has gone with Paul ambulance. We have to go in car.'

'What are you talking about? Who has been taken ill? Paul?'

'Victor. Collapse. Faint.'

Sandra got in front of Jane and held Peter's upper arms. 'What has happened?'

Kenny Crabbe left the musicians, came down from the stage, slipped an arm around Jane's shoulders. 'Your son is here, Jane. Go on to the hospital. Somebody fainted.' He passed a card into the pocket of Jane's raincoat. 'Call me. I will be there.'

Then, with a smile he turned away, back to New Celtic Alliance fund-raising.

Jane rushed out of the hall with Peter. 'What has happened?'

'We must drive to the hospital. Can you drive the car? Shall we get a taxi?'

'No, we'll never get a taxi at this time of night. I'll drive. What has happened to Victor, Peter?'

They raced down the road to the house, fetched the keys and got into the family car.

'Now tell me,' Jane said, as they started out on the fifteen-mile journey to the hospital. 'Tell me from the beginning.'

'So, Victor collapsed. One second, he was talking, then he went sideways. We caught him between us and put him on the floor.'

'Why? Was he unconscious? For how long?'

'No, he woke up right away. He had a pain in his chest, and it got worse and worse. I called for ambulance. Paul removed Victor's jacket. He was sweating.'

'Jacket. What was he doing in a jacket?'

'We were going to the pub. He put on his suit with the waistcoat and the jacket.'

'Which suit?'

'I don't know. He said it was his best suit. I never saw it before.'

Jane's memory scanned Victor's collection of suits. 'It's the seventies suit, isn't it? It's the Harris tweed suit. It's very heavy, made of thick wool. That's the one. He's been showing off his suit to you.'

'I don't know, Jane. What is Harris tweed? Victor likes the suit. He said it is very old, and he can still wear it. Not too fat to wear. We were just going to The Cornishman.'

'Was he drinking? What was he drinking?'

'Only a little whisky. He only had a little in a glass. We all had some. He just opened the bottle.'

'Oh my God. You mustn't let him drink. He takes pills.'

'Paul asked him. He said it was alright.'

'He was showing off, wasn't he?'

'He just wanted to show his suit, Jane.'

They arrived at A and E in the low period before the town's pubs and clubs turned out. Victor was on a trolley in the corridor, the ambulance men still standing around. Paul was slumped on a metal chair beside him. They were lit by a florescent light that was buzzing.

Jane rushed up to him.

Victor sat up gingerly.

'They are not doing anything for Victor, Jane. They are just making us sit in the corridor.' Paul was looking angry and glum.

Jane and Victor put their arms around each other. 'What?'

'We have been sitting here for an hour, Jane. The ambulance people are just looking at us. The security people are looking at me all the time, like I am a criminal.'

Jane let go of Victor. She looked down the long line of people and trolleys that stretched into the distance and around a corner. Victor slumped back.

'We'll go for a cigarette. Let's go.' Peter started to lead Paul away.

A security guard came forward. 'You can't smoke outside on hospital premises.'

'It's OK,' Peter said. 'We'll go outside the hospital, on the road. We'll be back, don't worry.'

The security man looked at Jane. 'Are you the wife?'

She nodded and swallowed. 'Yes, I am. I am Jane Everley, Victor's wife. What has happened to him?'

The uniformed guard walked away, punched in some numbers by the doors and let the young men out. Jane saw them melt into the lit-up ambulance bay through the shaded glass doors.

After a short while, the fluorescent light gave up. It seemed darker and quieter in their small patch in the corridor. Around them, people talked and groaned. The paramedics who had delivered Victor to the hospital still stood about, a little apart from them.

Jane sat on the chair that Paul had left. She leaned forward, grasping Victor's hands. 'I shouldn't have gone to Choir. Whatever happened to you, Victor?'

'Nothing happened. It was like I said. Can you get me out of here? I was just showing Peter and Paul my tweed suit.' He pointed to the trousers, jacket and waistcoat, all now folded neatly at the foot of the trolley. 'I poured them a drink from the decanter. You know, the Tesco whisky. I had a drink myself. I only had a few sips. They said I slid side-ways, and they caught me between them. I woke up on the carpet, beside my chair, with a pain in my chest. I don't remember any more about it. All these people keep asking what happened and questioning me about whether I feel safe at home. I'm not ill, Jane. Jane, listen.' He gripped her arm. 'Jane, they're suspicious of Peter and Paul. They want to know whether anybody asks me to do anything I don't want to do. Bloody cheek. I told them they're my cousins, visiting from Canada. Don't let me down.' He lay back again and stared up at the blackened, dead fluorescent lamp.

Jane looked around at the people waiting on trolleys and around trolleys. 'I think, we should stay for a while, just to find out if anything is wrong with you, if there is any underlying cause. Find out why you fainted. Then we'll go home. No harm in that. While we're here. Have you had anything to eat and drink?'

Some sort of hand-over seemed to be taking place between the paramedics and the hospital staff. 'We're off now,' they said to Jane. 'He's in good hands. They'll sort him out here. By the way, who are the young lads?'

'Cousins from Canada. Visiting.'

More time went by. At intervals, Victor's trolley moved noiselessly towards the side-wards, where people were being examined and helped. A great emergency, a traffic accident, came pounding through. Specialist staff came running and disappeared into the void at the end of the corridor.

The boys did not reappear. Jane wondered where they were and whether they had found a taxi and got home safely.

Finally, they were in pole position at the top of the corridor, ready to turn the corner. They could hear the drunks in the walking wounded hall, singing and fighting. A young lad with a battered face, black with blood, was lined up on a trolley behind them. His mother told Jane some dealers had beaten him up. Jane did not know what to say.

A skinny, middle-aged, demented woman kept escaping from the security guards, who were trying to keep her on a trolley. They kept saying, 'You'll never be able to get back all the way to Penzance tonight. There are no more trains.'

Victor said, 'That's what I mean. Look around you. It's mayhem here. There's nothing wrong with me. They've got real casualties to deal with. Can't we just go?' Victor got off the trolley in his underpants and started to put on his trousers and waistcoat.

'Why don't you go in before us?' Jane said to the young lad's mother. 'We're alright, waiting here a bit longer. My husband only fainted, that's all.'

Early in the morning, Victor was wheeled into a quiet side-ward, Jane following with her metal chair. There, they were left alone. Outside the windows, the sky was black. When Jane looked at the floor, she saw that blood had dried into the tiles and drained into the grouting. She wondered whether Victor was right, whether they ought to leave.

Victor was wired up to a machine. Bloods were taken; temperature, blood-pressure were being monitored. A doctor came with Victor's notes and went through it all with him again, where he was when he fainted, what happened, who called for the ambulance, who came with him to the hospital.

'My wife was at choir-practice. Paul came with me in the ambulance. Peter went to fetch my wife.'

Jane nodded.

The doctor went away. Jane heard a whispered discussion outside the curtains. She heard the words, 'vulnerable' and 'safeguarding.' Then she heard 'Stockholm syndrome', and 'no, you really can't say that, that's very rare.' She wondered where Peter and Paul had gone.

Sometime later, Victor was discharged. In the middle of the night, Victor had been wheeled away. There had been a chest x-ray taken on an old machine underground by a sleepy technician grumbling that he couldn't tell Victor anything, not on this old girl. Results were unclear, another young doctor said. There was to be a follow-up with the GP. The discharge notes described Victor having taken some whisky and having become over-heated in a heavy three-piece tweed suit.

Nothing had been done, it seemed, they were no wiser about the cause of Victor fainting, but they were glad to be away from there. As they drove out of the hospital, two tired figures emerged from the darkness of a bus shelter. Peter and Paul flagged them down and slipped into the back seat.

'We were worried,' Jane said. 'We wondered whether you had ordered a taxi home.'

'Those doors are one-way,' Paul said. 'We couldn't get back in.'

Awkward

Victor woke very early with a crippling chest pain. His little bedside table clock told him it was half past four. Confused about the time of day, he decided he needed a lie-in. Slowly, the pains began to subside, and he went back to sleep.

At coffee time, Victor was sitting up in bed, looking grey, clutching at his chest. The pains were getting worse, not better.

'That's it,' Jane said. 'I'm going to call for an ambulance. You're not right, not right at all.'

'But I've only just come back from there.'

'They didn't do anything for you, and what sort of diagnosis was that? You got warm in a tweed suit. It's laughable.'

She told Victor she would send him to the hospital in the ambulance alone. If he was on his own, she said, they might not keep him in a corridor for several hours, like they did the night before. They might admit him right away and find out what was wrong with him this time.

'I need you to be well,' she told him, as she packed his hearing aids, his spectacles, a book and a change of underwear. 'Don't worry, I'll come in, in the afternoon.'

At tea-time, Jane found Victor on a trolley again. She fetched a springy metal chair and sat down to wait it out.

'They've got fifty-six beds to find before they can admit me,' Victor said.

'Have you eaten?'

'No, in case they have to operate, I suppose. What's happening at home? I'm fed up here, can't we just go home?'

'No, Victor. We must just get some sort of answer as to what is wrong with you.'

'I'm an old man, Jane, that's what's wrong with me. Tell the boys they can have the house after we're gone.'

Jane sat up straight. 'What? Well, I can't agree to that. Only a few days ago, you couldn't wait to get rid of them.'

'When you're in pain, Jane, and you're helpless...'

Jane got up and went to Reception in the main hall. 'My husband is not at all well.'

'That's what we're here for. He's in the right place.'

'He's talking strangely. He's confused.'

'A doctor will be along shortly.'

Jane retreated. She sat on the metal chair again and held Victor's hand, while Victor hummed and whistled a wandering tune to himself.

'*A stardust melody, a melody of love's refrain.* Stardust. Hoagy,' Victor said, and tried again. '*The nightingale tells his fairytale.*'

He tried the phrase, over and over.

My God, I hope he's not losing his mind, Jane thought. What will I do? Surely, he doesn't intend to change his will? He can't. I have some rights, surely. Has he changed his will already, behind my back?

'I'm your wife, Victor, you can't.'

'*The melody haunts my memory.* What?'

'Nothing.' It would not be right to discuss his will here. What's done is done and can still be altered if he's done something stupid, she thought. He must get better.

Late in the evening, an isolation room was found on the third floor for Victor. A nurse sat outside at a desk, able to peep through blinds to the corridor. Jane was reminded of that hotel room in Moscow, where they were put up, oh years and years before, on one of Victor's cheap holidays. Bucket seats, they used to call them, advertised at the back of the Telegraph.

'One way of seeing the world, Jane.'

There had been a concierge on every corridor. They would walk into the room and tell you to be quiet when you laughed. The women, in their nylon suits, glared at your Parker pen and your Marks and Spencer lace. That was in the late seventies or early eighties. They were not long married then, still hoping for children. Wide-eyed, they gazed on a huge frozen lake, with people skating in muffs just like in illustrations. And all over Moscow, construction was going on. Cranes and hammering and banging. London was going through a deep, deep recession. Nobody's job was safe. They could have lost the house on Mount Road in Chingford then. Yes, it wasn't all plain sailing.

Victor slept and Jane tried to sleep in an upholstered, plastic chair beside him, sometimes laying her head down on the bed. There would be no doctor's visit tonight.

At midnight, Jane awoke, and Victor awoke. There were no more chest pains, and hadn't been since the morning. Just the constant, incomprehensible monitoring by the silent machine.

'I'm going home to sleep, Victor. I'll be back in the morning.'

Outside the hospital, walking to the carpark, Jane thought, am I going to be alone? I've never been alone. I've never paid the council tax, I've never read the meters, I've never had to think about the investments, buy or sell. I've never done anything like that. What do I do if he dies? What if he tries to give the bungalow away to the boys? Have they put him up to it? When did they get a chance to do that?

In the still damp pocket of her raincoat, she turned over and over Kenny Crabbe's card, not remembering what it was.

In the morning, the hospital rang. Victor can come home.

She dropped everything and went straight away. The boys were out somewhere. They'd said something about getting the local electrician in to look at their wiring and issue a certificate. She didn't leave a note. They would understand where she had gone.

She was expecting he would be dressed and waiting in the entrance hall. Instead, she was sent to a ward. He was sitting on a bed, staring at a wall.

'My pulse has been swaying about from 55 to 44. My blood pressure was off the scale. I've a spot on a lung. I've had two strokes which we didn't know about. Did we? I don't remember.'

'Goodness gracious, Victor.' She sat down on the bed with him. 'I've brought your trousers, shirt, tie and woolly.'

Why do I feel so angry with him? She thought.

'They won't let me go until they're satisfied that I can receive 'the appropriate care at home.' That's what they said. I said, I have a wife, locks on the doors and two burly young friends to look after me. They said, that was what they wanted to discuss. We must be careful what we say, Jane.'

She looked down at her hands. 'I suppose we must. Though, if they're 'illegals' isn't there a way of making Peter and Paul legal? It doesn't seem fair that they have to leave us. Not really. Well, they're difficult sometimes, Paul is, but they've never been any trouble, have they. Can't we sponsor them in some way?'

Victor dug her in the rib with his elbow. 'Here they come.'

Jane knew what was coming out of Victor's mouth next. The doctor and a woman with a clipboard pulled up chairs.

'Mrs Everley? I'm the duty doctor. We're going to discharge Victor today. He needs to go to his GP in a few days' time. He needs a follow-up x-ray, and we'll get him an appointment at the TI clinic. He's had a mild stroke or even two. He has multiple health issues, which will have to be addressed if he is to get well again.'

'There's something on my lung and my pulse is all over the shop. She knows. Can we go now?'

Used to petulance, the weary doctor carried on. With that unusual accent that you couldn't pin down, Jane wondered where he was from. She didn't want to ask him. It would seem rude and inappropriate and there had been such a hoo-ha in the newspapers about foreign health workers having to pay to stay and keep their jobs.

'... and the thing that has puzzled us is, Mrs Everley, there is a stress hormone that shows up in the blood. Victor, can you think of anything that is causing you such stress? This lady is a hospital social worker. Yvonne will ask you a few more questions.'

'And you can keep your black hands off me.'

Without missing a beat, the woman continued. 'So, can you tell me, is your pension enough to live on?'

'Yes of course it is. We have five pensions between us.'

She ignored the irascibility that was making Jane squirm already. 'I'm sorry,' Jane said. 'I'm so sorry.'

'Are you, perhaps, for instance, in debt?'

Jane said, 'We live modestly, and we're reasonably well off. We don't have a mortgage. Our car is paid for if that's what you mean.'

'Store cards?'

'No.'

'Nothing like gambling or an addiction? Alcohol consumption?'

'That's it. I'm off. Pack my bag, Jane.' Victor got to his feet and began looking for his socks and shoes. 'The bloody cheek of it.'

'No, really,' Jane said. 'Nothing like that. We don't smoke. We don't drink normally, at all.'

The woman lowered her clipboard. 'I should explain, Mrs Everley, the doctor is alarmed because in his bloods, Victor is showing dangerous signs of high stress. Stress is a number one killer of the elderly. If there is anything in your environment which is triggering Victor's stress, I am here to try and find it, and to help eliminate or relieve it. I'll give you my card. If you would like to contact me or any of my colleagues on the Safeguarding Team, you have only to pick up the phone.'

'Safeguarding? Really, there is nothing,' Jane said. 'He's always been impossible like this. He has high blood pressure. He is very independent. We both are.'

Jane took the card and put it in her raincoat with Kenny Crabbe's damp and crumpled card. The woman with the clipboard stood up. Victor was already by the door, hopping from one foot to the other.

Plombe Seeks Planning Permission

'What in God's name is he doing now?'

Victor rushed out of the kitchen, through the front door and out to the piece of waste ground where he always parked the car. He was in his tartan pyjamas and dressing gown.

He had been standing at the window looking out, when he saw a notice being nailed discreetly to the electricity pole at the back of the patch of ground. He knew instantly what it was.

Paul, still finishing his scrambled egg on toast, glanced at Jane, gestured with his hand to stay seated at the breakfast table and strolled out quietly behind Victor. Jane got up with Peter and looked out of the window.

The troublesome neighbour, Plombe, had just been down from Colchester for the weekend again. He had been hammering and banging outside his bungalow under builders' lights and under a canopy from late on Friday night, through Saturday and Sunday morning. The noise had reverberated through the ground, causing Victor to wander around the house, getting more and more agitated, looking for signs of a run of dirt, the precursor to cracking and crumbling.

'With a mundic house, you just can't go around disturbing the ground like that.'

Even Paul, who was bored with hearing about mundic as a building material, agreed with him.

By morning, Plombe's boundary wall, made of stone and earth, was down. In the afternoon, Plombe had suddenly packed up and gone again, leaving his wall in pieces all over the earth and his garden in disarray.

Now, there was a notice nailed up, stating that Plombe sought planning permission to build a garage on the waste ground between Victor's bungalow and his own.

Victor turned to Paul. 'This is not his ground,' he said. 'He has no right to ask for planning permission. If it's anybody's ground, it's my ground. I always park my car there and the old girl who lived here before always parked her car there, and she was a child when she came here to live. I'm the one who's got squatters rights if anybody has. Through habitual use unchallenged, Jane.'

Jane came and stood beside him. 'Well look,' she said, 'We'll have a look on the Land Registry site. If it belongs to Plombe, we'll soon find out, and if not, we'll complain to the Council.'

Victor looked down at his bedroom slippers. He thought the blue veins in his feet were looking prominent again. 'Oh, good grief,' he said. 'I'm still in my night-clothes. I'd better go in. You should have stopped me coming outside dressed like this, Jane.'

'Now, how was I going to do that? You took off like a rocket.' Jane laughed in the rare bright sunshine and guided him indoors.

'I tell you, Jane, that man will be the death of me.'

'Well, I hope not. Not yet, anyway.'

Peter grinned and agreed. 'Not yet, anyway.'

Victor sat at the kitchen table with Paul, thinking aloud, while Jane and Peter shared the washing-up.

'Why do I get so annoyed with that great big shit next door? Why didn't I go out and confront him about taking down that boundary wall?'

Why? Victor thought. I'm afraid, that's why. What if it is his ground and I can't park there anymore? Where will I put the car? Take down my own wall and park under the dining-room window? What would that look like?

'I've just had a thought. It's on the Parish Council agenda. That's a public meeting. Who do we know on the Council? Roy. Roy at the post office. He's on the Parish Council. Just go out and check for me on the notice board, Paul.'

Paul strolled down the road to look at the notice in the Post Office window and at the electricity pole.

When he came back, he filled a glass with water and sipped it. 'It's on the Parish Council meeting agenda, he has applied to the County Council for permission to build a garage.'

Victor blushed red. 'That man has no right.'

Jane turned to Victor and said quietly, 'Victor, anybody can apply for planning permission. They don't have to own the land to ask for planning permission.'

'But you see the bloody intention. Stupid woman. He's not put in an application for nothing. He intends to build on that waste ground and who is there to stop him? Roy and his Parish Council can't stop him. Have you seen what goes through the Planning Committee lately? And it won't stop there, oh no. First a modest little garage, then a plan to incorporate the garage into his bungalow, that's why the garden wall's been brought down, then permission to turn it into a granny annexe, then full planning permission for a brand new two-storey house, cutting off my light and ruining my only little bit of sea view from your attic, Paul. And I'm helpless. There will be nothing, nothing I can do. And, of course, everybody on the Parish Council will vote for him. That's nice, Mr Plombe. Have a garage for yourself on Victor's parking space. Victor won't mind.'

Paul thought a while, stood up and lit a cigarette. He waved the smoke away from Victor.

'No problem, Victor,' he said with a soothing tone. 'Don't bother Roy at the Post Office. Let this man have his planning permission. When Mr Plombe comes back, we will speak with him. We will all go and see him together. In the meantime, don't worry. Just park the car as usual. Peter and I will move the stones and rubble back, so you don't cut your tyres or trip over in the dark. And don't worry any more. You mustn't stress. It's bad for your heart.'

'Yes, Paul will speak with him. Thank you, Paul.' Jane felt proud of Paul. He was so much more relaxed and confident, these days, and so very supportive and kind.

'By the way, Victor, Roy said he wants to drop by later, when he closes the post office. Something about Christmas lights.'

Victor, who had been brooding with his head in his hands, looked up. 'Oh yes, the fairy lights. All the residents in Beach Road either give a donation to the committee or we help put up the string of lights across all of the buildings. It's quite a task, apparently. The lights go all the way down Beach Road and finish up at the Christmas tree in the children's playground in the Playing Field. They're at first floor level. You have to get up and down ladders. I'm not sure I'm up to it myself.

'Then there's another thing. Plombe. I wonder whether he'll refuse to have the lights running across his property. If so, the lights will have to stop before his bungalow and then be plugged in here. We don't really want the expense of running all those lights and having to switch them on and off every evening. We've enough to worry about. If we refuse to plug them in on our side, our name will be mud. Nobody will like us. Not that I worry about that, but we do want to fit in here, now that I've left the Yacht Club.'

'Yes, we do want to fit in. Oh, that this should happen, just as the women in the choir have started speaking to me.' Kenny Crabbe's orange face and hair in the glow of the streetlamp crossed her mind and was lost again.

Peter said, 'Don't worry. Mr Plombe won't object.'

Paul said, 'You won't have to give a donation or go up a ladder. Peter will help me. We will put up all of the lights for everybody on Beach Road. Tell Roy when he comes.'

'Well, that would help greatly,' Jane said. 'All the members of the Christmas Lights Committee are getting on in years, Sandra told me at Choir the other day. All that going up and down ladders. It is a strain.'

'No problem,' Paul said. 'I will fix the lights on Beach Road. I am a qualified electrician, not in this country.'

'You certainly are,' Jane said, 'and a very fine one too. I don't know why you don't get the English qualification. It would be easy for you, knowing as much as you already do. Let's have an early coffee and then you boys can make a start on Plombe's rubble.'

'Paul used to climb on the big pylons,' Peter said.

'No, I didn't. Enough with the fantasy, Peter. Tell the truth.'

Paul's Wonderful Community Spirit

Peter was chatting to the Major on the pavement. Paul was up a ladder pinning fairy lights to the front of the house a few doors down when another Social Worker pulled up in her car to visit Victor and Jane.

'And how is your health, Victor?'

Victor scowled. 'I was having a good day until you came along. What do you want this time? I'm watching my cousins put up the lights for my neighbours. I am in very good health, thank you very much. I have seen the GP and appointments have been made at the hospital.'

She was not to be put off, so Jane invited her in to have a cup of tea.

'I'm glad for you about the hospital appointments. But these cousins of yours puzzle me.

Are they about? How much longer do they have on their tourist visas? It can't be long.'

'I'm trying to persuade them to apply for a student visa,' Jane said. 'Paul is a talented electrician and builder. He put in this kitchen for me all on his own. He only needs another certificate or two to qualify in this country. They like it here by the seaside. And they've done a lot for us. There's plenty of work for fit young men. I don't know what we'll do without them. Ottawa has a very harsh climate, humid in the summer and perishing in the winter. But yes, they are packing up to leave shortly after Christmas, in the New Year.'

'I see. And have you ever seen their passports? Ever seen their visas?'

'Seen their visas? Why should we?'

'Where were they from originally?'

'Chechnya,' Victor and Jane said together.

Victor continued, repeating Paul's shibboleth. Have you any idea what they do to gays in Chechnya? The police beat them up and make them pick up ten other gays. They trick them. Some of the ones informed on aren't gays at all, just family men. Then, if they're lucky, the police hand them back to their families, expecting them to kill them. Only a handful get away. They go to safe houses and just a few are re-settled in countries that will take them, Canada or Belgium.'

'And these two are your cousins? Chechen cousins?'

'My dear, not everybody's grandfather was English. My grandfather settled in London after the first world war and took the English name, Everley. Lucky, that's all. The others stayed in Russia. I never knew much about them, until now.' A sob came up and just escaped notice. He held it down and swallowed hard. 'It's a matter of luck, what happens in families, you know.'

The social worker looked around at the neat kitchen, the pottery owl holding the spoons, the mug tree holder, full of matching, clean, unchipped mugs.

'Victor, let me tell you. I am neither from border control nor border patrol. If I see a crime, I'm obliged to report it. If I only suspect a crime, it is my job to suspect until my fears are allayed. Your health and wellbeing, your safeguarding as an elderly person with multiple health issues are my concern. If at any time you should feel imposed upon or oppressed in any way by your young people, if you ever feel that you are beginning to experience abuse or neglect of any kind at all, if they started swearing at you, taking your money or, God forbid, laying a hand on you, my duty is to empower you, protect you and prevent any harm coming to you. The team are only here to help.'

'I don't know what you are talking about. You've got the wrong family here. We're respectable people. I am a Chartered company secretary; my wife is a qualified schoolteacher with a DFE number. Do you know what that requires?'

The social worker stood up and pushed her chair neatly under the small kitchen table with the white plastic lace tablecloth. 'Well, I mustn't keep you from your Christmas lights. So nice when visitors help, isn't it.'

They went and stood at the front door. The Major was alone on the pavement, leaning on his stick, staring up at Paul when all three emerged into the December sunlight.

'So nice to see their visitors making themselves useful.' The social worker smiled with encouragement. It was an open-ended question.

'Good chap, Paul. Made of the sort of stuff the army needs,' the Major said.

There was no sign of Peter.

The woman got in her car, appeared to make some notes, and drove off slowly.

Turning back into the porch, Jane said, 'We've never told lies, Victor. We've always kept our noses clean. As professional people, we had to. You wouldn't even have Monica in the house, for some reason to do with probity. I feel very bad. That social worker didn't believe a word of what we said, and she won't leave it at that. We'll have to tell the boys. We can't get away from the fact that they are illegals. We could get ourselves into trouble.'

'Listen to me.' The muscles around Victor's jaw began to clench and knot. 'What if they are illegals? Most of the population of Britain are immigrants. Normans, Vikings, Jews. Even the Dutch drained Norfolk and stayed. There are stories of whole communities who get together to stop individuals like Peter and Paul from being deported. I remember a Chinese family in Chiswick where that happened. They ran the local Chinese shop. People didn't want to lose them. Why shouldn't Portmarrow be a village to do something like that? See what the boys are doing this afternoon for the people of this village? Up on a ladder all day fixing Christmas lights. They're white boys, after all. Well, Peter certainly is. Paul has brown eyes and sometimes looks a bit Middle Eastern. But no harm in that. Look what they've done for us, Jane. I've lacked trust, I'll admit it. And so have you. But they only wanted a place to stay, and we gave it to them, and we've had our reward. They've repaid us in buckets. They're like my own boys.'

'And I hope you won't do anything foolish like leaving them the house behind my back when you're sick.'

'What are you talking about now, Jane?'

Jane went back to the doorstep and looked out to the waste ground and the car. She surveyed the still shut-up bungalow next door.

'I haven't seen Plombe, have you? I thought he was down for the whole of Christmas.'

Victor came to the door, scowling. 'Who does he have to spend Christmas with? Does he have a family? I've never seen anybody with him. Good riddance, that's what I say. I hope he stays in

Colchester, or wherever he comes from. Anyway, I thought I heard his car the other night.'

'Oh? When was that?'

'A few nights ago. I don't know when. I thought I heard car doors slamming. I thought he might be unpacking his stuff. It was around midnight, I think, his usual time of quiet arrival. Must have been Friday. Yes, Friday. I saw the headlights sweeping in. They lit up the bedroom window, like they do. I remember now. I heard a bit of a scrape. I thought he might have touched our car. I looked later. There was nothing. Just a scratch. Probably had nothing to do with him. Anyway, if he'd been here, he'd have soon been hammering on the door, having a go at me for moving all the rubble back on to his garden. I'm glad he's not here. I don't want to see him. Probably lying low until he gets his planning permission. Or not. Any rate, I've got Roy primed to put a spoke in about the ownership of our waste ground. The Parish Committee won't like him trying to pull the wool. That should stall him.'

'We should live and let live, Victor.'

'I thought you would say that.'

As they turned to go indoors, they heard the big Coastguard helicopter go overhead. Then they saw two more, approaching from the opposite direction, helicopters from Culdrose.

'Air-sea rescue,' Victor said. 'Must be a big job. Coach-load of idiots caught out by the tide or something. We'll have to get used to it, living here. Funny time of the year to go walking.'

For tea-time, Jane made some scones. As the men spooned on the jam and cream, she said, 'The social worker was here, all to do with Victor's welfare again. We told the woman you were from Chechnya originally. I hope we didn't do wrong.'

Peter and Paul stopped, looked at each other and crumpled up with laughter.

'What's so funny?'

'You are.'

Peter got up, came around the table and tousled Jane's hair.

'Stop that. I've just had it permed. I don't like anybody touching my hair.'

Peter stood back, putting his hands up in the air. 'Okay, okay.'

Jane went to the hall mirror and put a comb through her hair. It was over-permed, crinkly and beginning to grey all over. The style was old-fashioned. These small, seaside salons, where the women talked nonsense. She felt aged, suddenly, not in control of her kitchen and her men.

'I don't understand you,' she said when she came back to the table. Smoothing down her apron, she still felt ruffled and foolish. 'There we were, trying to defend you. We were trying to stop people nosing around about you, that's all. We don't like telling lies, and we're no good at it.'

There was a pause.

'So, what do you want us to say, when people say you don't have a Canadian accent?'

She looked to Paul.

He sat back, unconcerned. 'I don't know,' Paul said. 'It's your lie. I wasn't there.'

Jane looked to Victor, who just looked down.

'Alright,' Paul said. 'How you handle a social worker. Do you need a social worker? No. Thank you, Mrs Social Worker, we don't need anybody.'

We've been too nice, too polite, Jane thought. We don't need a social worker. We didn't have to go into explanations and tell a lie. I didn't have to invite her in. Next time, I won't.

'We have a few days.' Paul took a sip of tea from the fussy little cup with red garden roses on it, gripping it whole, instead of slipping his finger through the handle. 'I have to see that electrician, Tremayne, about signing off the work here and giving you a certificate, Victor. He lives up in the Close. If there is any more to do, there is time to get done, don't worry.'

He picked up his cigarettes, lighter and wallet from the table, rolled up the sleeves of his shirt and jersey and walked out.

Peter shook his head a little and smiled. 'We'll get the electric done in time, Mama,' he said.

In time for what? In time for what? Christmas?

Some Enquiries are Made

The two Community Police Support Officers came to the door at just after eight in the morning. One rang the bell, and both stood back.

Victor came to the inner door in his pyjamas and dressing-gown. It was still dark outside. All he could see was two looming figures outside the porch as he fetched the key to the mortice lock from its hook in the hall and reached up to unbolt the inner door. There was no time to alert the boys in their dormer bedroom. He just hoped they had heard and had time to scramble into the loft space. If the police had come for Peter and Paul, he decided he would say nothing. Nothing at all.

Against the quiet of the porch, the road outside, the interior of the bungalow, the policemen's jackets were a fairy garden of beeps and disembodied voices.

'Yes?' Victor heard his own voice as from afar. He thought it sounded too studied, the vowel far too long.

'Mr Victor Everley? Could we come in? It's about your neighbour, Mr Ivan Plombe.'

'Ivan? Oh yes, a terrible business. We heard the helicopters. Thought it was just walkers stranded. Never for one moment did we think about suicide, driving a car over a cliff like that. It was on Spotlight. Would you like me to fetch my wife? I think she's asleep. I just got out of bed to make tea. When you're retired, there isn't much to get up for on a dark morning. I usually make tea just after the school bus goes, but it didn't go this morning. I suppose the schools may have broken up for the Christmas holidays.'

Victor realised he was babbling. The policemen were waiting for Victor to stand aside and let them in. One spoke, the other watched.

They stood in the hall. Victor hoped that the boys could hear the conversation and that they wouldn't panic.

'As I said, Mr Everley, this is about Mr Ivan Plombe. You may know that his car was found at the foot of Als an Marrow at the weekend.'

'Yes, I saw the helicopters and then the police cars went through the village on Saturday at a hell of a lick. Roy at the post office told me it was Plombe. Was the body in the…?'

'In the vehicle? Yes. Most people are working on the assumption that it was a suicide, but we can't make assumptions just like that, can we? We got to make enquiries, see.'

The second policeman nodded and added, 'Enquiries, door-to-door.'

'Did he die of the fall, or did he take tablets first? Was there a suicide note, Officer?'

'I expect our forensic people will be looking for all of that sort of thing. Then it will be up to the coroner.' The first policeman looked around. 'Why don't we sit down? You're looking a little shaken, Sir. We are tasked to collect evidence, door to door, just to get a fuller picture. He wasn't a full-time resident here in the village, was he?'

'Was he alive when he was found?'

'I understand not. He had been dead some time.'

Victor was still standing, staring at the light coming from the porch and the doorway.

He shook himself. 'Oh yes, do come into the kitchen. Would you like a cup of tea? I'll go and wake my wife.'

Victor went to the kitchen sink and drew a glass of cold water. He gulped it down.

'No, we won't have a drink on duty, thank you. Just a few questions and we'll be gone, let you get on with your morning.'

He has a bit of a Welsh accent, Victor thought. Bit of a Taffy, probably called Thomas, the way he said, 'assumptions.'

'As I was saying, he wasn't a full-time resident, was he?'

Victor sat down in his place at the small kitchen table. The first policeman squeezed himself and his beeping vest into Jane's corner, the other stood.

'Plombe? No, he came and went. The last I saw of Ivan, he was knocking down his garden wall. He wants to build a garage on the piece of waste ground outside, where I park my car. He's put in for planning permission. Why would you commit suicide if you…?'

The policeman waited for Victor to finish his sentence, but Victor had gone silent, staring out of the window at the slab-sided side wall of Plombe's bungalow.

The young man coughed. 'There's no knowing, no predicting,' he said. 'Suicide never does make any sense to healthy-minded people. How well did you know him?'

Victor spread his hands and looked at his fingernails for signs of dirt. 'Not well. Hardly at all. We were never invited over to his bungalow, and he only ever came here to ask us to move our car. He wasn't the friendly type. He treats his bungalow as a holiday cottage. I imagine that's what it is to him. Perhaps he'll retire to it, you know.'

'Well, he won't be retiring to the bungalow now, we can be sure of that.' The policeman grinned, then quickly wiped the grin off his face. He looked down to lower the volume on the chatter emanating from the contraption on his uniform.

'So, what are we saying? You didn't see much of him. Not friendly. A big bloke, would you say? A bit surly, other people have said. Only conversations were about car parking. Did you see him the night he committed suicide, allegedly?'

'No. What night was it?'

'On the Friday or Saturday morning early of last weekend.'

'No. I assumed he was in Colchester, where he lives.'

The policeman looked back in his notebook. 'What makes you think he lived in Colchester?'

'Well, I thought that's what he told us. His planning application has the address on it. You'll find the planning application number up on the electricity pole outside, on the waste ground, where he wants to build his garage. I looked it up on the planning site. I was going to put in an objection. The piece of waste ground is not his. It's not mine either, but…'

'He lived at an address in Staines.'

'Oh, well I don't know. Perhaps he told lies. You chaps should go to the address in Colchester, if you're making enquiries. Look on the electric pole for the planning number.'

The young policeman snapped his notebook shut and put it away. He stood up to go.

Victor accompanied them to the door. The house was still very quiet. No-one had made a sound.

'Sad business,' Victor said on the doorstep. 'I wish I could help, but what can anybody do?'

'Indeed,' the first policeman said. 'Suicide is no longer a crime, nonetheless, our job is to investigate, in case there is any doubt, any doubt at all. Now, I've left my name and the crime number on a card, which we will leave with you now. We've got a lot more people to see. If you can think of anything that strikes you as being out of the ordinary...' They walked away towards the next house diagonally across the road. Some wit from Yorkshire had called it 'Tideaway.'

Victor looked up at the string of fairy lights, which Paul had strung across Plombe's bungalow to the next. No-one asked Plombe's permission, and no-one will be able to now, he thought. He rubbed his hands together. But at least Plombe won't be building that garage.

Late in the morning, at brunch, when they were all eating fried sausage and beans on toast together, Victor said, 'Did you hear the policemen call? I didn't hear a sound from your bedroom. I was frightened it might be the immigration people at first, but it was just about Plombe's suicide.'

'No,' Paul said. 'Immigration don't send a pair of constables, they come with a lot of noise.'

'A lot of noise,' Peter said, 'I understand.'

'They weren't police, Victor.'

'They weren't?'

'They weren't even Community Police.' Paul grinned, picking his teeth.

'They were Support Officers.' Peter laughed and slapped the table leg beside him. 'You thought they were Immigration.' He laughed loudly.

'Oh Victor,' Jane said. 'You worry, all over nothing.'

'They couldn't even get an interview right. They were telling you the answers and giving away information about the case.' Paul looked at Peter and they laughed all over again.

'Well, I'm glad you two found my little fright amusing. How are you so sure they were Support Officers?'

'It was on the back of their jackets. Support Officer, no brain, no train.'

How come you know so much about our policing and interviewing techniques? Victor thought.

'Oh well, Plombe won't be needing his planning permission now.' Victor made himself look cheerful.

Paul poured himself some black tea. He popped a cube of sugar between his teeth and sucked a sip of tea through it.

'We can build a garage for you anyway. Something simple. Just a car port to keep the rain and sand off. You need it, especially in the winter, by the sea.'

'Oh, I don't know. Makes me feel awfully guilty, Plombe on a mortuary slab, not getting his garage and me getting a carport instead. Doesn't seem right, somehow. What would people think?'

Paul paused from buttering his toast. 'Why? Was it your hand on the accelerator?'

Jane, who had been listening to the conversation, said, 'Don't you mean foot, dear?'

'No.'

There was something about Paul's use of inflection, his seeming puzzlement at the end of the short word that bothered Jane. She thought she had misheard.

'By the way,' Paul said to Victor, 'I forgot to tell you last night. Tremayne, the electrician was happy with my wiring. We just have to modify the earthing and use a different circuit board. New regs, he said. We can't use plastic in the entrance hall because it's a fire exit. It has to be metal. Not a problem. We'll just get the bits, put them in and Tremayne will issue your certificate.'

'Really? That's very welcome,' Victor said. His face lit up with a big smile.

'Fabulous,' Jane said. She wanted to give Paul a big kiss, but knew somehow, he wouldn't like that. Peter would, but Paul wouldn't.

Victor In A Bad Way

No-one in the little mundic bungalow on Beach Road guessed how much Plombe's death affected Victor. It was like a tapeworm, eating away at his nourishment and his contentment. Staring at the darkened bedroom window night after night, he wondered, did he just dream that the powerful headlight beams of Plombe's car swept across the tightly closed curtains? Did he dream he heard car doors slam and a little scrape? Did Plombe drift down to his bungalow, start to unpack, change his mind, leave it all and drive the car west, climbing ever higher to the top of Westcliff, roaring over Als and Marrow some minutes later?

Did the momentum of the vehicle take him clear of the cliff, in the final plunge? Did it crash down on the ledges, taking out rock and vegetation? Did the weight of the engine cause the car plunge headfirst, or did it fall flat? Did he change his mind half-way down, or as soon as he went over the edge, or even before? Was he found with his foot on the brake? Or on the accelerator? Was the body flung clear?

What did Paul mean when he said, 'Why, was your hand on the accelerator?' He put that memory aside. What did it mean? The image of a hand on the accelerator slipped sideways as he fell asleep.

And me, did I have a hand in it? Did I have to resent him so? Was he a man in appalling despair, something which I failed to spot or to have any sympathy with, in any way at all? What sort of man am I?

After lunch, still brooding, Victor walked up to the Post Office to collect the new First Day Cover, which he had ordered in advance through Roy and which he should have felt excited about. This issue celebrated the historic British Airship R 36, already sold out and worth a percentage more on the second-hand market.

Roy spotted that he barely looked at it. 'Time you got a new hobby, Vic.'

'Why do you say that?'

'Not so interesting, this new issue?'

'I'll have a look at it later when I get home. I'll take this Tide Table as well.'

'Want an OS Map to go with them? Some local ones over there.' Roy pointed to a revolving wire stand.

'No, I've got a four-inch one at home, a real one. I don't use those new walking, running, and cycling things. I like the old ones, the field names and…'

'You can download them on your phone nowadays, Vic. And have music wherever you go. Rings on your fingers and bells on your toes.'

'What would be the fun of exploring, then?'

Victor barely noticed that Roy had called him Vic again. To Roy's mind, Victor seemed distracted and gloomy, depressed almost.

Roy glanced at the clock on the wall when Victor left to go up the road to the cliff path instead of down Beach Road towards his home. OS Maps sold well when a car went over the edge. The locals got used to the suicides, new people never did.

Victor was conscious that he was late setting out. According to the tide table, he could make it to the foot of Als an Marrow and back again before anybody would know he had gone. You couldn't see anything from the top. All he wanted was just to take a peek at the place from below. He thought it would settle his mind, stop his imagination running in all directions if he could just see the reality of the place. He knew that the remains of the car had been removed, lifted on to a barge and taken down the coast. There would be nothing left to see but gouges or scratch marks. But he must go and look.

Like taking flowers to a roadside tree where there had been an accident, he supposed.

Something like that.

The walk alone was soothing. No Jane by his side, no boys following along. Just Victor and the wind and the weak winter sun, and greyness. The chattering at the top of his mind began to hush.

The direct route to the foot of the cliff was along the beach, through the Seal Caves, not difficult, just slimy and straight through, without any deviation. He had his headlight with him and his back-up torch. It was unpleasant, forbidding and frightening, but the tide was right out. He just had to be careful not to break a leg in there, that was all. It needed concentration to stay upright and come through. Somebody, long ago, had staked a bar to the rock to cling on to.

Out into the light and air again, the sea still a long way out. No yellow sand, no sandy beach, just ground up rock, gravel and stone. A steep falling-off into the ocean.

He'd been through Seal Caves once before, but that time he had turned around and gone back again to the familiar, accessible sandy coves, where the naturists and naturalists hung about. He'd never before looked up to the top of Als and Marrow.

The sight was formidable.

Sheer rock, dolomite, was it? He must look up the geology of the place. Slabs of grey rock, uniform in colour bending over towards the foot of the cliff, impossible for a rambler to climb, punctured by green ledges, high up. You would never believe there was a coast road up there. Listen. You could not hear a car.

Where was our ledge? The easy climb down to the grassy platform, where we ate sandwiches. I with the ham and mustard and you with the egg and cress, Jane. Not visible here. Lost, a long way up.

A hushing, a shushing, a muttering and a booming but no words. Beyond words, the inexpressible ocean, the sun already in its slow falling. I have less than an hour to look around.

To look for what?

The vehicle has gone, taken off by crane and barge. They've done it all before, the salvage people, of course. They know how to remove the wreckage without a difficulty, without a fuss. There must have been others before this.

Whether by accident or by design, it all ended here, for a few.

And in the end, in a way, accident or design, did it matter which? Just one more life. In this vastness, all life ends.

Victor sighed heavily, emptying his lungs of old air, taking in new sea air.

I must look for remains of the vehicle. Even little pieces of headlight, red glass, white glass, plastic, little shards of metal. Has the sea taken everything? Everything? Everything leaves a trace of its passing. Nothing escapes. Material is never lost, only transformed, or taken away.

Systematic in his searches, Victor walked up and down, looking up for gouges in the green ledges, scratch marks in the rock. Looked among the little stones and gravel and pebbles. This ground where he stood, it was not a beach, could not be called a cove. It was blanked off to the west by sheer rock face. Even at such a low tide, there was only sea, no shale, no beach. Behind him, the already darkening shore and sea caves that would fill, and a cove beyond that would let him out, but only if… only if he went through the caves again. From that other cove, there was a stony path to the top.

Victor sat for a moment, the old breathlessness coming over him in tired pulses.

This breathing ocean. Walking by the ocean with an OS Map. Swimming and sunbeds. Red and blue and yellow bathing caps. Not here, not beyond Shag Rock, not beyond Seabass Cove. Just ocean.

'You're not well, Victor. You must stay on the ward, and we must find out what is wrong with you.'

Mortality. That is what is wrong.

Sunset already, a sun that went down on silence, no words, obliterated. Is there really no trace of Plombe? After the gibberish, the stamping up and down, my empty objections to the Parish Committee, is there nothing left of him? Just Plombe in my head?

Now it was dusk. Sudden dusk, the last of the sun's direct light blocked by the western cliff face, which almost in an instant it seemed, had turned from school uniform grey to charcoal.

He turned on his headlamp for use in the cave. Yes, it was dusk alright. The beam wobbled, then shone on a lone object, nestling among gravel and stone. A bunch of keys, untarnished, on a fob that seemed to spring up at him, shout for attention at him. He knew what those keys were and stood trembling, sea damps rising, sound of the waves now being different, beginning to growl.

He went and stood at the entrance to Seal Caves. It was a short journey to the other side, with the iron bar there for safety, yet the sound in the caves was different. The caves were filling. He turned away.

I'm trapped. Possibly. Where is the tideline? Can't see it. Didn't look for it before. Now I can't see it. Jane's got the mobile. Don't panic. Orientate yourself. Over there, Godrevy Light. Virginia Woolf's lighthouse, the lantern re-sited to a new steel structure on a rock. Solar powered. No men there now.

Map in my pocket of no use. Peppermints. Who knows I am here? Nobody. They will wonder where I am, where I went. Never mentioned coming here. They say, a body will reappear after a few days or a week or a month, bloated, somewhere along the coast, where wind and tide take it.

Trembling, Victor unstrapped the light from his forehead and played the beam over the rock, walking west, looking for a place to heave himself up onto a ledge and wait it out. Wait out the tide, like on that fishing trip with Roy.

No, there was nowhere to go. Not the caves, not a ledge. The tide would take him off some time in the early morning. The sea had given him Plombe's keys and taken away his life. This was a certainty.

'Jane!'

He shouted to her. The shout mocked him.

You could not swim round to Seabass cove, no. In this water, at this temperature, at this time of the year, no. You could try, and perhaps he should try, at the end he might try and die in the attempt. Or look one more time at the cliff face and search for a toehold. But he could never do it. He was not strong enough. His arms felt heavy. Heart trouble. Mortality.

He faced the tide and sat down to wait.

He had no god, there was no society, there was no explanation for what had befallen Victor. Jane was his rock, all this time. He knew what people meant by that now. The rock that stood in his way, the rock that stood up for him to climb, to cling to, to shelter under. In the face of time, there is no human nature, only pushing and posing and putting off and passing the time with planning permissions and objections to the committee, clustering our pride around them, teetering with our back to the void.

I don't have to look at it, nonetheless, and I won't.

In the gloom, he heard his father, still fit to bust with contempt for him. William John, who danced the Lambeth Walk and could not be fired because he knew where the Council drains were. 'Victory, Victor, victory at all costs, victory in spite of all terror, victory, however long and hard the road, for without a victor, there is no survival, Victor.' And the favoured, breast-fed milksop younger brother, Thomas, with the fecund wife and children to carry on the Everley line, sucking his blue-eyed blanket, smiling up to Daddy. Good luck to you all, dead or alive. I don't know what became of you or where you are.

And Ivan Plombe, whoever you were. Rest in peace, neighbour. I wish you no harm.

In my pocket, they will find my wallet, my driver's licence, my debit card, my sodden first day cover of the R36, the first British airship to carry a civil registration, which I never looked at and never shall, because now, it is too dark. That is, if my body reappears with its jacket, which it may not.

Sitting on the highest little mound of shale at the back of the cliff, he put his arms over and across his head and waited. Time passed. The sea crept ever closer, became more insistent on being heard with its chaos and its noise.

He shut it out, listening instead to the sound of his pulse, the irregular booming of his heart.

A new sound, different sound, a scrunching on the gravel made him look up in fear of Morgawr, a Cornish sea-monster, a seal, an unknown creature. In the luminous glow, there was a figure, human enough, bearing down on him.

'I never want to do that again,' the figure said. 'Come with me now.'

Paul. Victor recognised the voice, the tone. Another human being had come to be with him in this place, to go with him, out to sea, down to the bottom.

Leaning forward, he grasped Paul's knees and clung on with so much energy, Paul staggered, twisted and sat down heavily beside him.

He heard Paul say, 'Listen to me, Victor. We have to go now. If you stand up, I will get you off this place, but we must do it now. If you can't, I will leave you and then the Coastguard will come too late. Take hold of my arms and stand up.'

Victor heard only, 'I will leave you.'

As Paul scrambled to his feet, Victor reached out and caught Paul's belt. He clung on.

'OK, so listen. Just along here, this is where I came down on my ass. Listen, the last bit is a big drop. So, I am going to cup my hands together like this. You stand on my hands, and I push you up. You take the grass, roots, heather, stones, anything in your hands and you get up. Then you pull me up. Give me your light.'

Victor shook his head vigorously. It was his only light. He kept his back-up torch hidden in his zipped-up pocket.

'I need it to get us out of here, Victor. You were stuck here, now I am stuck here. We have to do this. Give me your headlamp.'

Pulling Victor along by the swelling water, buckling on Victor's lamp, he found the place where he had come down the cliff.

He cupped his hands together and squatted down. 'Up.' The shout echoed about the place.

Victor braced out of fear, found himself elevated, his chest against the sheer rock. He reached up a few feet and found strong, tangled roots. He pulled on a handful. They held firm. Fainting almost, he pulled himself up as Paul pushed.

'Now let me find a toe hold and grasp your leg.' Below, Victor saw the headlamp beam scan the rock.

'No. Paul, you'll pull me over. No.'

There was a pause.

'Alright. Get back. Sit back as far as you can go.'

'I can't pull. I haven't the strength.' There was a lightening stab in Victor's chest.

'Sit back, will you? Get back to the back of the ledge and cling on.'

Paul moved back, almost to the water, then sprinted at the rock. He came up and over, hurling himself flat in front of Victor.

Paul lay winded for a moment. Victor watched him, barely conscious of anything anymore. Then Paul sat up. 'We've done the worst. We can sit here all night. Spray will reach, but not the sea. But I think we can go on. I think we can go up.'

'In a minute. Let me get my breath. The pain.'

'Anyway, we can stay here. But in a minute, I will signal to Jane. Otherwise, she will call the Coastguard.'

'Jane.' Victor's life with Jane seemed far off. I've looked my death in the eye, he thought. I've been in the valley of the shadow. If I look down from this ledge, I can see myself there, a naked ape, rolled up in a ball, waiting for the sea. Where am I? Here, or still down there?

Still gasping a little, Paul said, 'I am no longer fit. Too many English pies and chips.' He pulled up his jacket and shirt, feeling for peeling skin, rubbing the foot that struck the rock that propelled him from the shale to the top of the ledge. 'I've scraped myself. What were you doing there, Victor?'

Yes, what was he doing? The afternoon seemed so far away and long ago.

'I came down through the Seal Caves. I wanted to see where Plombe had landed. I feel a terrible sense of guilt and loss, you see. It's my fault. I feel that I have killed him myself. I am responsible. How did you know I was here, Paul? I feel terrible to put you to all this trouble, risking your own neck. And incredibly thankful. I won't do it again.'

'I saw your headlamp as you came back from Seal Caves, playing along the rock. I knew you were looking for a way up and I knew you wouldn't do it on your own. Killed him, what do you mean, killed him?'

'It's all my fault. I drove him over the edge with my objections to his garage.'

Paul laughed at the black sky above them. 'You drove him over the edge, Victor? Is that what you are thinking?'

He lowered his voice. 'You didn't drive him over the edge. People don't commit suicide over permission to build a garage. No, Victor, I drove him over the edge.'

Paul pointed to his own chest. 'I. I got him to unpack his paddleboard from his roof-rack, I locked his house up, drove him over the edge and threw his keys after him.'

He slapped Victor on the back with affection. 'Hah! You've got me to thank. I'm going up the path a little now, to signal to Jane with your light. Don't move. You could fall off in the dark. Stay there. I will be back.'

I couldn't see his eyes. I don't grasp what he is saying, but I will hold his words in my mind, and I will think about them when I get up the cliff path, if there is one. If he comes back for me. I can't think about it now.

Victor grasped Plombe's bunch of keys in his pocket. With a grubby hand covered in scratches, grass and gravel, he moved them to an inner pocket, the one where he kept his wallet and the new First Day Cover. He felt his legs begin to tremble again, so he wrapped his arms around them. It was comforting, that way.

There was no moon. Darkness had fallen, with faint luminosity from the sea. The tide was running faster, up towards the flood. He could hear it chase him. He knew that below, his little dry mound had crumbled and spread beneath the waves. First the spray, then the little rivulets, runs and bursts of water, a fourth great wave to take him off, a floundering and a throwing up of arms, a smashing and pounding against rock, a giving up of the soul and a surrender to a slow death.

'Peter knows I've got you here and Jane won't call the Coastguard. Lucky, there was a gorse fire on the cliff, further up, Victor. The vegetation was burnt off in the summer. It doesn't smell too good, and you'll get black all over, but it means we can move up slowly. No gorse and undergrowth to stop us, you see. I'm going to stay by you as you creep forward. Keep your belly close to the ground. Don't look up or down. It gets steep in parts. We can rest, any time. No hurry.'

Victor emptied his mind and concentrated on the task ahead of him.

They reached the top at last. 'Lie flat on the grass. Rest.'

There was a breeze, the sea was a uniform calm, muttering about its loss, far, far off.

In time, Victor was able to stand. With Victor's headlamp, Paul signalled to Peter and Jane. They came in a great rush, in a haze of Pears soap and washing powder.

'I could kill you,' Jane said. 'It's a good job Roy had his wits about him and told me where he thought you'd gone, after asking for a tide table and no phone on you. You were only going out for your stamps. We had to go looking for you. We were worried to death. What a state your Musto jacket is in. You stink of bonfires. I could kill you, Victor Everley.'

Please don't. Please don't talk in that casual way about killing, Victor thought.

Secretly Trying The Keys

As the light ascended, Victor crept out of the bungalow in his pyjamas, walked the few steps next door, took the bunch of keys from his dressing gown pocket and opened up Plombe's sliding double-glazed porch door.

That's all I wanted to know, Victor thought. The keys work in the porch door. Do they work in the front door? The battered old nineteen-thirties wooden door had a mortice lock. If the key fitted, then these were Plombe's keys.

The old doorframe must have been warped. The key fitted but the lock was a little harder to turn. Needs some graphite. Probably the correct key, though not necessarily. There was a back-door key as well. Walk through the house and try it.

Halfway down the white narrow hall, with its smart framed prints of lighthouses of the world, Victor halted. Plombe's ten-foot stand-up paddleboard, pump, fin, paddle and carry-bag in red and black were staring back at him.

He checked the sightline. These objects could not be seen from outside the porch. To know the paddleboard was there, Paul must have been in this house.

Victor gasped for breath.

Hardly any need to go further, but Victor continued down the hall into the kitchen and tried the back door with the smaller, modern mortice key. It fitted and turned. So did the older little latch key, Plombe's attempt at double security at the back of the bungalow.

Victor felt his face begin to burn. How did it go? Paul's confession to Ivan Plombe's murder, as they rested on the first ledge on Als an Marrow after narrowly escaping the tide? His memory of Paul's exact words was vague. 'I got him to unload the paddleboard… and threw the keys after him.' Trauma, he supposed, the terrible upset of facing being drowned was blanking out the rest. He could not hear it in his mind anymore. He could not and did not want to visualise how Paul had got the car to accelerate over the edge of the cliff with Plombe in it.

He, Victor, was harbouring a murderer, a casual psycho, who only wanted to be helpful to him.

He remembered Paul's confident words. 'Plombe won't build his garage. We'll talk to him.'

'Christ alive,' he said aloud.

Like raising an orphan puppy that grew into a black bear. No, no comparison.

He heard a footstep behind him and stiffened, afraid to turn around. What would he say if it was Paul?

'What are you doing in here?' Jane, fully dressed for the day. 'Where did you get that bunch of keys? You realise you're trespassing? After everything that's happened, and the police may not be finished in here yet. You'll be incriminated. Let's leave before we get caught. I don't understand you, Victor, really, I don't. Ever since you got ill, you've been strange and unpredictable. I don't like it.'

He was so glad to see Jane.

'Yes, you're right, Jane. I never thought. Listen Jane, please don't tell the boys I have these keys.'

'Why not?'

'I can't tell you why. Just don't. Please. Our safety depends on it.'

'What?'

'Our lives may depend on you saying nothing about my having this bunch of keys. Jane, trust me. I will tell you later, when it's all over and the boys have gone, but Jane, please.'

'Why all this mystery? You know what?' she said. 'I'm sick to death of keeping secrets and telling lies. I'm sick of all this drama. Where did you find these keys?'

'At the foot of Als an Marrow, sticking out of some gravel. My headlamp found them, close to where Plombe's car went over the cliff.'

'Right. So, the first thing we do is take them to the police station and hand them in.'

'I don't want the boys to know.'

'Why are you looking so panicked? Alright, I won't tell the boys if you will agree to take these keys down to the police station. But I'm telling you something, I'm not putting up with any more drama from you, Victor. I've had enough of it lately.'

Jane went and stood outside the front porch.

Victor followed. 'There look, I've locked up the back door again, I only slipped the keys in the locks, I didn't touch anything, not even the doors.'

'No, but your footprints are all over the house and so are mine.'

'Only the hallway and the kitchen. I was just trying the keys to see whether they fitted.'

'Why, Victor? And what makes you think that keys you found on the beach would fit? Come indoors now, get dressed and have your breakfast. You'll catch your death out here in your nightclothes again. People will think you're demented, wandering around at all hours. I'll call the boys down for breakfast.'

'Please don't say anything.'

'I've said I won't. But we are going to the police station after breakfast. The boys will be busy with changing the electric meter, the electric will be off all day, this is a good chance to go to the supermarket and drop into the police station without saying a word to them. But I'm telling you, you'd better tell me what all this is about. I'm not happy about it, Victor, getting up at the crack of dawn and sneaking into Plombe's house like this.'

It was no better in the Police Station.

'So, you have these keys, which you found at the foot of Als an Marrow, which you say belong to your neighbour, Ivan Plombe, who committed suicide last week.'

'Yes.'

For some reason, the desk sergeant had insisted that Victor see the detectives who were dealing with Plombe's case and who had just come out of a briefing. He'd waited well over an hour, Now, he was sitting at a desk in an interview room by a radiator, feeling overheated in his winter coat.

'So, what made you think that these keys belonged to Mr Plombe?'

'I don't know. They were in some gravel. My headlamp found them. The light was fading, and I was walking towards Seal Caves to get to the beach before the tide flooded. I switched my headlight on, it's a really powerful beam, it was getting dark, they were poking out of the gravel. I put them in my pocket.'

'And why did you do that?'

'The keys weren't rusty, they were obviously somebody's house keys, then something told me they were my neighbour's keys. I thought I'd better rescue them.'

These detectives were friendly, Victor thought, but edgy. Very alert.

'Something told you they were Mr Plombe's keys. You knew Mr Plombe was dead?'

'Yes, and I knew that this was roughly where his car must have gone over the cliff. There were a few bits of glass and plastic and some metal bits from the car there. I thought this must be where it happened, and I thought these keys were probably his.'

'That's a bit of a leap, isn't it?'

The second detective laughed out loud.

The first detective corrected himself. 'A bit of a leap of imagination, isn't it? You thought the keys came out of a car that is no longer there.'

Victor sat back and sighed. 'Perhaps it was.'

'And are these his keys?'

'Yes, they are. Before coming to you with them, I tried them in the doors. They do work, well the middle lock is stiff, but that may be because the door is old. They're his, alright.'

'I see. Mr Everley, as I recall, there is no beach below Als an Marrow. When you were at the foot of the cliff, on that narrow strip of gravel, racing to get back before the tide came in, what made you think that these were Mr Plombe's keys?'

'I don't know. They looked like they might be them, and they were where Mr Plombe's car went over the cliff and they looked new, not rusted by the sea.'

'Were you already familiar with your neighbour's keys?'

'No, not particularly. His keys look a bit like mine. Our bungalows are similar, we both have a thirties style original front door and a double-glazed door to the porch.'

Victor took his own set of keys out of his pocket. 'You see? We have the same kind of front door key, with the lattice top as decoration. It's unusual. Somehow, I knew they belonged to Plombe. Then there was the fact of the bunch of keys being shiny, not rusty, and being in the same area as the bits of glass and metal from the car, well, somehow, I knew. I only tried them out this morning to satisfy my mind that they were the keys. Then my wife suggested I bring them in to you, because I'd gone into the bungalow.'

At last, the detective looked satisfied with Victor's explanation.

'And so, you went back through Seal Caves and on to the beach and home?'

'Yes.'

'It gets dark by four o'clock at this time of the year. Darker at Als an Marrow. What was the tide doing?'

'It was flooding. I had to hurry up.'

'But you made it through Seal Caves.'

'Yes. Just. I had my headlamp and a backup torch. I've done it before.'

The detectives looked at each other, as if to say no, that doesn't sound right.

The detective who took the lead in the interview leaned forward, placing his elbows on the desk. 'Seal Caves flood at the beach end first.'

'I know. That's why I had to hurry up.'

There was a pause. An electric fan started up somewhere. It was hot and stuffy here.

Victor said, 'Look, I felt guilty. I feel dreadfully guilty. I feel I've contributed to Mr Plombe's suicide. I was prepared to make a stink about him trying to build a garage on the waste ground between our properties. I was going to object to the planning committee. I didn't think it was right for him to ask for planning permission like that. I mean, I always use that waste ground to park my car. The old lady who lived there before us, she used it as well. That piece of ground was not claimed by anybody. It was just the entrance to the field beyond, full of bungalows since the nineteen-seventies, but it was a farm gate entrance, originally. I have the use of the strip of ground, and I was outraged. I didn't think it was right that Plombe should turn up, pull down his own garden wall overnight and apply for planning permission, just like that, knowing that I used the ground, I live here all the time, and I have nowhere else to park my car, to keep it off that busy road where wing-mirrors get smashed off all the time. But I didn't want anything to happen to him, not like that.'

'Not like what, Mr Everley?'

'I didn't want him to commit suicide.' Victor felt that he was about to start blubbing like a child in front of a headmaster. 'I didn't like his attitude, but I didn't wish the man any harm.' Victor's eyes were filling with tears. His nose was beginning to weep. He fished around in his overcoat pocket for a handkerchief or a piece of tissue. There was nothing in his pocket but a dry-cleaning receipt.

The second detective got up and found a box of man-size tissues in a filing cabinet. He put the box down in front of Victor. 'Let me tell you this,' he said, 'completely off the record and you can make what you want of it. We detectives, we're not the Helmets. We're a different breed. We exist to clear up the messes that they make. We're all graduates and we've all seen a bit of life. A lot of us have an MPhil or an MSc. We treat the public with respect, and they respect us. You'd be surprised what people tell us when we approach them nicely.'

Victor was still wiping his nose. He kept his head down. What did that mean? What were they after? He felt mentally penetrated. Destabilised.

There was more silence.

The desk sergeant came in and whispered in the ear of the leading detective, then went out quietly.

The older man stood up. 'Your wife is waiting. She says she has been to Tesco and wants to go home now.'

Victor got up from the chair. 'I can go?' His legs and back felt stiff. 'Do you want these keys?'

'The desk sergeant will book them in and give will you a receipt. You're free to go.'

'Thankyou.'

The relief of being out in the open air again was joyous. Victor said, 'Jane, I wish you hadn't made me do that.'

'Why not? They're not our keys and we've been in Plombe's bungalow.'

'They think I'm a nutjob or a thief and I've caused them to be suspicious of me.'

'Well, you haven't done anything wrong, have you? You've just handed in the keys, though I can't imagine why they wanted to talk to you all this time. You've been in there three hours. I told that policeman on the desk it wasn't fair. I've got a freezer-full of shopping dripping all over the boot of the car, including ice-cream.'

'I didn't tell them I was trapped by the tide and Paul rescued me. I didn't want to draw attention to Peter and Paul.'

'Why not? I understand that, but why have you become so secretive over these keys?' Jane went ahead of Victor to open the car doors. 'I'll be glad when all of this is over and the boys have gone, love them though I do. I shall miss them dreadfully, but we seem to be constantly enmeshed in lies, lately.'

Victor sat in the passenger seat. 'Listen, Jane. Can we have a little drive? Can we go and park by the river? By the tennis club. I want to say something to you while we're on our own.'

'Whatever is it, Victor?'

'Just drive and I'll tell you.'

By the time they reached the Memorial Park, Victor knew that he was not going to be able to tell Jane what he was certain he knew about Plombe's 'suicide.' He would have to make something up.

'Now, what is all this about, Victor? I need to get home and put the food shopping away.'

This was a bleak corner in the winter. In the circular flowerbeds, the bedding plants had been dug up. All that remained were the big palms, peeling, grey and sickly. Behind them, the tennis club was boarded up for the winter. A few cans were rolling around, dripping into puddles in the tarmac.

'I don't want to stay here,' Victor began. 'Cornwall is not all it's cracked up to be. Do you like Torquay and Paignton? I do. More our sort of people there. I've got no social life here. The yacht club turned out to be not a very nice place. I thought I was going to enjoy being Treasurer, but it didn't work out like that. People were prejudiced and stupid.'

He stared at the river, thinking of the last meeting in the library and committee room. What a pompous little ape he himself had been, falling back on his years of experience in the boardroom, using it to make a grab for power in the tiny, provincial yacht club, exposing a little corruption and self-interest by the members and the staff, who retaliated by simply rejecting him. What did it matter?

'Cornwall has knocked some spots off me. I've learned a lot over the past few months. Jane…'

He turned towards her, gripping her arm. 'Jane, I don't want to stay here. I want to go. Sell up. Now that the bungalow is done. It's looking good, all refurbished, with a new kitchen and bathroom and a new en-suite in the dormer bedroom. We could advertise it with a good estate agent in the spring, even a London estate agent. What would people give to live in a place like ours, eh?'

He laughed, a bitter cry coming up from some deep reservoir of fear. He gripped Jane's hand. He interwove his fingers into those pliant little fingers of her small paw.

'Or we could just put it back in the auction, take our chance with the price, put a reasonable reserve on, so we don't lose any money. Nobody would know about Plombe or the boys. We have enough in the bank. We could get somewhere modest in Torquay, not on the front of course, although we could get a flat. A flat with a sea view would be good. A retirement flat. They have carparking and security and wardens. They even have carers for when we get older. They're much more our sort of people in Torquay.

'It's raw here. I never knew. I never suspected how raw. They're not like us, the natives. They're suited to the place, but we're not. We haven't the…'

'We haven't the what?'

'I don't know, Jane.'

He looked into her face and saw a complete lack of comprehension.

She untangled her fingers from his.

'Only you've been saying that rather a lot lately: I don't know, I don't know. What don't you know? I know you've been greatly affected by what Plombe did, but that was what he did, not what you did.

You're not responsible for what Plombe did to himself. It's not your fault. I don't know why you think it could possibly be your fault. And besides, you may not have been making friends, but I have. When you went to hospital and they had their benefit concert with the Irish people, everybody was really friendly towards me. I feel I'm getting somewhere here. Anyway, you've got Roy: he's nice to you, he took you fishing and… I know you've had a shock, getting trapped by the tide. It was a close shave, and I don't suppose you're over the fright yet, but thank goodness Paul was there to rescue you without any fuss or involving the police and the Coastguard.'

He looked out across the grey river. Flood tide again, flooding up towards Tesco, creeping up towards the Cathedral, the National Carpark. He could never think of the inexorable movement of water in the same way again. He knew that he could never tell her what Paul so casually told him, that he had murdered Plombe as an afterthought, as a friendly gesture, because Plombe had tried to grab Victor's carparking space.

They would never escape Peter and Paul now. They were trapped, he and Jane. Trapped until Peter and Paul decided to move on.

They would never move on. Why would they move on, when they had arranged things so neatly in Portmarrow for themselves, with their Christmas lights, their grateful village, their refurbished bungalow by the sea and two foolish monkeys to cater to their every need?

And what would Paul be capable of when he discovered that Victor had been to the police with Plombe's keys? Another little accident for himself and Jane? Or would that be an accident just for himself alone? Jane could go on cooking and baking and sewing and mending for them until she made a will, died and left the bungalow in their names.

'Jane, you must promise me that you will never tell Peter and Paul that I went to the police station with Plombe's keys.'

'I've told you I won't, but I think you are being ridiculous. You need to buck up your ideas and pull yourself together, Victor Everley.'

Victor Investigates

'Where have you been? Why were you out so long? Why don't you tell us what you are doing? We have been waiting for you. The electrician could not wait any longer. Anyway, the new earth stake and fuse board have been replaced, everything is finished, and this is your new electrical certificate. Look after it. They don't issue another.'

'Oh Peter, that's lovely. Wonderful. Help me put the shopping away before the bags start dripping.'

'Why do you need all this food and all these bottles, Mama?'

'It's Christmas, Peter. We're going to invite all the people we know to drop in on Christmas Eve. All our neighbours on Beach Road. That's when the choir comes around to sing carols.'

'Carols.' Peter thought about the word.

Paul appeared to think about it too. 'On Christmas Eve? That will be OK.'

Victor was studying the Electrical Installation Condition Report. He had no idea what he was looking at, but it looked authentic enough. Privately, he'd seek out Tremayne, the electrician, just to make doubly sure he had the right piece of paper. The boys need not know he was doing a final check. He needed that paperwork to place with the deeds, to sell the bungalow, to get away.

To get away. That was his urgent project. Get away to safety.

Over the course of two days, Victor sat in his chair with his newspaper, brooding, waiting for an opportunity to get up to The Close and find Tremayne, the inspecting electrician.

How come Paul had all that knowledge of re-wiring a house? He had about him the air of efficiency and the sure-footedness of an expert. He had the focus and dedication of a person who needed this job, but nobody had paid him, except in giving him a temporary home. Who was he?

Victor thought back to Peter's first evening, when he missed the mini-bus and asked whether there was an allotment nearby where he could get into a shed for the night. Understandable: shelter was fundamental to survival. To be out all night in the autumn rain, it could mean pneumonia and death, even at Peter's age. How old was Peter?

They had come a long way since then. The boys had saved his life twice, but still he longed to be free of them. There was something entirely wrong about the situation, never knowing who they were or where they came from.

Peter and Paul had put their trust in him to say nothing about them. Surely, they could tell him where they originated? Surely there was a way of making it possible for them to come out of the shadows and stay in this country, get jobs and stand on their own feet?

Why should any of that matter to Victor, anyway? The refurbishment was complete, and they were all moving on, every one of them. The bungalow would be occupied by someone else. And Plombe's bungalow too. Perhaps both bungalows would be purchased by a speculator, somebody who would flatten both buildings. Perhaps four brand-new, showy, square edifices with plastic cladding on the upper storeys would rise in their place, obliterating forever the contentious, unclaimed field entrance, the cause of Plombe's unthinkable death.

'You're spending a lot of time in that chair lately, staring into space.' Jane was in front of him with his morning coffee.

'I'm still not very well. I start gasping as soon as I get up.'

'Time you went to see the GP. You need to move about, because you'll start putting on weight if you sit there all day, and that will only make it worse.'

'I know. Make an appointment for me, would you? You're very scratchy lately, Jane.'

'You don't need to be so dependent on me. I've got things to do, with Christmas just around the corner. You can make the appointment yourself.'

'I think I will.'

That was the way. That was the way out of this house. A walk up to the surgery with a diversion to The Close. Nobody here had to know. If one of them tried to accompany him, he would plead the need for privacy with the doctor, and he would say he was only going to be a few minutes.

The receptionist on the phone told him there were no appointments available for a week. He speeded up the process by saying that he was breathless all the time and thought something was very wrong. He was told, in that case he could sit in the surgery and wait until a doctor was free.

He wandered into the kitchen. 'The doctor can see me now, Jane. I'll just change my shoes and walk up there. I'll get the bread from the baker on the way back. Anything else needed?'

He slipped out of the house, strolled down towards the surgery, and diverted left up the old mineral railway trail, cutting through a gap in the fence to the little group of nineteen-fifties council houses. The Close was up here somewhere.

He asked some children playing in the street, but they didn't know a Mr Tremayne.

He saw an old couple come out of one of the houses in The Close. He'd counted twelve houses in the cul-de-sac, so they must know where Mr Tremayne lived.

They both looked puzzled. 'No. We bin up 'ere thirty year. No Tremayne 'ere.'

'Are you sure? He's an electrician.'

'Somebody's 'avin you on, my 'an'some. No Tremayne up 'ere.'

'Oh well. I'll ask at the post office.'

I can't believe this, Victor thought. A barefaced lie. And what about my certificate? Wherever Paul got it from, perhaps it's not valid. They must have got it from somewhere. Somebody signed off the work. I mean, they wouldn't have changed the fuse board and the earthing if somebody hadn't made them do it. So, where is Tremayne? Perhaps Paul got the address wrong. But then, Paul went up here the other day to see Tremayne to make an appointment to get the work signed off. The electrician was supposed to have been here, that day I handed in the keys at the police station.

Back through the gap in the fence and on to the mineral railway path, he stood for a while to catch his breath, staring at the viaduct and the grim stone-built terrace of houses across the valley. This may be a seaside village with tourism now, but ugly metal tin-streaming sheds and the daily grind of heavy industry were only just buried beneath the surface.

You know what? He thought, I'll be glad to be gone from here. There's something alien about this place. Something not very good. The people are… I'll never make friends here. But then, I never did make friends. They used to say I was stand-offish at London

Bridge, but you always need to be independent when you have responsibility. The sea air is good here, it's quiet, but there is something closed in. And something abandoned, like this little narrow-gage railway that took ore down to the ships in the harbour. It's a place where heavy industry has come and gone. That old couple in The Close, for instance, in a council house built for labourers. Oh well. Time to move forward and leave it all behind. Chalk it up to experience.

There were no customers at the post office. He found Roy staring into space, waiting for the van to take away the day's bags and all the Christmas parcels.

Victor said, 'Roy, I'm looking for an electrician called Tremayne, up at The Close. I can't find him there.'

'Let's have a look.' Roy looked up the postcode. 'What number?'

'Fourteen, I think. I counted twelve houses up there, but I couldn't find the other two.'

'No, there aren't fourteen houses up there, only twelve, Vic.'

'Are you sure? Well, what other houses could be mistaken for thirteen and fourteen?'

'There aren't any other houses up there. It's just a little cul-de-sac. They replaced a row of tumbledown quarry workers' cottages in the nineteen-fifties. Here, you can see on the Google map.'

A frisson that reached down Victor's arms and into his fingers settled into a loud palpitation in his chest.

'You alright, Vic?'

'Yes, Roy, I'm fine. Where does Mr Tremayne live, then? Tremayne the electrician.'

'Well, I'm not familiar with the name in this village. Let's Google electricians.'

Victor went and stood by the rack of Christmas and New Year cards, so that Roy could not see his face. I've been had, he thought. What do I do now? I'll have to tackle Paul about it. No, I won't, I'll let it pass. I'll wait for them to go at Christmas, it's only a week away now, and I'll say nothing. When they've gone, I'll find an electrician to check the electrics and issue a certificate or have some modifications done, whatever is necessary. The electrics will be alright for now. I won't say anything to Jane, I'll just lie low and wait. Best not to challenge Paul.

He thought of the bold and confident Plombe, his abandoned paddleboard waiting for him in the silent hallway with the pictures of lighthouses of the world. The bumptious Plombe, dead and gone, just like that.

No, I won't say anything.

Roy called across to him. 'No, there aren't any Tremayne, electricians, none that I can find locally. It's a Cornish name alright. Have you a phone number for him?'

'Yes, somewhere, I picked up his business card somewhere. I can always find another one. There are plenty of electricians about. Doesn't matter. Are you stopping by with the choir on Christmas Eve, by the way?'

'Certainly. Wouldn't miss that for the world.'

'So, what did the doctor say, Victor?'

'Oh, the surgery was full of people coughing and spluttering. I decided not to wait any longer. I've made an appointment for next week, anyway.'

Peter was stringing up newly made paper chains, chattering and laughing with Jane. Every year, Jane used to bring home paper chains from the primary school where she worked. She must have bought coloured paper squares and glue in town the other day. Paul was lolling about on the sofa, fiddling around with his mobile.

'By the way, Victor,' Paul said, 'Mr Tremayne is coming over with his invoice for inspecting the electrics and issuing the certificate.'

'Really?' Victor was caught off-guard, unable to control his surprise. I must be more careful with my reactions, he thought. I really must.

Paul looked up sharply. He seemed to scrutinise Victor carefully. 'Yes really.'

'When?'

'Today, after work. He wants cash.'

'Yes, no problem.' I really must hide what I am thinking, Victor thought. But then, this brave young man has saved my life twice. Why would he ever want to harm me? Perhaps that confession about killing Plombe was a joke? He said he never joked but always told the truth, because people never believed the truth. Perhaps, after coming down that cliff after me, at the risk of slipping and falling off, perhaps he was all hyped up and just joked about Plombe. Or am I living with a very dangerous killer who could strike at any time if he knew I had been to the police station with Plombe's keys?

Don't let Paul know I have been up to The Close to a house that doesn't exist, to a Tremayne, electrician who doesn't exist and who is coming here after work.

Tremayne came with his invoice, just as Peter and Jane were tidying away after supper. Victor kept him at the door while he looked carefully at the piece of paper. But Peter was right behind Victor.

'Come in, come in,' he called.

Tremayne stepped inside the porch.

Tremayne Electrical Installations, with a Newquay address and telephone numbers. City and Guilds BS7671 Part P Compliant. It looked authentic enough.

'I thought you lived up at The Close,' Victor said.

'This is not Mr Tremayne, this is Sandy.' Paul stepped into the porch behind Victor. Victor could feel his breath on his neck.

'This is a Newquay address.'

'Tremaynes are everywhere.'

Sandy was mute, staring at the wall.

Victor read out the first item. 'To supply and fit 1 x 18th Edition Metal Consumer Unit Incorporating 1x twin RCD and Surge protection.'

He read out the second item. 'To supply and fit 1 x Earth Rod. I thought we purchased those things ourselves, Paul. You installed them already, but they had to be changed for the certificate.'

'No, I left it to Tremayne's to supply the right parts. I didn't want to buy the wrong things again with your money.'

The other items, 'To carry out an Electrical Installation Condition Report' and 'To provide a Domestic Electrical Installation Certificate' were straightforward. Payment terms, Cheques payable to, and Direct Internet Payments, with bank numbers were on the bottom of the invoice.

'Right, so I'll put this through the bank. Thank you for bringing the invoice.'

Got them. I can check these numbers for authenticity, Victor thought, his old instincts from a long working life in commerce rising up to claim precedence over his fear of Paul's disapproval.

Sandy stiffened. 'I want the cash,' he said. 'I was promised cash. I was told to collect cash only.'

No-one moved.

I'm not going to give him seven hundred pounds in cash, Victor thought. Who is he? Who is this Sandy?

'So, you are the person who made these changes and then issued the certificate, did you?' Victor was trying to remember the signature on the certificate that he had already put away with the old deeds to the house and other certificates, certificates he needed to sell the house and get out of here.

'No,' Sandy said. 'Somebody else from Tremayne's did that.'

'I know what I can do, I'll write you out a cheque,' Victor said. 'What's your surname?'

'Angove, but I have to bring back the cash. A cheque's no good. Sorry.'

'And in this house, I don't keep seven hundred pounds in cash. Sorry.'

The atmosphere had become tense. Sandy turned to go. He reached for the handle of the front door.

'So, do you live at The Close? Number fourteen? I can get the money in the morning and bring it to you.' That will give me time to check the numbers on the invoice and ring Tremayne's, Victor thought.

There was a gasp from Peter. 'I can pay. I will go upstairs and get the money.'

Peter turned and ran upstairs. He came down with the money and counted out seven hundred and four pounds.

'Receipt? Sign on the invoice as 'paid?' And put the date.'

Sandy Angove took Victor's pen and signed paid. He handed the precious piece of paper to Victor, who could not stop himself looking triumphantly towards Paul. I really should not do that, he thought, as Paul steadily returned and held his gaze. I really ought to keep myself in check, or the whole thing could rebound on me.

When Peter and Paul got their coats and wandered down to the Cornish Arms to play pool for an hour, Jane got up and switched off Abandoned Engineering.

'Now, what did you do that for, Jane? I was watching that.'

Jane stood in front of the television screen. 'Listen, Victor. You'd better pay Peter when he comes back. That was very rude of you to let him pay your bill like that. You know they haven't any money.'

'Haven't any money? The young man didn't seem to have any trouble finding seventy crisp notes in tens to pay somebody we haven't seen before. So, where did this vagrant of ours get this money, he gave away so easily? How much have you been giving them?'

'Ten pounds a week each. That's pocket money, Victor, for soap and razors. A child would get more. And look what they do for us for those ten pounds a week. You should be ashamed.'

'Soap and razors.' A vivid memory of the soap on a rope in the shower upstairs in the dormer bedroom seized hold of his mind. 'They haven't been here seventy weeks. So where did he get his seven hundred pounds?'

'Perhaps he had savings.'

'They go to the post office all the time. I'll bet they have an income of some sort that we don't know about.'

'What if they do? What has that got to do with the fact that you didn't want to pay, and Peter just gave the man cash out of the generosity of his heart?'

Victor sat up. 'Where's that receipt, Jane?' He scrabbled around in his pockets. 'Where is it? It has the details of Tremayne's on it. I want to do some checking. For God's sake find it.'

'Find it yourself.' Jane folded her arms.

'What?' In all the long years together, Jane had never spoken to him like that.

'You owe Peter seven hundred and four pounds. Send him to the post office with your bank card in the morning and give his money back.'

Victor stood up, still looking for the signed receipt. 'Don't be stupid. I'm not giving him my pin number.'

'How else is he going to get his money out? I'd trust him with my card and pin number any day. In fact, I do. He collects their pocket money every week.'

Victor stood still. 'And have you checked your balance each time?'

'Yes of course. He brings me back the card and the ticket with the balance on it. I'd trust him with my life, Victor.'

Defeated, Victor slumped back down in his chair. He had gone very pale, thinking of the steep cliff, the void, the darkening strand below. 'Open the window, Jane. There is no air in here. I give up with it, I really do. How much more are we supposed to give them? You deal with it. I can't any longer. I don't think this is going to end well.'

'Don't be such an idiot, Victor.'

Jane left the lounge and went to look for the receipt. It was crumpled up in a ball by the waste-paper basket in the dining room, as though someone had chucked it and missed. She brought it to Victor.

I'm done for, Victor thought. They don't give a damn whether I check on their story or not.

He took the ball of paper to the kitchen table and smoothed it out in front of Jane. The bank details at the bottom were torn out, but the telephone number remained at the top.

'I don't care what you say, Jane. Never mind the money. I'll ring Tremayne's in the morning and find out who this Sandy Angove is, who claims to live in a house that doesn't exist. I need to know whether the electrics have been tested or not, whether they have been certificated or not. I don't need to be told lies; I need a certificate that I can hand over to a conveyancing solicitor.'

'I wish you wouldn't be so combative all the time. There's probably some explanation you haven't thought about.'

Locked in the Dining Room

It was lunchtime in the Everley dining room again. The tension of the evening before had eased only slightly. The very air was charged, and Victor could not stop himself from causing trouble. He wanted to gain ascendency in his own house, bring things to a head, prove he was right. Peter and Jane were in their own world, gossiping and chattering about Christmas, discussing glittery things and the old practice of keeping a plum pudding under the bed to rot down for months. Leaning back in his chair, gazing at Paul, who was smoking in the house again, Victor had a vision, a cartoon drawing of a plum pudding with fuse wire sticking out of the top, lit and throwing up sparks like a Bonfire Night sparkler of the kind that children hold in their gloved hands. I know I'm stirring the pudding, he thought. I know it's dangerous.

'I rang Tremayne's first thing this morning,' Victor said.

The others stopped and looked at him. Paul did not move from his casual position in front of the old bottle-gas heater, but raised his eyelids to gaze at Victor, a long, unswerving, brown-eyed gaze.

'I spoke to the receptionist, then to a person they called Old Man Tremayne himself. They don't have an employee called Sandy Angove, living at fourteen, The Close, Portmarrow. They don't have any Angoves at all. Nobody from Tremayne's has been here to certificate this property. Would you believe it? This means, the certificate is worthless, and seven hundred and four pounds have disappeared into some con man's pocket.'

Jane looked as though she was about to speak, but Paul sprang out of his chair and grabbed Jane by her left wrist.

'Come with me.'

He strode to the dining room door, took the key from the lock, pulled Jane through the doorway and locked Victor inside with Peter.

'We won't be long,' he said.

Victor heard the front door and the porch door close. For a long minute, he stared at the dining room door, not thinking, not feeling anything at all, except that a small voice somewhere towards the bottom of his mind said, 'I told you it would come to this.' It left him with a profound, numb terror.

'Listen,' Peter said to Victor. 'He won't harm Jane. He's angry that we've been cheated, and you blame him. He will put everything right. I know him. He gets angry. He is sensitive. He does not like being called a cheat.'

Victor recovered and sat up. 'On the contrary,' he said. 'I don't call Paul a cheat. I simply say that whoever this Angove is, he is not an electrician who works for Tremayne's. Neither has this Sandy Angove ever worked for Old Man Tremayne. Mr Tremayne told me he is the head of the outfit. He started the business out of an A40 van in 1968, year of revolutions, he said. He seems real enough. He wants to see that invoice with its number. He thinks it must have been copied, a cut and paste job. Somebody could have got it out of a skip. Either that or somebody in his office has some sort of scam going. It could have happened before. Whatever is going on, he wants to nip it in the bud.'

'Sorry?'

'In gardening, Peter, or in growing tomatoes, you pinch out the small buds so that the best ones will grow and ripen to a better fruit. If we let all of the buds flower and grow into fruit, all of bad and mis-shaped fruit, the crop will be small and disfigured. If we let only the best grow and prosper, we get a great crop and that means we build a great farm. It's like eugenics. In management, we use metaphors to make a point, like cutting out dead wood to create a productive enterprise. That's the glory of the English language, Peter. Have you got a language like that? Where is my wife?'

Victor strode to the dining room door and rattled the doorknob until a small grubscrew fell to the floor, unnoticed. 'What has Paul done with my wife? Where has he taken her?'

He turned back to Peter. 'Well? How is he going to get out of this one?'

What is more to the point, said the steady voice in the back of Victor's mind, how are you going to get out of this one, Victor, Victor, Victory? You're playing the only hand you have and you're playing against yourself.

'I think, Victor, we must be calm and let Paul sort out this Sandy Angove. Paul will do it. You can rely on him.'

Peter was still at his place at the table. A glistening film was forming over the Cheddar cheese and pickle on his plate.

'Well, he'll have his work cut out, Peter dear. Number fourteen, The Close, doesn't exist, chum.'

Peter looked down. 'How do you know that?'

'I'm not a complete idiot, Peter. I'm not Jane. You don't get to be a Company Secretary, starting from the Walthamstow gutter, without knowing a trick or two, doing some checking up for yourself. You think I'm a fool. No, I'm not a fool. I'm ahead of you foreigners, every time.'

Panting, he moved back to his chair by his old electric three-barred fire. The room felt chill.

'Where is Jane? What is Paul doing with Jane? Why has he done this?'

'Jane will be fine, Victor. Paul won't harm her.'

There was nothing more to say. They sat still while the sun moved around, casting transparent moving shadows through the battered Cornish cordyline trees outside the window.

Victor sat picking at his fingernails. 'You know, Peter, when I retired from life in the office, I thought I was in clover. I thought I could take my little bounty and my wife, and I would come down here to live and everything would be well, and I would be so happy. I'd put off living, you see. That's what retirement is. They give you a watch. It represents getting your time back. But it's cruel, Peter, because they've already sucked the life out of you with their corporate games. You've worked and slaved for them, saving them millions, yes millions. Those lazy, gravy-sucking Eton messes. Yes. With your intelligence, with your ability, you make millions for them, but you can't afford to live in town, not in their town, no. You walk to the tube, you rattle around underground, rubbing noses with other poor devils like you, then you get the bus and finally you get home to your tiny little house and garden, stinking of traffic. You can't open your windows because of the stench from the buses and lorries. Your wife has been struggling all day in a classroom with a bunch of abusive kids, kids with displaced parents crowding at the gate who don't speak English. When you don't have any children yourself to carry on after you. Oh, I know. What don't I know about it?'

He paused for breath.

'Let me get you some tea. Paul gave you a shock. But Jane will be alright, don't worry. They will be back soon.'

Peter got up to go to the dining room door.

'Oh, I can't go to the kitchen to boil a kettle.'

'No, your good old mate went and locked the door on us. Why has he locked the dining room, Peter? Am I dreaming this?'

Peter came and stood by Victor. 'Listen, Victor, everything will be alright. You've done good things, and everything will be alright. When you do good things, they come back to you. My family used to say that.'

'Where are your family now, Peter?'

'I left the village. I ran away and then they said the village was bombed and gassed.'

'But who by, Peter? Are you a Kurd? Why don't you tell me? Why the mystery? You see, this is why I can't trust you. When I go and look for Angove's house, it doesn't exist. Then there is Plombe. Where did he come from? He said he was from Colchester, then it turns out he was from the other side of London. Paul won't tell me anything about himself. Surely you can give me a name, a town, a country. I seem to be wandering around in a miasma. There's no ground under my feet, only a stench rising. Jane is the only person who has a history. And now she's changed. I hardly know her.'

Victor lowered his head. 'I'm feeling faint,' he said. 'I feel dizzy.'

Peter went to the window to open it, thinking there might be undetected fumes from the mobile gas fire. 'Victor, there's a woman just coming through the gate. Do you know her? She's carrying a bag for laptop for work.'

'What does she look like?'

'She's a black lady in a suit.'

Victor got to his feet and looked out. 'Oh God, it's that coon from Social Services, checking up on us. I don't want to see her. Shut the blind, Peter. Pull the curtains.'

'She's here now, at the porch.' Peter slid into the shadows, between the curtain and the wall.

Victor began to whisper. 'I can't talk to her. We're locked in here. How would we explain that? She's suspicious of you. Just keep quiet, Peter.' He slid down in his chair.

The bell rang, then there was a knocking on the glass door of the porch, a pause and a scuffle of feet on the gravel under the window. A shadow passed over the sunshine that was beaming through the glass.

'Mr Everley? Victor?'

Victor stayed very still.

'Victor? I can see you.'

Victor pretended to be asleep.

'Victor? Come along now. I've come to see if you're alright, if you are wanting anything. Are you alright now? Are you going to let me in?'

'I'm asleep,' Victor shouted. 'Go away. Leave me alone. I'm napping. I always have my nap in the afternoon. Go away.'

He thought he heard her click her tongue. 'Very well. I will come back in the morning.'

'Goodbye.'

There was a scuffle, a scrunch of feet and a squeak of the gate.

'She's gone.'

'But not for long, Peter. You see why I just want to get away from here? I've had enough of this little village, Peter. I don't want to live here anymore.'

'Really?'

'Listen, Peter. We'll give the house to you. You and Paul. You can have it. You've done so much to it, it's yours anyway. We don't need it. We can go and rent somewhere. It's better. It's better that way. Because when we get old and ill, if we have nothing, then the Social Services will look after us free of charge. They have to. In this country, if you have a house, they make you sell it, and they put you into a care home with other old people. There's piddle in the carpets, plastic over the chairs in these care homes. I've seen it. Listen to me, Peter. Tell Paul. You can have it. You can have the house. If you won't take it now, you can have it when we're dead. Or, I know: I can take out a lifetime mortgage on it and give the money to you to buy a little flat of your own. That way, nobody can bother you. You'll be safe. You can get jobs and live under the radar. You'll be in the clear for the rest of your lives, as long as you stay out of trouble. There's freedom here in this country, just so long as you stay out of trouble. Jane and I, we...'

There was a scraping of a key in the front door lock, some chatter and laughter. Jane unlocked the dining room door and suddenly she was standing there, holding up the key.

'Paul, you locked them in by mistake,' she said.

Victor stood up and turned to face the door. Paul was loafing behind her in the hall, smoking in the house again.

'He lives in number twelve,' Jane said. 'Angove, he lives in number twelve with his mother, not number fourteen. And Paul made him give seven hundred pounds back. There you are, Peter. Here is your money back.' Her eyes shone bright as she took a wad of banknotes out of her pocket. 'I'll get your other four pounds from my purse.'

Victor thought for a moment. 'Yes,' he said, 'but we still owe Angove or somebody for the fuse board and the earthing spike.'

Paul came forward. 'Oh, I wouldn't worry about that, Victor. Angove will put that down to experience, you know.'

'Yes, but I still need the electrics checked and a real Certificate of Compliance.'

'It is real, Victor. Angove is a qualified electrician, he told us what to do, we did it and he issued a certificate.'

'But is it a real one, Paul, one I can use?'

'Yes, it's real, Victor. You just didn't have to pay for it.'

Paul smiled, Peter smiled, Jane smiled happily.

Victor put on his smile. 'Now let's have some tea, Jane.'

That evening, Victor accompanied Peter and Paul to the Cornish Arms. When Peter was at the bar, he said to Paul, 'Remember when you told me you got Plombe to unload his paddle board? We were on the cliff, and I have to admit I was still terrified. I thought I was going to die, fall off or something and you were there for me. It has sort of bothered me ever since. Why did you get him to unload the paddle board before he drove off and…?'

'The paddle board?' Paul leaned closer to Victor. He lowered his voice and looked around. 'These paddle boards, well the beach cleaners, the volunteers, they collect hundreds, thousands of them after a season. They stack them up high, faded, broken. If these boards are left in the sea, they break up in tiny pieces and they end up in the stomach of little sea creatures. They're not made of wood. The bass you go fishing for, they eat them. And the small dolphin pups, they love to crunch them up and swallow some pieces. Then they get stuck inside and they starve to death. I hate that.'

Victor Back on the Trail

'Listen, Jane, tell me again.' Victor was whispering in the bedroom. 'What happened after Paul grabbed you by the wrist and locked Peter and me in the dining room?'

Jane dropped the pairs of tights that she was sorting out in a drawer and sat on the bed. 'I don't know, well, he handed me my Musto and said we were going up to find Angove.'

'Then where did you go?'

'We went up the road and up the tramway.'

'Did you go through a fence?'

'Yes, we did, it came out into The Close.'

'What happened then?'

'For goodness' sake, Victor, why do you need a blow-by-blow account of everything? He asked some kids who were playing in the road, and they said Angove lived with his mother in number twelve.'

'Did he expect there to be a number fourteen?'

'I don't know. I'm not sure. What does it matter?'

'It matters because he told us that Tremayne, not Angove, lived in number fourteen. If you remember, he said the other day that he was going up to fourteen, The Close to see Tremayne about signing off the electrics.'

Jane raised her voice. 'Well, he got it wrong, didn't he? But it's all sorted out now.'

'Shush. Be quiet. I don't want them to know we're discussing it.'

'Why not?'

'Because somewhere in all of this mess there is a big lie, and I want to get to the bottom of it.'

'You're paranoid, Victor.'

Victor sat on the bed. 'Paranoid I may be, but there is something wrong with all of this electric business.'

Jane sat beside Victor and looked into his face. 'What is it, Victor? What is wrong with you?'

Victor tried to look away.

'I'm afraid of them, Jane. I can't put my finger on it, but I'm afraid. They're aliens. There's something wrong with the whole set-up here.'

He sat upright. His face reddened. 'And I don't care for being locked in my own dining-room with the other one while he marches you off somewhere. Look at it from my point of view. That woman came from Social Services while you were out with Paul. She looked through the window straight at me. She knew I was hiding. If I was in my right mind, I should have said, call the police, call the police because I'm locked in my own dining room by that guest of mine you were worried about. But I didn't. Instead, I hid from her. I pretended to be asleep. Next thing I knew, I was telling Peter they could have the house, and we would go away; you and I would leave. I would put a lifetime mortgage on the house, and they could buy their own flat with the money, live quietly and keep out of trouble. I don't know what comes over me sometimes. I should have told that social worker to call the immigration police. So, Jane, I don't know what is wrong with me, but I do know that I need help.'

From a fierce whisper, his voice had descended to a low muttering. 'I need some perspective, Jane. I'm going up to The Close and see what I owe Angove or whether I owe Angove money. Paul has intimidated the poor man into giving back the price of the certificate, but I do owe him for the components that were purchased on my behalf.'

'I'll go with you.'

'No, I'll do this on my own, if you don't mind. But I won't tell them. I want to take back control of my own affairs, slowly, slowly, if necessary. And if we can get through Christmas, Jane, I want, either for them to leave or for us to leave.'

He grabbed her hand and began to speak in fervent little bursts. 'We'll go. Start a new life somewhere else. Torquay. That's the place. It's nice there.'

Jane looked at the closed curtains, the little chintz covered slipper chair, the dark wardrobe. 'You're not yourself, Victor. Why wouldn't we get through Christmas and why do you hate this place so much now? Ever since Plombe drove himself over the cliff.'

'Yes, quite so. Every time I look through that window at the side of Plombe's bungalow, I think about it, about what happened.'

'But you can't dwell on these things.'

'No, but it makes me feel sick to the stomach. Don't you understand?'

Sophistry, Victor thought. Why can't I tell her the truth? Why can't I tell her what I know? When I tell the truth, Paul said, nobody ever believes me.

While Peter and Paul were sorting out some long planks of wood which they got cheap from one of the small builders in the village, Victor sneaked away on the pretext of going out for a loaf of bread and a newspaper.

He climbed up the tramway against a rising wind, got through the fence, walked the length of The Close and before he could doubt himself or change his mind, he went through the gateway and knocked on the door of number twelve.

A small, fierce dog started up a yapping. No-one came to the door, so he tried knocking again.

Let's just get to the bottom of this, he thought.

An older woman opened the door a little way.

'Good afternoon. Sorry to disturb you. I'm looking for a Sandy Angove. I think he is an electrician and lives here.'

'My son, yes. I haven't seen him today. He went out last night and hasn't come back yet. I'm expecting him any time. He's not in any trouble, is he?' She glanced around and behind Victor.

'Oh goodness no. Fact is, he did some work for me. I'm Victor Everley.' He held out his gloved hand. 'I live on Beach Road. He checked some new wiring and issued me with a certificate, but I haven't paid him yet. I thought I would chase him with the money.'

The woman brightened up and opened the door a little further.

'Well, I don't know what to say, Mr Everley. You might find him at Tremayne's.'

'No, I tried him there. He doesn't work for Tremayne's.'

She looked surprised and annoyed.

'Oh well, I can't help you, then.'

'And you don't know where I can find him?'

A younger woman, holding a little child, came and stood behind her in the doorway.

'Not now, no. He went out last night. He should be back before long. I can't answer for him. He works all hours.'

Victor thought for a moment. 'Does he? Mrs Angove, when you see him, will you tell him, Mr Everley called with his money and that Mr Everley would like him to call in at the bungalow where he did the certification work for me.'

As Victor turned away, the terrier broke free and skidded out of the house, snapping at his heels.

Victor kicked out at the dog's neck. 'Please keep your animal under control,' he said with a firm voice. He saw that there were holes in the front door and that old gloss paint was flaking from it. As he walked through the gap between rough concrete posts where a garden gate should be, he thought how blessed he was to have his own little double-glazed bungalow by the sea and that now, he must be strong and regain what was his.

From the high ground on which The Close was built, the sea was a distant grey backdrop. You could barely hear it. The perpetual westerly wind tugged at his city coat in gusts that threatened to topple him. He looked up at the bare, quarried hill behind him. Nothing but fallen rock. 'Torquay next stop,' he said to himself, 'where you can't smell the elemental rock, and the palm trees all stand upright in neat rows. Jane and I, we have a future in Torquay.'

As he got back through the wire fence and on to the steep path, there they were, standing about, waiting for him, the three anxious Musketeers. Jane, you can't keep your mouth shut about my whereabouts, not for a moment.

I'm going to brazen it out, Victor thought, as he met Paul's eye.

'Where did you go, Victor? You were only going for your newspaper and bread.' Jane came forward, fussing, tucking in his scarf.

'You know very well where I went. I went to see Sandy Angove to pay him what I owe him.'

'But he paid me back,' Peter said. 'He gave the money back to Paul.'

'Yes, Peter, but that doesn't make it right. I still owe him, or I owe somebody, for work done. I still owe him for the inspection, and I still need to track down whoever provided me with a certificate and a bill on Tremayne's paper. Why did Sandy Angove use Tremayne's business stationery when he has never worked for Tremayne?'

Jane had her exasperated look about her again. 'I don't know, Victor. Perhaps it's something to do with the tax office. Perhaps he doesn't have a job. Perhaps he is drawing benefits and shouldn't be working. The point being, the job is done and we have a certificate.'

'But have we?' Victor looked pointedly at Paul. 'If somebody could produce the elusive Sandy Angove, I would believe it. He seems to have done a bunk as well.' He led the way rapidly down the track, back to the bungalow. He was determined now to say whatever was on his mind, to challenge whatever he felt like challenging and to take the screwed-up piece of paper, the supposed bill and receipt to show Old Man Tremayne as he had said he would.

'Right,' he said as he opened the porch door and let the others in. 'I'm going to see Old Man Tremayne on Monday morning at Newquay with this counterfeit bill and receipt, as I promised him. He was as curious about it as I am.'

'I'll come with you.'

'That's fine by me, Paul. Anybody else want to come? Make it a coach party?'

Peter and Jane shook their heads and looked down.

'As long as you aren't planning on locking my wife in the dining room with Peter.'

'No, of course. Not on Monday.'

'Not on Monday,' Peter said.

Everyone laughed, except Victor.

'And now I'll have a look at the pieces of timber you've selected for that carport you've so generously decided to erect for me. Where are they?'

Victor Suffers A Defeat

Paul reached down, pulled the lever and bumped forward the front passenger seat where he had been sprawling since the start of the hour-long journey to Newquay.

For much of the journey Paul appeared to be dozing. He is self-contained, Victor thought. He never says more than he has to. The wrinkles around his eyes with a single line down each cheek showed an outdoor existence and long exposure to a hot sun. Or perhaps he was just a little older than he appeared. His movements were always decisive and economical. Victor remembered how, even on the dark cliff-face, Paul was able to stand up confidently from sitting right down on his haunches. One had to be able to do that from childhood, from long practice. And then, there was the business of getting down and up Als an

Marrow. Nobody could do that. No normal person, except perhaps the highly trained. The way he sprinted full tilt at the rock face and came up and over, scrabbling at the vegetation. The way his heart rate returned to normal in double-quick time. Paul had been one of the super-fit, Victor thought, and not so long ago that his body had forgotten. Special forces? But what was he doing here in Portmarrow with little Victor and Jane?

Even asleep, Paul seemed alert, like a bird or a wild animal. Who was this person in Victor's car?

'Nearly there?' Paul wiped the sides of his mouth and looked in the vanity mirror which was embedded in the visor.

'The sat nav says we are a minute away from Tremayne's, Paul.'

'Good.'

'I'll do the talking,' Victor said.

'Go ahead. I will just listen.'

'By the way, I meant to ask you this before we go in: where did you find Angove?'

Angove? In the Cornish Arms. You must have seen him there, Victor. He's nearly always there.'

'Can't say I did. I do wish he'd reappear now. I expect his mother does, as well. She was worried about him. He normally turned up in the morning, she said. Perhaps he's home by now. What do you think?'

Paul shrugged his shoulders slightly and looked out of the side window.

'That must be it,' he said. 'Down this road.'

The sat nav had taken them to a small industrial estate with medium-sized, purpose-built metal sheds down an overgrown side-road. The first thing Victor noticed was that there were very few cars parked at the small units and that there were no lights on in the front offices. Where was everybody?

'Oh goodness, Christmas holidays. I think they may be shut for Christmas.'

Victor got out, pocketing the key.

Paul stayed in the car.

There was a notice, roughly scrawled, blue-tacked up on the reinforced glass door, with instructions to contact the Liskeard office for urgent enquiries. Emergency cover only. Happy Christmas and see you in the New Year.

Pity, Victor thought. I should have telephoned first, before coming all this way. It's a fruitless eighty-mile round trip.

He went back to the car. 'Shut for Christmas,' he said. 'I should have thought about that before setting out. Christmas Eve is only a few days away.'

'It doesn't matter,' Paul said. 'I've never been to Newquay, so let's go into the town. I'll buy a pasty for you. We can sit by the sea and have a discussion. It's not cold outside.'

Victor sighed. 'You're right,' he said. 'The sun is warm. Best not waste the day. I'll buy you a pasty.'

'No, no, I insist. Pasty is on me.'

They sat on a bench on a tall cliff, the old hotels and road to the airport behind them. Each clutched a peppery pasty, which they nibbled at. The wind tugged at their clothes. Moving shafts and sticks of light penetrated grey rain clouds, creating brief diamond swords on the sea. Victor pulled his coat around him and tucked in his scarf.

'The meat is tough,' Victor said.

'Potato is not the best.'

'The pastry is not like Jane's, eh?'

They sat in silence for a while. After the disappointment at Tremayne's, Victor saw that there was little more to do before Christmas. He felt that Paul could so easily solve the mystery of Angove, but he hesitated to ask about it. There were always these voids, he thought, these voids in information and understanding. How could he make it all different, close the gaps, smooth things out?

'Have you really not been to Newquay before, Paul?'

'No, I have never been here.'

'Newquay is a Victorian railway town, a Riviera town. It wouldn't have existed but for the branch-line. Its great advantage was the headlands on which the landowners could build the grand hotels, and the cluster of different beaches. Nowadays, it's a world surfing capital.'

Paul did not seem impressed. He did not show much of a reaction.

'There is a story about one of the hotels behind where we are sitting. After the first world war was over, the survivors of the town, the soldiers of the Duke of Cornwall's Light Infantry, they had a big dinner there. The dining rooms were full of people. On that first anniversary of Armistice Day, they vowed they would have a dinner there every year at the same time, for as long as they lived. They never wanted to forget what they had been through and the comrades they had lost, you see.

'Well, time went by. People died of natural causes or in accidents. Every year, new names were read out and remembered. Then came the sixties and seventies and people didn't want to attend so much. They wanted to forget the two world wars. They had bills to pay, and the dinner was just another expense. It must have been disconcerting to hear about old friends dying. I suppose too, people got bored with it.

'Then in the nineties, there was an economic slump and a big falling off. Many had died. Most had died. The hotel wasn't looking as good as it used to. People had got accustomed to hotel food; dressing up and going there wasn't such a treat. A lot of the old soldiers, most of them were in nursing homes and on their last legs.

'It all came down to a small round table of five, with carers and relatives to inhibit them. They didn't have much to say to each other.

'Finally, it came to the last evening. It was a wet night, wet enough to catch your death. The last two turned up in wheelchairs. The hotel had changed hands a few times, but the staff remembered the form. The food was laid out as usual. Not much was eaten. By all accounts the last pair glared at each-other across a small table for two in a corner by the service door, each waiting for the other to snuff it, both Cornishmen of 'other ranks.'

'There was no longer anything to say. They now lived in a world that knew nothing of them. They'd both buried even their children.'

'I know somebody who lives in a wheelchair, Victor. You will meet him soon.' Paul screwed up the paper around the final piece of his pasty, the lump of pastry known as the Pope's nose. He flung it at the herring gull that was stamping up and down and staring at him, keeping its distance.

'All they knew,' Victor said, 'was that they were the survivors. And that it was not over yet. Somebody, one of the two, had to survive to become the victor.'

Paul looked at Victor carefully. 'Is this what your name means, Victor? Survivor?'

Victor puffed out his chest a little. 'No, it means the conqueror, the winner. Valiant, Victor and Vulcan were fine bomber aircraft. I was christened Victor after the last bomber in the series, in 1958. I expect they'll bring out a First Day Cover of all of them one day. They brought out one of the Vulcan only a few years ago. I have one of the Valiant, from the first flight in 1982.'

'Is that so?' Paul looked out to sea and back again to study Victor's face. 'But Victor, there is never any victor. Survival is not victory. Neither of those men at the last dinner even survived.'

'In the end, no, I suppose not.'

'And their hotel behind us, where they ate all those dinners, is boarded up, ready for demolition. It says, New Luxury Flats, Victor. So, everything changes and is forgotten.'

'Yes, Paul, I suppose that's how it is.' Victor gave a great sigh.

'So that is the story, Victor, the real story. Nobody survives. Even the plants, you know, they give us oxygen, keep us alive to decompose as food for them when we are dead. We don't farm them, Victor, they farm us. Every bit of life you see in front of you, it will die, one time or another.'

Overcome by an emotion he did not comprehend in himself, he reached out to rest a hand on Paul's knee.

'You know, you have such an interesting perspective on things. I would never have seen the plant kingdom in that way. We think of plants as being so much less than us, just there for us to eat or admire. There is so little we know about you, Paul. We'd love to know, for instance, what you used to do before this, before you met us.'

'Well, this, for instance.'

The cliff and the sky swung around. Victor found himself on his knees, his pasty on the turf two feet in in front of him, his arms together, straight, above his head. He felt his bowel void out.

He heard Paul say, 'Oh dear, Victor, did I hurt you?'

He was conscious that Paul was still seated on the bench, and that he had let go of his wrists, though shock had kept his arms in the same position over his head.

Paul guided his arms down.

'Lie down flat, Victor, on your face. Cross your legs at the ankles. When you are ready, uncross, roll on your knees and then you can stand up.'

What wretched thing has happened to me? Victor thought. He lay on the ground, his face in the rough grass of the clifftop. What has gone so terribly wrong for me? This pointless visit to Newquay, challenging a man I cannot take on.

After a while, Victor got up, arms feeling wrenched, but nothing broken.

'Is that a public toilet over there? I need to clean myself up,' Victor said.

As Victor moved away, the gull moved in quickly, snatching up the food that lay on the ground. Paul kicked out at the bird, but it was already on the wing.

When Victor reached the grim little pebble-dashed public toilets building, he saw that it was padlocked due to vandalism. Facing into the wind, he went around the side, where no-one could see, took off his trousers, wiped himself clean as well as he could, leaving the soiled underpants behind.

Cold shock had now left Victor breathless. The salt air was crisp and clean, the sea grey and murky. I must get back home, Victor thought, back to Jane. I must quietly get my papers in order, ready to take my wife and myself away to safety.

When he got back to the car, he saw that Paul was waiting by the driver's door.

'I'll drive,' Paul said. 'You're not well enough.'

'You can't, Victor said, 'I'll have to drive the car.'

Paul stared ahead, his hand on the driver's door handle. 'I have international licence.'

Really? Victor thought. How? Why? When?

Paul drove them home efficiently, with concentration. The words kept going around in Victor's mind. Who are you, that you drive on the left-hand side of the road without hesitation, like an Englishman? He was embarrassed by the farmyard stench his trousers were giving off. He wanted to apologise to Paul about the smell, but he could not find the words. When they arrived, he must get past Jane quickly, clean himself properly and put his soiled clothing to soak in the bath. He felt he had meddled with actions and with motives he was not meant to understand, and he had come off the worse for it. He would not challenge Paul over the matter of the electrical certificate again.

When they were almost home, he turned to Paul. 'Please, Paul, don't tell Jane.'

Paul glanced in his direction. 'No, I won't tell Jane. I never tell Jane, do I?'

Victor Accused

The carport was almost up. Victor stood with Jane at the boundary between the two bungalows, where Plombe's garden wall was now nothing more than a shallow indentation in the ground. The rubble from the former wall lay neatly spread in the carport, waiting to be covered by a concrete base.

'It's still not right, though,' Victor said. 'I've no legal claim to that parcel of land.'

'Oh, stop fretting.' Jane gave him one of her glances and walked away towards their own front door.

Victor followed her into the kitchen. 'You're scratchy again. What's wrong with you now?'

Jane began to put on her pinny, ready to begin cooking, fumbling with the ties.

'What's wrong with me? With me?' Her voice was rising. 'Shouldn't I be asking what is wrong with you?'

Victor leaned against the kitchen counter. 'What do you mean by that?' He was displeased with the way she constantly frowned and tutted at him these days. 'This is supposed to be a nice time of the year, coming up to Christmas, but all I'm getting is frowns and sighs and sarcasm.'

'Then answer me.'

'Answer you what? I don't know what you are talking about, Jane.'

'Oh yes you do.'

'What?'

Jane began scrubbing at some potatoes. 'You think I'm blind, Victor?'

'What? For goodness' sake, say what you mean.'

'Tell me this,' she said, jabbing the air towards him with the peeler. 'Where are your underpants?'

'What? What underpants?'

'Do I have to spell it out? All right, I will. Your underpants. You get in the car with Paul, and you go to Newquay for a nice day out, on some pretext. When you come home, you put your trousers to soak, and your underpants are missing.'

Victor felt himself blushing. He studied the clean new tiles on the kitchen floor. 'I had no idea you took such a close interest in my underwear.'

'I do when an item goes missing. You go out wearing underpants, you come home without underpants. What is the explanation?'

There was a silence while Jane continued to rip at the potato in her hand.

'Why do you want to know, Jane? Are you sure my underpants are missing? This is a ridiculous conversation. I'm not listening anymore.'

Victor took a step towards the lounge, where he intended to hide behind his newspaper.

Jane put down the potato and the peeler. 'You turn your back on me, and we're finished.'

'What?'

'It's not much of a life anyway, is it, with all your lies and all your secrets. I'm going, Victor. I'll stay for Christmas, but after that, I'm going. Monica's thinking of leaving the club and getting a flat. I'll go and live with her. I won't stay here in a house full of lies and deceit.'

'Lies and deceit? The only liars and deceivers I know are those two out there.' He pointed in the direction of the carport. 'And you're the fool who brought them here. I'm the one who's been trying to find out the truth about the electricity certificate. You don't seem to give a damn. You'll swallow anything those little oiks tell you.'

Jane lowered her voice. 'Sorry, Victor, you can't cover it up that way. I may be stupid but I'm not blind.'

There was a pause. Victor looked up at the new plaster ceiling, with its two neat rows of energy-saving spotlights. He lowered his voice. 'I truly don't know what you're on about, Jane.'

Jane blushed down to her neck. 'Right then, I'll spell it out. I'm talking about your affair with Paul.'

'My affair?' Victor's hands closed into fists.

Jane put down the potato peeler. 'There, I've said it. You don't have to explain anything. I will stay to do Christmas for you. People from the choir are coming on Christmas Eve. But after Christmas, I'm off somewhere. I don't know where yet. I'll let you know.'

Jane left the kitchen and went into the bedroom, closing the door behind her.

'Just a minute.' Victor stormed into the bedroom. 'What are you talking about? My affair? With that little bastard? Are you insane all of a sudden? What in God's name have they been saying to you?'

'Then where are your underpants?'

'Behind a public toilet in Newquay.'

Of all the things he might have said, he said entirely the wrong thing, he thought. But surely, even Jane couldn't be so bloody stupid as to think things like that about him.

Jane had retreated to her side of the bed and was sitting with her back to him, dry-eyed, smoothing down a pillow.

He stood in the doorway, bellowing. 'I shat myself, if you want to know. I tripped up, fell arse over tip and shat myself. It was cold, I am old, it was the shock of falling. Now are you happy?'

'No. No, I'm not. I don't believe you. I don't believe anything you say. There's something going on between you and Paul.'

He sat beside her on her side of the bed. He lowered his voice. 'Listen, after we discovered that

Tremayne's was closed for the Christmas holidays, we sat on a bench on the cliffs. Paul bought us a pasty. It was a cold day, if you remember, windy but pleasant. As I went to get up, I fell. That's when I shat myself. Listen, will you? Perhaps I am not very strong or very well, perhaps there was something wrong with the pasty, but that's the truth. Then I went over to the public toilet, but it was closed, locked and barred. I went around the back of it, because there was nowhere else to go, I took off my trousers and pants, I shook out the pants, cleaned myself with the dry parts that were not soiled, then threw the pants away. My trousers were still smelling badly. I apologised to Paul. He was very good about it. He drove us home because I was so shaken. I felt ashamed and I didn't feel like explaining myself to you. I simply put the trousers to soak.'

'Well, if you say so. I don't know what to believe any more.' Jane smoothed down her skirt. 'But I won't stay here after Christmas. I'm going away on my own.'

His outrage sank and dissipated into a grey misery.

'Look, we'll both go away after Christmas. We'll have a holiday before deciding where we want to live. Then we'll sell up and go. Begin again. Forget all this.'

In the long wardrobe mirror, he saw himself gesture with his hand. 'We've never been apart for more than a few days, have we? Since we first met outside that dancehall. What was it called?'

She hesitated, reluctant to be drawn down into the sentimental journey she did not want to take with him. She felt her resolve to be alone slide away.

'The Flamingo.'

'The Flamingo.'

They sat in an exhausted silence. He was afraid to go on, in case the memory was too fragile, insufficient to keep them still gummed together. There they were, reflected in the mirror, flesh under the skin much reduced but still alive after all these years, still bound together, as it should be.

Jane began to weep silently. Victor bowed his head and waited for the sad little storm to pass.

'We'll get through it,' he said. 'Somehow. We've always done before.'

He became aware of two figures standing together in the doorway. After a while, Paul came into the room and sat on the bed, close beside Victor. As the mattress took his weight, it depressed, so that Paul seemed to lean into Victor, though he was sitting upright. He threaded his fingers together and cracked the knuckles. Peter came and sat beside Jane. Unseen, Peter wound his foot around the back of her ankle.

'Mama,' he said. 'Dinner time. What are you cooking?'

Paul is Violent

'That's it. All we have to do now is wait for the Choir and all our neighbours to come.'

Jane set down the last bowl of her home-made mince pies on the dining-room table and looked around. All was well. 'I never thought we'd make it to Christmas Eve, but we've got here. We've made it.' She slumped down on one of the hard little dining-room chairs that had been placed around the sides of the room.

Throughout the bungalow, the clutter had been cleared away into the bedroom. There remained a little corridor around the perimeter of Victor and Jane's bed, so that they could creep about and lie down.

'The room looks so much larger in here, we ought to leave it like this.'

'We should have built a garage, but there was no time left,' Peter said.

'We've run out of time,' Paul said. 'Never mind. Carport is good but can't store anything.'

Jane looked up. 'Yes, the carport is good, indeed it is. It certainly enhances the value of the property. I'd never have thought about it, but for you. I don't know whether Victor has thanked you properly yet. But thankyou both, from the bottom of our hearts.' Jane smiled, a broad smile. 'You've done so many good things for us. We shall miss you dreadfully, and we shall never forget you, but needs must.'

Paul stood up. 'Yes, we have agency work, and we must go.'

'And you're still determined to go immediately after the Christmas meal is over?'

Peter opened his mouth to speak, but Paul answered for them. 'Yes. All arranged.'

There was a pause. To fill the emptiness, Jane got up and began to fuss with the flowers in an over-large glass vase. 'Remind me to take all these vases back to the church vestry immediately after Christmas before anybody notices they have gone.' Then she blushed. 'Oh, but you won't be here. You see how I've come to rely on you, Peter. Anybody want a glass of wine before they all pile in? Where is Victor, by the way? Not that we can't manage without him.'

'Victor? Victor went to get some beer. A pin of beer. What is that?'

'That's a small barrel, Peter. The men might like beer. I forgot that. The ladies might like a glass of wine, but one dip of my mulled wine from the bowl in the hall is lethal enough for anybody.'

Jane laughed; her cheeks flushed. She took off her red knitted cardigan with its Santa brooch and hung it neatly over the back of her chair.

'Just going to check the lights in the carport.' Paul went outside.

'I didn't know you've rigged up lights in there too.'

'Oh yes,' Peter said, 'And fairy lights, so people can see, and have a smoke there. Car is parked on the road for this evening.'

'But... where is the power coming from? Have you run a cable from the hallway? Somebody might trip, Peter.'

'Trip?'

'Fall over, on the cable, as in trip-hazard.'

'Trip, no. No hazard. Cable comes from Plombe's house.'

'Plombe's?' Jane got to her feet, her eyes opening wide 'We can't go in there. That's Plombe's house.'

'Plombe is dead, Jane.'

'Yes, but that doesn't mean we can go in there. We really can't go in there. That's trespass. We could get in a lot of trouble doing that. It belongs to somebody else now. The police might still be going in and out of there, collecting evidence. We still don't know it was suicide. I mean, of course it was, but they still have to make their enquiries to be sure.'

Peter smiled his blue-eyed smile. 'But you went in there, Jane, with Victor. Sit down, Jane, drink your mulled wine. Nobody will notice the cable coming from Plombe's house. Cable is underground.'

Cable underground?

The room seemed to chill. Jane reached for her cardigan. Peter got behind her chair, took up the cardigan, put it around her shoulders. He put a little pressure on her shoulders, close to the neck, her knees bent, and she sat down. He came around and stood in front of her, his smile never fading.

'How did you know Victor and I went in there?' Her hands felt jumpy. With her left hand, she held down the right hand which gripped the stem of her cabernet wine glass. 'We can't just purloin somebody else's electricity supply. That's illegal. It's a criminal act.'

'Well, drink your wine, Jane. It's nearly Christmas. The people will come soon. They will like the lights.'

Jane stared at the coloured paper chains hanging down the wall, chains that she and Peter had made so happily one afternoon, now hooked around the dining-room mirror above the fireplace. She was trying to think, but already she felt hazy, deprived of air to breathe. Had Victor told the boys she followed him into Plombe's house in the early morning? Did Victor tell them she made him take the keys to the police? That would be just typical of Victor to be so inconsistent, swearing her to silence and then spilling the beans himself. She wanted to ask Peter whether they knew where Plombe's keys were now, but something, some instinct prevented her.

She should never have gone next door after Victor, that morning. They should never have agreed to have the carport built on a disputed piece of land. What would it look like to people? In her mind, she tried a few answers to their questions about the lit-up carport. She saw herself smiling brightly to friends and neighbours: 'Oh yes, we've put in a bid for Mr Plombe's bungalow too. Well, it only makes sense. It would be a larger plot and the possibilities for expansion would be endless.' Or, 'Oh yes, the carport is just temporary. We'll take it down after Christmas.'

She must buttonhole Victor and confront him about telling the boys they had gone into the bungalow, after swearing her to silence.

But what did that matter, in the face of this? They were taking power from Plombe's bungalow to light the carport, and people might find out.

She shifted in her chair. 'So, how were you getting in and out of Mr Plombe's bungalow?' Her voice sounded weak. She cleared her throat.

'Keys. We have keys.'

She heard Paul as he strolled back into the house and stood at the doorway to the dining room. Jane had just risen from her chair, her cardigan around her shoulders.

'Paul,' she said. 'Paul, we can't take power from Mr Plombe's house. Peter said you'd rigged up an underground cable from there to the carport for the lights. You'll have to disconnect and run a cable from our porch. I know it's a trip-hazard but. . .'

Paul looked down the dining room table and chose a silver platter of small eats. He reached forward, took up the tray and brought the sharp edge down on the bridge of Peter's nose. The doily and the little puff pastries scattered on the carpet. Peter yelped, grabbed a handful of paper napkins and held them against his nostrils.

As the paper turned bright red, Jane guided him to the newly tiled downstairs bathroom. She was trembling.

'He doesn't mean it,' Peter said, his head over the sink.' He's sad to be leaving tomorrow. He has been so happy here.'

'Please don't talk, Peter. Hold your nose and look up. Everything will be all right. It will stop bleeding in a minute. I'll fetch a key to put down your back.' Jane had gone automatically into primary school teacher mode.

'A key?'

'An old wives' tale. A cold key stops the bleeding.'

As she retrieved the old lattice-topped brass key from its nail in the porch, she glanced across to the waste ground. Paul had done as she asked. The lights in the carport were out.

Victor saw the fairy lights go out in the interior and on the roof of the carport and wondered what had happened, what failure of wiring had caused that. He was standing still in the road, with his pin of beer under his arm, when he saw a figure rushing towards him.

'Do you remember me? I'm Rita Angove, Sandy's mother. I was just on my way to see you.'

'Mrs Angove. Yes, of course I remember you. Mrs Angove with the little dog. You live at number twelve, The Close, not number fourteen, as I was told. What can I do for you?'

'Sandy,' she said. 'You haven't seen him, have you? Only, it's Christmas Eve and he hasn't been home.'

'Not since we last met. When I came up to pay for the work, he may have done for me?'

I'll be darned, thought Victor. I knew it. He's done away with him. He's murdered him. Well, I won't let you get away with it so easily this time, Paul my lad.

'Only, you see, Sandy would never miss Christmas with his girls. I think there's something wrong, Mr Everley. He goes away to work, yes, but he comes back, you see, especially for Christmas. He always wraps their presents himself. Where else would he go?' She began to rub the backs of her hands.

Only, I must be careful, Victor thought, or he'll do me in as well.

'Well, let's think,' Victor said.' Have you been to the Cornish Arms? I'm told, your son goes in there.'

She shook her head. 'He would never go there. We're Methodists, born and bred.'

'I see, but are you sure? These younger people don't uphold the same strict standards…'

'Anyway, I've been there, on the off chance. I've been everywhere I can think of. You think you know your own son very well, but when it comes to looking for him, you haven't a clue where he might go.'

'Does he have a workshop? Somewhere he trades out of?'

'No, nothing like that. Do you think I should go to the police, Mr Everley?' Her face began to crumple into misery.

Victor thought about it. 'I do think so, yes, if he hasn't been seen and if it's unlike him to stay away at this time of the year. I take it, you've been to his friends?'

She looked up and down the road. 'That's it,' she said. Diane and me, we've been trying to think what friends he has. Diane doesn't know and I don't know... the children are crying for him. They're breaking their hearts. We can't feel to do anything about Christmas without him. There's something wrong, I know there is. His phone's been on, but he doesn't answer.'

'If his phone's been on and he not answering, if there is any charge left, the police could trace where the phone is. But there may be no need for that. Look, I know somebody who knows your son. Let's go and ask him,' Victor said. 'But then, if my friend Paul can't help, I'd go straight to the police, if I were you.'

He led the way to the bungalow, where light was blazing through the open door. Jane was fussing around Peter in the bathroom, Paul was in the dining room, tucking into the canapes. No sign of the Choir and neighbours yet. Victor put down his small barrel of beer and picked up some canapes that were scattered on the floor.

'What's happened here?'

No reply from Paul.

'Try to restrain yourself from hoovering up all the food left on the table before the guests arrive. Anyway, come in, Mrs Angove.'

She hesitated outside the dining room door. 'This is my cousin Paul, Mrs Angove. He may know where your son is.'

'Have you seen my son? Are you a friend of his? He hasn't been home for days. He never misses Christmas Eve. Something's wrong, I know it is.' The words came streaming into the room, shrill, driven by fear.

Paul turned, to look her square in the face. 'I don't know him,' he said. 'What is Angove?'

'Sandy Angove,' she said. 'This man here says you know him.'

'I don't.'

Paul turned away to the canapes. 'This food fell on the floor,' he said. 'Not suitable for guests, so I am hoovering it up.'

Victor put his hands in his pockets and gripped the linings. He felt his arms and legs go rigid. He wanted to sock Paul in the face.

'You don't know him, dear?' Mrs Angove turned away and went out of the front door.

Victor watched her go. She looked up and down the road in a daze before bending her shoulders and walking on towards the beach. Go to the police, Rita Angove, he thought. Go now, while there is power in your son's phone and while there is still a chance. He lifted up the pin of beer and looked at the label.

'Don't pull stunts like that, Victor,' Paul said quietly.

'Stunts like what, Paul? She'll go to the police station next. What will you say when the police come here?'

The house had gone quiet. Victor could hear a tap running in the bathroom. He moved to go and turn it off. He wondered whether Jane had taken Peter into the bedroom or upstairs to the dormer room.

Paul stood in the doorway. 'I got your seven hundred back for you.'

'This isn't about seven hundred pounds, Paul. A mother is looking for her son, who is missing.'

'I hope it is, Victor, about a mother looking for her son. There are a lot of mothers looking for their son in the world.'

'This is England, Paul, not some fly-blown war zone. Everybody is accounted for.'

Paul moved away from the door. As Victor went to the bathroom to turn off the tap, he found Jane at her position beside the sink. Peter was bent over. She had her hand over his back and shoulder. She looked up at Victor, closed her eyes and shook her head. 'Don't ask,' she mouthed silently.

A bump and purple gash had formed on the bridge of Peter's nose by the time the Choir came to the door. The four of them stood in the hallway, Peter and Jane side by side, Paul and Victor behind them.

There were no greetings, no glasses of mulled wine taken. The men stood four deep and began to sing in an undertone, *Lo, he comes an infant stranger of a lowly mother born.* What on earth is this? Jane thought. She stood with a fixed and frozen smile until the unknown carol ended.

The men stood back. The women shuffled forward. Together, they filled the pathway, the front garden, they spilled into the street. *Hark the glad sound, the saviour comes, the saviour promised long,* the combined choirs sang, with clipped line-endings and frequent repetition. *Let every heart prepare a throne.*

At the solemn, festive sound, Paul turned away and went upstairs to the dormer bedroom.

The singing ended as soon as it began, in the same clipped, shouty style. It was tuneful and grimly joyful, but alien to Jane, something she did not remember them ever rehearsing. They trooped indoors politely, drained the orange juice and water, and prepared themselves to re-assemble in Skinners' Row.

They are different, Jane thought, so very different. She saw Monica chatting with Victor and was glad that they were getting along.

Before the choirs left, Sandra appeared in front of her in the kitchen. 'Jane,' she said, 'a word.'

'Sandra. I hope my little do has warmed everybody up, ready for Skinners' Row.'

'Jane, the choir won't be needing you after Christmas.'

'Really? I thought we were short of contraltos.'

'No, we're fine.'

'What about Monica?'

'She's a soprano. She's fine.'

'I see. Would you like to tell me why?' Rejection is a vile thing, Jane thought.

'It's a committee decision, Jane, it's not up to me alone.'

'No, I don't suppose it is. Just when I was getting somewhere with the music, and I like coming to Choir.'

'There's nothing wrong with your musicianship. You learn quickly. I've always liked you and I always argued to keep you in the choir.'

'Did you? Well, what is it then, Sandra? At least have the goodness to tell me, after I've worked so hard to put all of this on for you, baking trays of mince pies and…'

'Your husband didn't help, taking in people from goodness knows where.'

'What?'

'And there's all the goings-on at night, the comings and goings and the lights going on and off.'

'What? But they've been fitting a new kitchen and bathrooms for me. They completely rewired the bungalow for me.'

'And at night? And what is this carport they've been building on Plombe's land?'

'It's not Plombe's land. It's our land.'

Jane stared into space as Sandra left the kitchen. She felt hot and tearful suddenly. All those months with the gentle Peter and the difficult Paul, were they being watched and judged by a racist community, all this time? People who did not understand anything. She returned to the dining room, glad that the choirs were getting ready to leave. Not one word of thanks, she thought. Not one word. I won't be doing this again for them.

An orange head of hair peered around the door. Kenny Crabbe. Jane bumped into him as she came out of the dining room with a jug, wondering where she was going to find more orange juice and water.

'Kenny,' she said. 'How wonderful to see you. I didn't expect to see you again and wondered where you were. You should have brought your musicians.

We could have had some cheerful music. I'm sorry I had to leave your concert so early, that evening. Victor had a stroke and was at the hospital. Nothing terminal.' She gasped. With his shock of almost orange hair, he looked wonderful, indeed he did. 'But Kenny,' she said, you don't have your instruments with you. I was hoping you would play for us, get rid of this dreary Methodist droning.'

'Ah, the Merritt carols. They take some getting used to, I'll grant you that. You need to know a bit about them before you can begin to appreciate West Gallery singing.'

'The West what?'

'They had no organ, you see. Sometimes they had a fiddler, or whatever they could get hold of. Only thing was, they had their voice. Celts are clever with their voice. Four-part harmony was not enough for them. Merritt gave them a fugue. That'll be what you find so different.'

'Well, I was just expecting *Once in Royal.*'

'No, you won't get that here, Jane. They came out of the fields and the barns, their holes in the ground, with archaic tones in their throats and their refuge was the chapel.'

But he seemed distracted. He was not laughing or even smiling. He was looking at her strangely, she thought.

'I've just been chucked out of the choir,' she said. 'It's such a shock You've no idea.' Hot tears were beginning to form in her eyes.

'That may be just as well.'

'Just as well?'

He grasped her arm. 'Put down that jug,' he said, 'and come with me.'

'Kenny, I have guests to see to and the orange squash, I'm not sure, I think I have some more somewhere.'

He walked her around the side of the building, into the shadows. 'Listen,' he said. 'I've been here a quarter of an hour, walking about your lovely little bungalow and listening out and thinking. I don't know how to put this, and I don't want to alarm you, but there is something very wrong here. Listen. Get your passports and money and get out. Go. Go now, go tonight, for your own sakes.'

'What? Kenny, I can't possibly go with you. You are wonderful, Kenny, a lovely man and highly talented and a great entertainer, but I have my life here, with Victor. I couldn't. It's out of the question. I couldn't possibly go away with you.'

He stared at her.

'No, you daft, ignorant woman,' he said. 'I'm a Catholic man, I've an old wife, six grown children and two in the cemetery. Will you listen to me?'

He grasped her arms and shook her. 'There's death in this house, I can smell it. I've been in a few tight corners, and this is one house I would sleep with my boots on. Do you hear me? I've never been wrong. There's wickedness here. Pure evil distilled. Get your passports and your money, get Victor away. Get on the next plane out of Newquay. Don't hang around the airport, get the Dublin plane, if not, then the plane to London. Dump your car, get the London plane to Spital, or even the night ferry, the Eurostar, or the coach from Victoria. Then Spital to Dublin by air. There's a guesthouse outside Dublin I can send you. They'll look after you. I'll let them know you're coming right away. From there, they'll find you somewhere quiet, keep you out of the way of it. But don't think you can come back.'

'Out of the way of what, Kenny? Don't be ridiculous. Whatever has come over you? All over being thrown out of a choir? Because of some ignorant, racially prejudiced country bumpkins? I don't need them. They don't frighten me. There's law and order in this land. I have the Christmas dinner to make tomorrow. It all depends on me. My boys are leaving tomorrow. There's so much to do. I'm safe here. This is our home. We've paid cash for this house and we're not going to leave it on the hysterical whim of some Irish folksinger. Sorry, I don't mean to be rude, Kenny, I know you mean well, but there's nothing wrong here.'

He dropped her arms. 'Alright. I tried. Maybe I'm damaged by forty years of war and all this collecting for the widows. War is a killer. You begin to see things in the shadows that aren't there.' He turned and strode across the garden, past the darkened carport, through Plombe's gate. For a moment, the streetlamp licked his hair into an orange flame before he disappeared into the night.

Strange man, she thought. All the Irish are strange. The Cornish are strange, but the Irish are something else. Now where was I? The orange squash. In the back of the cupboard, I think, possibly. We never drink it, and the boys got tired of it. I wonder where the boys are. Gone to the pub, I suppose. Not their sort of party.

The men and women of the combined choirs were leaving, stuffing mince pies into their blazer pockets, another peculiar Cornish tradition, Jane supposed, as the bowls of pies emptied. She ignored them and did not go to the door to say goodnight. She'd finished with the choirs and their strange harmonies.

Monica was sitting in an armchair with a glass of punch, staring into space. Jane went up to her. 'You OK, Monica?'

'Your husband just insulted me again,' she said. 'I didn't mind the racism, I didn't even notice it, but now he thinks I was dipping the till at the yacht club. Well, I wasn't. If anybody was, it was the old steward, and he's gone. What am I going to do now? I've never been accused of such a thing in my life.'

'Where's Victor got to?' Jane looked around but did not see him. 'Don't worry about him, I'll deal with him. I'm leaving him when Christmas is over. There is so much to do before then. Are you still moving out of the club flat? I'm looking for a flatmate.'

'No, no I'm getting along very well with the Commodore. I think I'll be staying at the club a little longer. Hope springs eternal, as we say in this country. Unless your husband comes back and ruins everything for me.'

'Oh Monica, he won't go back to the yacht club. In fact, he's thinking of moving to Devon.' She laughed. 'Kenny Crabbe, the singer, just asked me to live with him. I said no, of course. Too Irish. There will be better offers than that.' She laughed again. I'm getting tiddly on my own mulled wine, she thought.

The Major had buttonholed Victor. They were drinking whisky by the fireplace in the dining room, their backs to the square-tiled grate and electric fire. Jane heard the Major say, 'No, planning permission and all that lark is about to be abolished. Tory government, Victor. Deregulation, free for all.'

Jane saw Victor smile, one of his bitter little smiles. He ought to be pleased he can have his garage now, she thought, then perhaps he won't be such an old curmudgeon. I wonder where the boys have gone, she thought again. Well, this is hardly their sort of scene.

The last people to leave were neighbours from Tideway across the road, people she had never met before. At least they did not stuff pies into their pockets. Before they went out of the door, without thanking her or saying goodbye, of course, she went up to them and said, 'So, does your house mean 'The Hideaway' in Yorkshire dialect?' She was met with a blank stare. When they had gone, she shut the door.

Christmas cake had been trodden into the new grey wool carpets but mercifully no wine had been spilled. Victor was all for clearing up before they went to bed, but Jane said no, she would have to get up early to dress the turkey, make the brandy butter and do a hundred small things to make Christmas Day memorable.

The boys were still in the pub, or wherever they had gone. She locked up. They would be able to let themselves in with their own keys. Tomorrow was going to be such a long day, she thought, but it would be so worth the effort to give them a good send-off.

Yes, But Why?

'Jane, are you asleep?'

'Yes.'

'Are you still feeling tiddly?'

'No. What is it?'

'I wanted to hear what happened when I was out, when you were in the bathroom with Peter and there was blood everywhere. Not that I'm being nosy, of course.'

Jane sat up and went to put on the lamp.

'No don't,' Victor said. 'Leave the light off. I don't want them to know we're talking.'

'Oh, don't be so paranoid. Anyway, it seems such a long time ago now. We've had the reception since.'

'Well?'

'Oh, well, Paul bashed Peter on the bridge of his nose with the sharp edge of a tray, you know the silver tray I normally have in the hall for letters. It was full of pastries. He just brought the edge of the tray down on his nose. It cut his nose, opened up that scar on his face, made it bleed inside and out and then a big lump formed. I hope there's no permanent damage. Peter's afraid of hospitals.'

'Did he?' Victor sat up and leaned on an elbow. 'I tell you, Jane, I can't wait for them to go. All this violence. You never know when it's going to break out. He's a powder-keg, that young man.' Victor lay down again and stared at the ceiling, thinking of his wretched self, lying nose-down in the grass on the cliff-top at Newquay, with the smell of grass and of his own ordure.

It was nowhere near dawn yet. There was light from the streetlamp and the string of Christmas fairy lights on Plombe's bungalow, he supposed. He thought the lights must be powered from his own supply. He didn't know where to switch them off. It was too late in the night to think about it now. He'd have a look in the morning.

'So, what was it all about?'

'What? The violence? He threw his fish and chips at the wall, didn't he. Do you remember? Frightened the life out of me. I don't know, Peter must have just said something that didn't suit.'

'Do you remember what it was that Peter said?'

Jane was half asleep again. 'No, I don't really.'

'What was the subject? Can you remember that?'

'No. Oh yes, I do. The carport. They had the carport lights working on Plombe's supply. I only said that that was stealing, and Paul had to switch it off and take the supply from here instead. With that, he attacked Peter with the tray.'

'Typical. I'll be glad when they've gone. Then it'll just be you and me again.' Victor's hot water bottle had cooled rapidly. He wrapped his legs around Jane's.

'They had the carport lit up for people to smoke out there, Victor. It was a nice idea.'

'Yes, of course. I saw the car had been moved to the street and I saw the lights go out when I was walking down with Rita Angove. I hope she found her son or at least went to the police. I wondered what happened. What a worry. His girlfriend and he have children, you know, two daughters.'

'Oh well, he's probably turned up by now. It's Christmas, after all. Happy Christmas, Victor.' Jane sighed and prepared to turn away.

'Jane, do you think they listen to us? They certainly watch our every move, and they seem to know about everything we do.'

'I don't know, Victor. How could they do that? I'm tired. I have to get up early to clean the place again before I do anything towards producing a meal.'

'I'll help you. You know I will. What time did they say they were going?'

'Well, I'll get the Christmas dinner on the table at about seven, so they might go at nine or ten. They don't want dinner any earlier, they said. I did ask.'

'I wonder what they are doing for transport. There won't be any trains or buses. I'd be surprised if they were able to book a taxi for Christmas night. All the drivers will be exhausted and home with their families. It would cost a bomb to be driven anywhere on Christmas night. It would be worth driving them myself to wherever they want to go. Then we'd be sure they were gone.'

Jane sat up again. 'I've been thrown out of the choir, by the way. Sandra announced it to me after they'd eaten all the food. Then when they went, they started stuffing pies in their blazer pockets. That's the yokels for you.'

'Oh Jane,' Victor said. 'You know I never liked that Sandra woman.'

'And that cheeky Kenny Crabbe wanted me to go away with him.'

Victor laughed in the darkness. 'I'm not surprised. I'd go away with you any day.'

'Would you, Victor?'

He said no more. She was on the point of slumber.

Victor woke up at three, to the faint, intermittent sound of high-pitched drilling. I'm dreaming, he thought. I must have been. Or Jane has been snoring. Or it is those horrible little toads? What are they up to now? Very quietly, he got out of bed, shuffled into his backless sheepskin slippers. It was like a dentist's water drill, he thought, as high-pitched as that. Enough to waken and strike terror into the hardest of men. What is going on?

He turned the handle of the door and crept into the hallway. Nothing. No sound. I must have been dreaming, he thought. I must have.

He went into the lavatory, waited a minute, and pushed the plug in. I'm sure they listen to us. I'm sure they know every movement we make.

He shuffled back to the bedroom window and listened. No sound. Could the drilling sound have come from the direction of Plombe's bungalow? No. How?

He got back into bed.

And how did they manage to break into Plombe's electricity supply?

They can't hear my thoughts, he said silently to himself. I can ring up anonymously to report them. If they haven't gone tomorrow, by Boxing Day, I can ring the police. I can ring the immigration people and get them removed with lots of noise. But until Christmas Day is over, for Jane's sake I will go on playing ball. I can't ruin her Christmas, not so late in the day, not now.

He was going to nudge Jane again, to ask how those tykes got into Plombe's bungalow, but Jane was falling into a deep sleep now. She needed her rest.

Early on Christmas morning, Victor dressed warmly, let himself out of his own front door and walked briskly around to the back of Plombe's bungalow. Really, he thought, if the boys are listening to my every move, there is no point in hiding what I am doing this morning.

He was scrutinising the back door when Paul came around the corner.

'Just looking at Plombe's back door,' Victor said. 'Doesn't seem to be broken into or disturbed at all.'

'Why would it be?'

'I was just wondering, Paul, how you got into Plombe's bungalow to use his supply to light the fairy-lights on the carport.' Victor tried a casual smile, but his cheeks felt as though they were performing a grimace, muscle by muscle.

Paul looked bored already. 'Oh well, you know, it is easy to change the barrel of a lock.'

'Yes, but he also seems to have an old mortice lock in the door, which he would have used as double security, I suspect.'

'Mortice lock is not so easy, but this is old mechanism, not a good lock. I have keys.'

'Would that be Plombe's keys?' A second set, rather than the ones you hurled down the cliff, which I picked up and took to the police? Victor wanted to ask but dared not.

Paul shook his head briefly. 'I have keys, I will leave with you when we go tonight.'

'Oh Paul, I don't think I want Plombe's keys. They're not mine and could get me into trouble.'

'But I was thinking you might need keys to sort out the cable which comes from this bungalow to the carport. But no matter. Some person like Angove could sort out the cable. He is always in the pub.'

I hope he is, I hope he will be in the pub as before, Victor thought. I hope nothing has happened to him. But Victor hesitated to say anything about that either.

Paul began to wander down the narrow path to the front of Plombe's bungalow. 'Let us look at the front door,' Paul said. 'As you see, nothing disturbed. No broken locks. No sign of cable to your new carport.'

Victor exhaled heavily. 'If I were to keep the carport, whoever buys Plombe's place or whoever inherits it from Plombe, would definitely claim it because the power supply goes from Plombe's underground supply directly to it. So, it's of no use to me. All that effort of yours for somebody else to enjoy, Paul, and my car permanently parked under the dining room window or parked in the road.'

Paul shrugged and glanced at the fresh rubble on the ground under the wooden structure. 'You could get Plombe's bungalow, then there would be no argument about cables.'

'Get? How? We haven't enough put by to get hold of Plombe's place. It's a nice thought, but it can't be done.'

'I meant to ask my friend in the village to lay concrete,' he said. 'But so much to do before Christmas. If I did not go with you to Newquay to see Tremayne about that invoice, it would be done in time. Sandy Angove could re-route the supply to your supply. But perhaps you will not need a carport.' He smiled again, a relaxed smile, no grimace. 'Or we could just dismantle.'

I see why I was charmed by you, Victor thought. Despite what you are.

'Well so, let us go and see what you have for traditional Christmas breakfast.' Paul put his arm around Victor's shoulders and led him indoors.

'By the way.' Victor halted in the porch. He turned and looked Paul in the eyes, a few inches from his face. 'Did you hear any drilling last night? I could swear I did. Shook our bed. I am sensitive to anything like that. A house made of mundic block is a delicate structure.'

'You know,' Paul said, 'this is a mining place. All the time, they are looking for lithium. They don't tell us what they are doing, so they do it at night, in case we don't like it. Mining can lower your property value. Perhaps you could get out. Go to a nice place like South Devon. I like the red fields with the very green grass. Even the sheep, they roll in the earth and look red. I like them.'

How do you know? How do you know so much about me and my plans? Victor thought.

'On Christmas Day, we don't have breakfast, just a cup of tea, because Jane prepares the goose, which is so big it needs a lot of cooking on a low heat. So, we have brunch at ten o'clock. There is a choice of smoked haddock and pancakes with maple syrup.'

'Haddock is fish? Perhaps a little of each, Victor. What do you suggest?'

'Me? Haddock every time. We go for a walk in the morning. There is a mid-day charity dip: that is a swim in the sea. The sea is still warm at this time of the year. Most people go in in a wetsuit. We'll go and have a look at that and put a few coins in the tin for the Lifeboat. Then home for The King's Speech, a cup of tea, a piece of Jane's Christmas cake, then final preparations for our Christmas dinner.'

'And this happens all over England?'

'All over the Christian world, where Christians gather. But families do it differently. Some wait for the evening to open presents. Some rip them open in the morning. There are countries where presents are opened on Christmas Eve, but we don't have any of that foreign nonsense here. Some have their Christmas meal at lunchtime and then settle down to the King's speech. The way we do it, it takes pressure off Jane. She doesn't have to get the meal on the table until seven in the evening.'

'Yes, seven is a good time.'

After brunch, the boys disappeared upstairs to do some final packing.

'They really are going,' Jane said over an extra half-cup of coffee.

'I wonder what state they will leave the room in. Last time I was up there they had a dozen or more big cardboard boxes. All for fuses, Peter said. He said they would use them for their own packing when they left, but I think they got rid of them. I saw them outside, flattened, ready for recycling. Anyway, they only have their clothes and phones to take away with them.'

Jane looked sorrowful. 'Yes, it's terribly sad. They ought to have more possessions at their age than that.'

'Oh, I don't know. What is their age, anyway? They're not weighed down by goods and chattels, like us. Besides, they chose to leave their own homes and come here, looking for a better life, or whatever it is they think they are doing.'

'I'm not listening to you,' Jane said. 'It's Christmas Day and I am not listening to any negativity from you. At all.' She turned away from Victor and began checking her timed list of tasks. 'Now,' she said. 'I'm going to slip away from the Charity Swim early, on my own, so don't let the boys follow me. I'm going to come back here and dress the dining room table. I've polished all the silver, I've managed to get the rust marks out of the white linen, it's all looking good. Can you keep them diverted until at least 2.15? We'll have tea in the lounge after The King. I'll lock the dining room door, so nobody fiddles with my table decorations and place settings. We've never had anybody with us at Christmas before, have we? We should do it more often. It's going to be a wonderful day, a day to remember all our lives.'

She came up to Victor and adjusted his red Christmas woolly. 'You won't ruin it all by starting an argument with Paul or by being sarcastic about immigrants and things, will you.'

'Goodness no,' Victor said. 'Why would I do that?'

She checked his expression for sincerity.

Christmas afternoon turned out to be gentle and mild. The sea was almost flat calm. Volunteers had cleaned the beach of seaweed and detritus that had been carried to shore by strong currents and huge waves following the autumn gales. This was a perfect afternoon for a Sponsored Swim.

Peter and Paul were walking along the strand towards Shag Rock, heads bent together. Sitting in the lee of the harbour wall with Roy, Victor wondered what they had to say to each other. Did they discuss their past, or were they planning a future for themselves?

'By the way,' Roy said, 'when those two first went to stay with you, I got confused about what language they were speaking. Do you remember?'

'Yes, I do. I remember the day very well. I was collecting my new First Day Cover: I don't remember what it was now. It was a good one, though. I couldn't wait to get it home.'

'Well, I know what they were speaking now. I wasn't confused at all. One was speaking Romanian, and the other was speaking Hebrew. It was the same the other night outside your house, at your party.'

'Really?' I wonder what it all means, Victor thought. 'That means, they both know both languages. So where does that place them in the world? They're just simply not illegal immigrants, are they?'

Roy threw the dregs of his tea into the sand beside him.

'Let me guess, Roy. Peter was speaking Romanian, Paul Hebrew.'

'Yes, you're right. Where there's a choice, a person will speak their own language, if they are sure they will be understood. I used to see that in Israel, all those years ago.'

'Oh well, whatever they are, they'll be gone tonight. I can't say I'm sorry. Jane will miss them, but I certainly won't. They're too much of a handful. Do they have a sort of allowance, or anything? You know, from our government.'

'You know I couldn't tell you, if I knew.'

'They're always at the post office, regularly.'

'Yes, they are. Sorry, it's time to change the subject, Victor. I am the postmaster.' He folded his scarf behind his head and leaned against the granite wall. 'Though probably not for much longer.'

'Oh?'

'They're closing sub post offices all over. I'm up for review, so I'll probably be next. I'll get my lump sum, stick a plastic conservatory on the back and bolt the front doors for good. I can make a few bob selling bass round the back door of The Atlantic; they're fetching a lot of money for a night's work.'

In the distance, Victor could see against the sun that Peter and Paul had turned at the tideline and were making their way back across the beach. Swimmers without wetsuits were coming in, towelling off water and sand, being handed their warm clothes and hot drinks. All well organised, Victor thought.

'Roy,' he said. 'We're thinking of going, selling up and moving to Torquay. Well, it's a nice town. We've given it a go here, but it's quite hard to make friends. Not that we need other people, but without the boys, we think we'd like a new start.'

'I did wonder what you were doing. This whole business with Tweedledum and Tweedledee. You're not the sort of person to take in…'

'It's not me, it's Jane. She wanted to keep them here. And they've been good to us, in their way. Well, in many ways, to be fair to them. They've practically rebuilt the house for us.'

'This is not my business, Victor, but, really, have you asked yourselves why?'

'I ask myself every day why I've been so blessed.'

'No, Victor. Do you ask yourself why they moved in on you and rebuilt your property?'

Victor felt the familiar blanket of dread fall over him. He shrank into himself, thinking, what if? What if? But he could not fasten 'what if' to anything imagined. The sun went on shining, the boys went on strolling along the strand, casually picking up flat pebbles with which to skim the water; the bathers went on chattering, drinking hot tea, moving up the beach.

'There you go.' Victor raised his voice at Roy, looking into his eyes with sudden aggression. 'It's this sodding community, with its naked prejudice and hatred of foreigners that fears them. Not I. Peter and Paul have done nothing but good for me. They defended me against Plombe; they got my money back when Angove tried to cheat me and hid away from me so I couldn't find him. They put up the lights for the committee, where people are too frail or too frightened to climb a ladder. The Major is always saying that Paul is just the sort of man this country needs. We have an aging population, you know. We need our foreigners to pay our pensions. And another thing: I believe there is good in the world. Yes, good. I believe that man is fundamentally good, and youngsters are good.'

'Wow wow, hold on to your hat. Where did that come from, old friend? Why so angry?'

Victor subsided. 'I don't know, Roy, I've had a stroke, you know. My heart is not right. I can hear it at night. My pulse is uneven. I need peace and quiet. I need to get away. We want to go to Torquay. Why don't you go with us? You could sell up too. You could do with a friend. You'll be on your own here, sitting in your conservatory all alone, fishing in the dark on a ledge, the sea licking up at you. It's dangerous work. A rogue wave can take you. It's a young man's game. You can't do it forever. Why should you have to sell fish around the back of a hotel, a good man like you? The Post Office should give you a proper pension. If you'd invested regularly in first day covers and Japanese prints from early on, you'd be worth a bob or two by now.'

Roy was half sitting up, looking at Victor strangely as the boys strolled up.

'Just been told off for throwing stones when swimmers are in the water,' Peter laughed, while Paul sat on a small rock beside Victor.

'We'll go home now,' Paul said, 'to help Jane.'

'Oh,' Victor said, 'Jane wants us to stay out a bit longer, at least until quarter past two, while she is setting up the table. I've got our beef sandwiches here.

And there's ham and chutney.' He handed them around.

'We'll walk a little way up the cliff, then, to the Heuer's hut.'

'Alright. Don't be late. We have to see The King at three o'clock. Jane wouldn't want you to miss that.'

The boys moved on. 'There you are,' Victor said, as they moved out of earshot. 'Good as gold. I'm proud of them.'

'If you say so.'

They sat in silence for a while, Roy with his eyes closed, leaning back against the sea wall again, Victor looking out at the lifeguards as they went on counting heads in the water, at the inshore lifeboat standing off. He gazed at the men in the rib, waiting to pick up anybody in trouble. Yes, it was certainly a community that looked after its own.

The sun was in its descent. The beach began to empty of people. The lifeguards began packing up their unused gear.

Roy opened his eyes and sat up. 'What time is it?'

Victor looked down at his old, everyday watch, the one he wore when he went for a walk. 'Ten past two, time to pack up and go home. Jane will be ready for me now, with more ham and the home-made pickle and chutney. Will you join us, Roy, for our Christmas dinner at seven? We'd be honoured. There's plenty, believe me. We've got this enormous goose from Butcher Braddon that Peter brought home in his rucksack. There's certainly room for one more around the table.'

Roy hesitated a moment. 'No,' he said. 'Thankyou. I've got my pheasant in the slow cooker. Everything is ready. I just need to do a few sprouts. I've got my afternoon and evening mapped out.'

'If you're sure. Look, I'm sorry I got annoyed earlier on. Everybody misunderstands my youngsters and their intentions. The only thing I wish is that they would tell me where they are from and what their position is in this country. Not knowing puts me on edge all the time. But there we are, I suppose I shall know one day, or perhaps not. Perhaps they will disappear tonight after the meal and never be seen again. That's the fun of it.'

Victor did not smile.

Roy packed up his flask, put it back in his bag with his waterproof and his see-through rain hat.

What an old woman Roy is, Victor thought.

As they turned to go their separate ways, Victor said, 'By the way, Roy, if anything should happen to me, you'll see Jane is all right? I mean, she doesn't know anything about insurance policies or how to sell a house or Japanese prints or anything about money. The Japanese prints alone would fetch a tidy sum. I don't want her to be diddled. She doesn't know anything about auction houses, how it all works, and she's never been to see a solicitor in her life.'

Roy looked down at the sand in front of his feet. 'I'll tell you something,' Roy said, 'I've been here a while. Portmarrow is a valley of ashes, where dreams come to die, where they make buildings out of scoria, mine waste, mundic block that trickles into the dirt when water touches it, concrete block that bursts open from minerals busting to break out. Radon gas comes up out of the earth and slow poisons you. You have to be a native, genetically modified over the generations to survive the radon. It's why they don't like double glazing and always have their picture-glass thin windows open, night and day. You know what

Portmarrow means? Death Port. Port of the Dead. You know what Als an Marrow means? Death Cliff. Cliff of the Dead. Nothing grows but heather and gorse. No birds nest up there, just a few poisonous adders slithering around in the undergrowth. I'd point her in the right direction,' he said, 'if ever she needed my help, but don't leave her in that position. Take yourselves to Torquay, just as soon as this Christmas is over.'

They crossed the carpark and shook hands at the bus shelter.

'I climbed Als an Marrow, all the way to the top.'

'Then, you're one of the very few. Have a good Christmas,' Roy said. 'Next year in Torquay.'

Jane was in the kitchen when Victor changed into his slippers and came indoors.

'Everything is almost ready,' she said. 'Have a look in the dining room.' She handed him the key from her apron pocket.

When he looked at the table, with its white linen and its silver and gold cutlery, he felt it struck entirely the wrong note for the boys. 'Oh, I don't know, don't you think it's a bit formal? You know, considering their background. Why don't we tone it down a bit? They may not like this at all. Don't you think it's a bit intimidating as it is, with these silver napkin rings and candlesticks?'

'Oh. Well, what do you suggest?'

Victor began to collect up the cutlery and the cut glass. 'I think they would just like the table mats and the beer mugs, don't you?'

He began to fold up the crisp linen tablecloth.

Jane walked out of the room and sat at her place in the kitchen.

'Where have you gone now?'

Victor poked his head around the kitchen door. 'Jane?'

'Go ahead, Victor, do it your way. Anything for a quiet life.' She went into the lounge and took up a magazine. I spent days on getting the linen clean and the silver polished, she thought. She got up and started moving her ornaments around in the glass case.

He scurried around the dining room, putting things away. He took out the box of unscratched table mats, the ones with scenes of the Norfolk Broads, windmills and water. Out came the Sheffield stainless steel cutlery. Away went the silver and gold pieces of cutlery, back into their plastic covers and into the rosewood canteen. He put the candlesticks into the back of the cupboard. As a final touch, he found some red paper napkins and folded them into flat triangles, leaving them on the side-plates. After a moment, he collected up the 'Vienna' bone china side-plates, with their gold trim, and put out the plain white second set from John Lewis.

'That's better, Jane,' he called to her, 'so much better. They'll feel more at home now. Do you want to look?'

There was no reply. He found her lying on the bed, her back to him.

'That's good,' he said. 'You have a little rest. I'll carry on here.'

The sun dipped down further, casting blocks of shadows over the village from Westcliff, as far as the Als and Marrow headland, all the way down to the children's empty playing field, where the swings, chained together in pairs for the winter, danced and hung in strange formations. The boys did not return for The King at three nor for their piece of Christmas cake and tea at a quarter to four. Disappointment fell on the house. All the little parcels of Christmas gifts still lay under the tree.

At last, Jane said in a small voice, 'Have they left? Are they not coming back?'

At five, when it was dark outside and the wind was rising again, Victor climbed the narrow stairs to the dormer bedroom and knocked on the door. He could hear nothing but his pulse thumping. He knocked again softly and stood back as the narrow door swung open.

A westerly squall smacked against the window with a spattering of rain. Victor walked forward and closed it tight. There was no double glazing here, just thin glass in a decaying wooden frame and a rusting, long bar-catch made of wrought iron, curled at the end, holed evenly. I really ought to have had a double-glazed unit put in for them, he thought. It must have been draughty up here. They never said anything, never complained. They could have said something, but they were never ones to complain.

The room was clean and tidy. The twin beds were stripped, the bedside lamps unplugged, the leads wound up neatly in elastic bands. Even the rug between the beds was rolled up in polythene, leaning against the wall. There was a cheap, stained rucksack of medium size at the foot of each bed. We could have provided them with two better ones, he thought.

They're packed, he said to himself, ready to go. Just a few clothes, no extra coats, no change of shoes, nothing in the pockets of the rucksacks.

The wardrobe was clean and empty inside. I misjudged them, he thought. All this time, I thought the worst of them.

The little light, wooden bookshelf still held some tourist books on Cornwall, all upright, in their original positions, a walker's guide, pictures of some historical attractions, some National Trust publications; and on the top, Jane's doily and Lladro sculpture, Jester and Ballet Dancer. All clean. Not a speck of dust.

He almost tip-toed into the en-suite bathroom. Again, all neat and clean, the shelves empty, no marks of toothpaste, no smell of aftershave. The plastic shower-mat, still drying, was rolled up and held by the grab-handle in the shower unit.

The fake piece of Semtex, the soap-on-a-rope that had given him such a scare the last time he had been up here, when there were wires everywhere and when there was gypsum plaster drying pink and red, the soap-on-a-rope was gone. Only the damp bathmat was still on the white-tiled floor in front of the bath, an oversight, he thought. He rolled it up and placed it by the wall.

The lavatory was spotless. So was the lavatory brush and stand. Nothing but the cleaning materials remained in the vanity unit's cupboard.

They've done Jane proud, he thought. She'll have nothing to clean when they have gone.

Before he shut the door on the room, he looked around in satisfaction at the smooth walls and ceiling painted matt, the new bull-nosed skirting boards glossed to perfection. I couldn't have asked for more of two strangers we sheltered who became our true friends, he thought.

Humbled, he went down to Jane, who stood at the bottom of the stairs, waiting.

'They haven't gone,' he said. 'Their bags are packed, and the room has been cleaned. Their bedlinen is in a couple of big plastic bags. I expect they'll bring that down with their rucksacks when they're ready to go.'

A Christmas Game

Victor and Jane heard a key in the door at nearly twenty to seven.

Jane flew into the hall. 'Where have you been? We were so worried.'

Peter and Paul looked a little windblown. Their coats and shoes looked damp.

'Well, come in and sit by the electric fire. Or shall we put on the gas fire? Victor, push the gas bottle heater into the lounge.'

No no, electric fire will be OK. Leave it in the dining room, please. Uses too much gas. We didn't get very wet. We went up on the cliff and right up on the coast path. We went too far, then realised it was getting dark, so we came back down on to the road.'

'Then we realised we have gone a very long way.'

'Very sensible. You should have telephoned. Victor would have come out and fetched you.'

'No, no, it was all OK.'

They trooped into the kitchen. Jane looked at the clock on the cooker. 'You missed the tea and Christmas cake and The King, you bad boys. We didn't open our presents; they are all still under the tree. That's a shame, but we are on schedule to start serving up just after seven.'

'We're in for a feast. Let me show you the table,' Victor said. He took the dining room key out of his pocket, turned it in the lock and flung open the door. He turned on the lights.

He went forward into the room to yesterday's pin of beer standing on a side table. 'Come in, dear boys,' he said. His voice was far too loud. He began to draw off a pint of flat beer. 'Have a sup of this.'

Peter looked around. His shoulders began to sag. 'Oh,' he said. 'It isn't what I thought it would be like.'

'Not what we expected,' Paul said.

'No?' Victor turned off the little tap. His tankard was half full.

'Sorry, I was hoping we were having a Christmas meal, with all the trimmings and white napkins and all the silver things on the table, like Jane said. Paul, you see, he hasn't had anything like that. Last Christmas, he was walking down a railway track with a cheap orange blanket over his shoulders, in the rain with dozens of derelict people, never knowing where he was going or what was going to happen to him, what was around the next corner. Barbed wire fences and bright lights. That is all he has known. You see how it is for him.'

Victor glanced at Paul, who was staring at the wall over his head.

'Why, of course, of course, how foolish of Jane. She got it wrong, didn't she? Help me get all the silver out, the cutlery and the candles. Let's do it now. We'll even have the silver rose bowl and the little silver wren that weighs an ounce. It's in the cupboard somewhere, Paul will like that, you'll both like that. The candles look lovely when they're lit. I can't think what could have come over Jane.'

He picked up the tablemats, flinging them into the sideboard, digging deep for the best silver.

'And wine with the goose. Sorry, but some wine from your cellar under the stairs, if you will trust us with the key.'

'But of course we trust you with the key. Here, take it, my boy. Choose a good one. Don't be sparing on Christmas Day.'

He sounded false to his own ears, like some pantomime Dickensian patriarch.

Victor heard Paul go into the lounge and turn on a raucous television talent contest. Under his woolly Christmas jumper with its red-nosed reindeer, he felt his shirt begin to stick coldly to his back. He slapped at a bead of sweat which was crawling down the side of his face as Peter returned with the two investment Chateau Lafites and the anniversary champagne, gifts from Jane, never to be opened.

'Here, help me unfold the linen tablecloth and turn up the napkins. We need four place-settings in our usual places, Peter. I'll show you how to make a rose by folding the starched linen. It's easy enough.'

Out came the canteen of gold and silver cutlery. Back, roughly in the drawer, went the Viners of Sheffield. The pieces danced and skittered together as the drawer jammed and Victor banged it shut. I'll put it back properly tomorrow, he said to himself, before Jane notices and thinks any of it has been scratched.

They were putting the finishing touches to the table when there was a shunting and scuffling at the front door. Victor went out into the hall to see what was happening. In the gloom of the streetlamp, he saw a fat, bald man with grey whiskers, propped up in a wheelchair. Paul was pushing against the new carpet and rugs.

'Help me,' Paul said. 'He only has one arm to drag himself along.'

Victor noticed that under a pungent blanket there was no sign of legs. He stood back as Peter and Paul spun the wheelchair and propelled the man through the dining room door.

'This is Dr Reagent,' Paul said. 'Have you met?'

'He's an intellectual,' Peter said. 'He doesn't speak much. Always thinking. Call him Reg. Everybody does. Quite the fanatic for geology. Born in Brazil, nurtured in Caracas, summarily blown out of Sweden. Nobody wants a one-armed geologist. And yet, one often sighs, 'Give me a one-handed geologist.' You employ them generously to tell you where the oil is, you spare no expense, the ungrateful geologist rewards you by saying, 'On the one hand there may be oil, it might be here, it might be there, on the other hand there may not be so much, or then again, there may be plenty.' So, give us a one-handed geologist every time, eh Reg?' He smacked the bald man's head.

'You have stolen my lines.' The bald man was soft-spoken. He looked up at Victor, with eyes that flashed and danced and laughed. 'Your humble servant, sir,' he said.

Victor was staring at Peter. Your language is suddenly impeccable, he thought. Fluent as a native speaker, more fluent than that. Stagey.

He glanced across at Paul, whose jaw was working, whose teeth were grinding. He looked like a coiled spring, Peter staring at Paul like a small animal in headlights.

It was as though a shaft was opening up before Victor. He gripped the back of a chair.

Victor was sure he knew the bald man; sure, he had seen him somewhere before. That grey face with the bushy grey beard and sideburns. 'I'll just go and tell Jane there is one more for dinner. Peter, can you fold out the extension to the table and rearrange the linen? We'll need another place setting.' He had an impulse to flee from the room, flee from the house, get far away, jam his fingers into his ears.

'We don't want to put you out,' Peter and Paul said almost together. 'Only, Reg would be alone in the cold on this night of all nights. And we're leaving immediately after the brandy and cigars, let us assure you of that. Don't trip over our bags in the hall.'

Victor was already hurtling down the hallway towards the kitchen, the twin voices rising, pursued by an invisible djinn that exuded from the wheelchair.

He heard manic laughter. Was it deep inside his own mind?

In the kitchen, he sprawled over the worktop, his hands shaking. He loosened his tie. He felt the buttons tighten on his shirt, constricting his chest. His arms had become heavy.

'Whatever is the matter? You're going red, white and blue in the face.' Jane left her gravy-boat and came across to him.

Something is happening. I don't know what it is, he wanted to say, but I want us to flee, flee now, but I'll never get us past the thing in the hall.

He hauled himself up, through gravity that had redoubled itself and was grasping him, pulling him towards the floor. He steadied himself, clinging on to the mixer tap while he drew a glass of water. He gulped it down. 'We have another guest.'

Jane brightened immediately. 'Have our boys brought a friend back? Bless them, always thinking of someone else. That's wonderful.' She wiped her hands on her pinny and rushed to the dining-room for the greetings.

Alone in the kitchen, Victor heard, 'Your humble servant, Madam.' That Victorian expression. That Dickensian tone. I am in a Jules Verne novel, he thought, on a journey to the centre of the earth. Pinch me, somebody.

As he trudged back up the hall and peeped through the doorway, he heard Jane simper, 'Poor duck,' as she wheeled Reg to Victor's place at the head of the table.

Peter was pouring some of the anniversary champagne into a glass flute for Jane. Victor saw Jane wrap her hand around the stem and lower her head.

Her cheeks flushed, she called to him over her shoulder. 'Our goose is cooked, Victor.'

And then the chorus, as though they all knew their lines so very well. 'Bring on the bird!'

All was ready. Victor wheeled in the goose on the hostess trolley and began sharpening a carving knife. Peter stood on a chair and with a metallic blue phone, he took a photo of Victor and the goose. As the plates were handed down the table, Victor said, as casually as he could, 'Whose phone is that? Yours are black, aren't they?'

Peter looked at Paul, who said. 'This? This is Angove's.'

Victor paused, dread forcing his arms and hands to a standstill. 'What are you doing with Angove's phone?'

'Angove doesn't need it.' Paul had taken up his gold and silver knife and fork. Light flashed along the blade. He reached forward for the gravy boat. From the top of the table, Reg watched him carefully.

'Why not?'

'He's under the carport. Hah!' He picked up a bread roll and threw it at Peter. It hit him square on the forehead.

Everyone, including Jane, guffawed.

Victor thought, am I the only one here who thinks that this is a strong possibility?

For the last hour, he had sat at the bottom of the table, occasionally mopping his brow, watching and listening. After all the guzzling and the passing of the steamed vegetables, the sauteed brussels sprouts with chestnuts covered in Cornish butter, the honey-roast parsnips, the glazed baby carrots with thyme, after the bad behaviour witnessed, the table-fight with Jane's home-baked bread buns, missiles that landed on the floor, that high pressure table-manners rage, held in for well over an hour, now finally left him. The goose and port gravy sat heavily on his gut and Victor wanted only to sleep. He wanted to prop himself up on his elbows. Instead, he sat back, rigid against his chair.

Jane had changed the music on the stereogram and Peter was now waltzing her up and down, around the dining room, down the hall into the lounge. He could hear their shrieks as she fell against the cabinet of glass animals.

Down the table, he caught Paul's eye. 'Our bags are in the hall, our dirty linen is by the washing machine,' Paul said, clipped and distinct.

'You constantly monitor and check my thoughts,' Victor heard himself mumble. He stopped himself from saying more. Halt. I must not, I must not, he thought. I must not be truculent, I must be well composed, and at that fleeting idea he laughed quietly to himself.

He allowed his eyes to close, because the part of him that constantly monitored Paul's language, the intonations, the accents, heard the detail better that way.

They were muttering together, Paul with this Reg in the wheelchair. He couldn't hear. Something about some bloke who just wanted to make big bangs and finally banged himself to death, after Birmingham.

He mourned the investment Chateau Lafite, purchased for him by a loving wife with a dream, to be held indefinitely, never to be opened, wages saved up for months to buy and to hold this. Opened, spilled, glugged, and almost gone. He pulled the second, the last bottle towards him. Just a little taste, he thought. He looked around for a glass. Any piece of the Waterford crystal would do. And mercifully none of that was broken. Yet. The night was young. He took one of Jane's glasses and filled it, sipped and sighed.

Very nice. Not worth all the scrimping and saving, though. Like a lot of hopes and dreams. The unopened bottle was always the best. A bottle of expectations.

'The best is yet to come.' He raised the glass to the muttering pair.

They did not hear him; he hoped they didn't. A little voice, somewhere in his head, said to him, the stopper is not yet out. The genie. The genie is still in the bottle.

Sipping the dregs of the Chateau Lafite from his wife's crystal glass, two bottles at £2,000, thinking, you can't drink fine wine with food, he felt himself fall into to a daze. He woke suddenly, an elbow on the table, his chin in his hand.

Paul and Reg had not moved. They were head-to-head about something intense. He stayed in his position, his eyes closed, listening. The Blue Danube had stopped playing. Listen, listen, Victor, listen.

'I told him, I said, take my word for it, you'll never outrun Semtex.' Reg banged the parquet floor with the leg of a crutch and croaked out a laugh, followed by a fit of coughing. 'It kills me every time,' he said. 'I told him, honestly, two pounds of plastic explosive taped to the back of a five-litre plastic can of petrol makes a marvellous rolling ball of orange flame. That's all you need.'

Paul sat up, laughed, and glanced down the table at Victor.

Victor did not blink.

Paul relaxed a little, cricked his head, this way and that, plonked his elbows on the table, threaded his fingers together, cracked the knuckles and settled again to hear the rest of the anecdote.

'So, after that little debacle, when I lost a fine man, he had lovely long, fine pianist's fingers, so he did, I said that's it, you must always have a second power supply.'

The second power supply, Victor thought. The carport. Plombe's.

Victor half rose, a stab of pain, a glass shard under a rib. He shifted position.

From a grey mist, the pair seemed to peer down the table at him.

'Burps. I've got the burps. Pardon.' Victor attempted a comic laugh and a belch.

The dancing pair came to the door, Peter's arm still around Jane's small waist.

'And now for the pudding! Who's going to set fire to it? Victor?'

She's engulfed in a flame of her own, Victor thought, while this house collapses around her head.

'I'm out,' Victor said, waving the last empty bottle of premier cru, to try and convey to her the idea that this, this precious stuff has been consumed too, but she seemed not to notice or care.

'I've got the brandy; I just need the matches. Where have you put them, Victor? This pudding has been under the bed since October, boys, wrapped in a Glass cloth tea towel, everybody. It's been steaming for four hours and now it's hot and ready for eating.' She began scrabbling around in a drawer of the sideboard. 'Where are they?'

Victor patted his pocket.

'Give her the matches, Victor. Let her set fire to her pudding and then give the matches back to me.' Paul was staring at him.

Victor got to his feet, pulled out the box of matches from his trouser pocket and handed them over to Jane.

'There's a big bowl of strawberry trifle for those who don't like Christmas pudding.' Jane lit the six red candles in the silver candlesticks. Her eyes sparkled. She turned out the lights. 'Here it comes. Oh, but first, everybody move places. Victor, you go up and sit by Reg. Everybody else, shuffle around. Talk to somebody you haven't talked to before.'

That'll be difficult, Victor thought, but I'll be glad of a conversation with this surprise guest of ours.

Jane went into the kitchen to serve up the puddings. She began singing snatches of songs.

Peter appeared to listen carefully. 'What is she singing?'

Victor answered in a pointed way, addressing Paul. 'Oh, you won't know it. It's an English folk song. Do you have folk songs in your culture? It's about a useless hunter who makes an attempt on six does and fails to shoot every single one of them, but he's very merry about it in his ineptitude. He thinks hunting the merry little doe is fun. A doe is a female deer.'

'I know that one,' Reg shouted. He began to sing, 'Jacky boy?'

'Master?' Jane answered in a reedy little treble voice from the kitchen.

'Everybody has a master,' Reg said to Victor. 'Everybody.'

Jane brought in the pudding, poured brandy over it and set it alight to murmurs of appreciation.

Victor watched the blue flame as it chased its tail and ended in a puff of fragrant smoke.

'Volatile, isn't it?' Reg was leaning towards him, grinning.

'What? The brandy? Yes.'

'Fifty percent at least. You have to add SO_2 to minimise aldehyde accumulation, as cold as poss, less than 75F to minimise fusel oil formation. Then you distil as fast as you can. Use white grapes.'

'Is that so?'

'Goes up nicely, doesn't it? Imagine a cellar full, or the hold of a wooden ship packed full of the stuff, in leaky barrels with iron hoops.'

'The Marie Celeste.'

'The Marie Celeste? No. Those were barrels of denatured alcohol. Are you a chemist yourself, Victor?'

'Goodness no. I was just an office boy. In shipping, though, all my life. Retired now. And you?'

'Geology,' Reg said, 'but you already know that. Got into mining quite young. Before my time, they used to 'shoot the rocks.' Some of the old men just about remembered it. First, they used to tamp in the black powder, set a trail alight and then run like hell... oh but you know all of this.'

'No, I don't. This is a mining district, but I don't know anything about it.'

'Frankly,' Reg said, 'I just liked big bangs. I love the old kinetic disassembly. I never got over the fascination of the quick chemical reaction, that vigorous outward release of energy, those high temperatures and hot gases. Could never get enough of them. Endless fascination. One minute, you behold a gentle scene, the next second, boom, it's all around your ears. But what I hate, I absolutely despise... the embarrassingly over-wired. The unnecessarily big bang. The Cornish have it, of course. They used to laugh themselves silly over the Irish car bombs, all those unnecessary pounds of explosives. Retired now, of course. Something fishy about the Beirut blast though. That wasn't just bags of fertiliser decaying, I tell you. I said so, the minute I saw it. Everything needs a det, unless it's completely unstable, like your old, degraded nitro. And that Plasco building, that was controlled demolition. And those twin towers. When you know enough, you can make a building do a ballet dance, Victor. It's an art. It's a real art. They've got military grade thermite that you can't make in your own laboratory. It's your actual nano-thermite, think of that. And nowadays, you can even paint the stuff on.' Reg smiled happily. 'But you know the worst,' he said, 'the absolute total let-down you see at the fireworks displays. The damp squib.'

You're just a bloody bore and conspiracy theorist, Victor thought, with your whiskers and your one arm. You couldn't have been much good at the job, either, looking at the state of you. Where have your legs gone? Were you born like that, or are you just inept?

'Who will have a piece of my pudding?' Jane looked around the table, holding up a gold-rimmed china bowl. 'Turn up the lights again, please, Peter.'

'No, leave them, just as they are, dear lady, just for a minute. Your pudding looks so nice and round. It looks like a perfect cartoon bomb, with its red candle. Such a pity to destroy it by eating.'

Jane giggled. 'A cartoon bomb. I'm flattered, Reg. But eat it we must. It's been waiting long enough.'

'Does it have nuts?' For the first time, Paul looked concerned.

'Yes, almonds.'

'Then I won't. With my allergy, almonds are a killer.'

Really? Victor thought. If only I'd known. Have a Snickers, dear boy.

'Have some trifle, then. I'll take the almond flakes off the top for you.' Jane went to pick up a crystal bowl.

'No. I'll have blue cheese later.'

'That's a whole Stilton there on the sideboard,' Victor said. 'The best. In my grandfather's time, they used to sell the imperfect ones on the stalls in the East End that the hoity toities wouldn't eat.'

'Who?' Paul looked at Victor in his penetrating way.

'The knobs, Paul. The knobheads, who had to have everything perfect.' His voice sounded a little pointed. I've got to stop this, he thought. I'll have to rein myself in. Just a little while longer.

There was a brief silence.

'I'll have a little pudding and a lot of trifle,' Peter said.

'Will you, dear? That's a little piggy. You shouldn't have two puddings.' Jane dished up two generous puddings for Peter.

You're rattled, aren't you, Victor thought, looking at Paul in the face. You've just exposed a weakness of your own, a simple physical weakness that you didn't mean to, and now you're in a stew. Well, suck on that. You've been exposing my weaknesses since the day you got here. And you're leaving at last.

Are you?

Reg had two pieces of 'the bomb', as he insisted on calling the pudding. Victor watched as he consumed the brandy butter, licked his fat lips, wiped his moustache with the napkin Paul had tucked into his collar and continued excavating at the base of the pudding until it fell open, exposing the hidden sixpence that Jane had left in it for Peter to find.

I don't suppose we'll see that again. We'll have to find another one for next year, Victor thought.

Reg pocketed the sixpence.

Having spooned down the two puddings, Peter moved along the table, where he sat heavily on Jane's lap. He put his arms around her neck. 'What happens next?' He whispered loudly in Jane's ear.

'Peter, you're crushing me.' Jane pushed him off. Peter's nose caught on her Santa brooch. Blood began gushing from his nostrils again and he retreated to his chair, where he began to stir the trifle, faster and faster, harder and harder, until Jane shouted, 'Stop. You'll shatter the crystal bowl.' He put his arms on the table and put his head down, closing his eyes tight, wiping his nostrils with his Santa jumper.

That looks like vomit and cochineal, Victor thought, looking at the ruined trifle. How much longer will this have to go on?

Paul shouted across the table at Peter, 'Stop that bleeding. I hate blood.' He uttered some sort of oath which Victor had not heard before, and threw a starched white napkin at Peter.

Victor muttered, 'So you like a dry slaughter, do you?' He thought no-one could possibly have heard, but both the eyes of Reg and Paul turned sharply and looked at him.

'What happens next is,' Jane said, doing her best to ignore Peter's and Paul's bad behaviour and the blood on her Santa brooch, 'we bring out the Stilton and port. Who's up for that?'

The men nodded yes, looking back at Peter. Peter stayed in the same position, his right hand tapping the table.

Victor got up, turned up the electric lights and began to stack the greasy plates on Jane's old hostess trolley. He wheeled away the worst of the debris into the kitchen.

Rearranging the table, Jane got up to begin the washing-up.

'No, no, stay,' Paul said.

Jane hesitated. 'Victor is in charge of the Stilton and port,' she said. 'He always does that for us. Of course, we've always been alone before. He has a little by the fire while I start the dishes.' She sat down beside Paul, flattered to be included and relieved of the task.

Victor came into the dining room. 'Yes, stay, Jane,' he said. 'Now, this is the little glass you need and, thank you, Jane. Jane has placed the decanter on my right. I am going to serve the man on my left, that is Paul, and Paul, will you continue to pass to your left, and so on, to Dr Reagent, through Peter, who won't want any, through Jane, who doesn't like it, until the decanter comes back to me. The port must never, never go across the table, don't ask me why. Starboard is right, port is left at sea, so perhaps it has something to do with that. Just one of our little British customs, eh, Reg?'

Reg wavered on the point of speaking. Victor saw the uncertainty in his face. For just a moment, he felt in charge of the evening again. Yes, you really don't know anything about civilisation, do you? Any of you. If not for Jane and me, you'd be out there in the mist and the fog and the rain, looking for a home in a bus stop or an allotment shed. Welcome to England, dear boys, my Engerland. Have a nice life.

Peter awoke sobbing. The slow tapping on the table became a banging. The dreadful sound of Peter wailing chilled Victor to the bone.

'Whatever is wrong?' Jane went to him and stroked his hair. 'Whatever is wrong?'

'Yes, what's wrong with you, Cry Baby?' Reg shook him by the arm while Paul gave him a double kick in the shins under the table.

Peter continued to cry, a long, primitive howl that seemed to have no end.

'Oh God.' Reg spoke to Jane. 'He always does this when we get near the finish.' He sat up straight in his wheelchair, waved his arms about and bellowed over Peter's bawling in a pedantic style,

'I weep for you, the Walrus said,

I deeply sympathise.

With sobs and tears, he sorted out

Those of the largest size.'

'Stop it. Don't abuse him,' Jane said. 'Leave him alone. He's weeping for his family. He's had a terrible life. You're a bully. You should be ashamed.'

Under a look from Paul, Reg put his head down and began fiddling with the gravy-stained napkin around his neck.

'He's tired out,' Paul said. 'He'll be alright in a minute. What time is it? It's really time to go, if we are to put some distance between ourselves and the bridge. We must begin work at the Greenwich Observatory tomorrow. And the Post Office Tower.'

Reg leaned forward. 'The Observatory is so historic. With priceless exhibits. The seat of English civilisation, I always say. Wouldn't it be a splendid thing to hear the Muezzin's call from the Post Office Tower? I've often thought so. So multi-cultural.'

'Oh, don't go,' Jane said. 'There's brandy and cigars yet.'

'Yes, don't go,' Victor said. 'You said you were going after my brandy and cigars.' He made an effort to control the sneer in his voice.

'You're right, Paul,' Reg said. 'Right as usual. It's been a wonderful evening, dear friends. It could never have come off better. Let's hope we don't get the old damp squib, eh, Victor? We'll take the brandy and cigars with us for the journey. We'll have a coffee in the service station on the way, if it's open on Christmas Day.' He looked down at his watch. 'But it's almost Boxing Day already. We must leave, Paul.'

Reg eyed the bottle on the sideboard.

'But first,' Paul said, 'a game to cheer Peter up. He is suffering at the thought of leaving you. Let us leave on a high note.'

'Yes, we must do that,' Reg shouted. 'We must leave on a screamingly high note. What shall we play?'

Paul got up. He went behind Victor and stood by Jane. 'Let's play a game.'

'What game?' In a panic, Victor scrambled to his feet.

Peter rushed forward to Jane. 'He's not going to hurt you,' he said into her ear, holding her around the small of her back and her shoulder as Paul slipped two cold, metal hand cuffs linked by a chain on her wrists, behind her. They could not have been uncomfortable, but when Jane looked over her shoulder and tried to bring her right arm forward to see what had happened, the other arm followed. For a moment, she staggered. She looked to Peter, but Peter was already in the hallway, gathering up the two rucksacks.

Victor faced Reg. 'What is Paul doing?' He found himself standing tall, not seeing what had happened to his wife.

'The thing is,' the man in the wheelchair said gently, 'Live practice is the only way, you know, as is live ammo to your squaddie, so . . .'

Victor felt a dart of pain behind his eyes. He saw the lights and the candles and their reflections in the silver and on the crystal glass. They seemed to be trying to burn themselves into his memory.

As Reg spoke and looked away, Paul slipped on to Victor's wrists a similar pair of handcuffs, looping an extension chain around Jane's.

'These are loose,' Paul said. 'They are on a small timer. They will fall off after four minutes, don't panic.'

'Clever device,' Reg said. 'These boys scour the trade fairs to find things that they can adapt. Gives them time to get me out.'

Victor rounded on Paul. 'Out of what? This is no game. What are you doing? I'll call the police. It's time I did.'

Reg shook his head in sadness.

'To the minibus,' Paul said to Reg.

'Doctor Reagent.' Victor moved forward, pulling Jane backwards behind him. Through the fog in his consciousness, he felt her stagger and stopped himself from further movement forward. 'Reg, what is happening here?'

'A game, just a game, old sport. We are going. After four minutes, the cuffs will fall off and you are free to go. Just don't touch the window, whatever you do. You're all wired up, you see. Ditto the door. For the love of Mike don't touch the door. Don't try the ceiling. The only way is through the fireplace wall. And even then… And now, I'll say adieu. It's been a wonderful experience for these two reprobates. They say they've never been treated so well, all these months of puddn and pie. And thank you, madam, for this evening's goosey goosey gander. It's been just wonderful, that's the only way I can express it. Wonderful.'

Paul looked at his watch. 'While you're yapping, we have three minutes, forty-one seconds.'

'Oh, pardon. Silly me.' He looked up at Paul, and then at Victor. 'Paul has to change over the power supply before you can get out of it. And we must get out of it before we go up with you. Hah!' He glanced up at the John Bull Toby jug, took up the little silver wren, an RSPB purchase back in the 1970s, and the Georgian silver pineapple, bent at the top. He put them where his lap should be.

Paul snatched them up and put them back on the sideboard, where the little bird fell sideways. He stood it upright. 'We don't steal,' he said.

'Paul.' Victor heard himself shout as Reagent was propelled out of the doorway in his wheelchair. He saw the dining room door close in front of him, but the key was still on the sideboard where Paul left it with the phone. He took a step forward and Jane stumbled against his back. He tugged at his wrists, as he heard the porch door close and then the outer door close and lock on its latch.

After the whirlwind, a silence fell on the room. The candles continued to waver and brighten, the electric lights continued to burn steadily. Jane had gone quiet and seemed to be in a daze. Victor heard her uneven breathing, her little sobs, and moans. He reached back and found her fingers.

'It's only a game,' he said. 'I'm sure it is.'

'They'll be back,' she said. 'They said it was a game. Peter said he would never leave me. He said that I could go to Bristol with him. I was planning on at least visiting him in the New Year. This is a game, isn't it, Victor? Isn't this a game? I do hope they come back soon.'

They listened. From the street outside there came no sound.

Victor looked around. 'I don't think we can sit,' he said, 'not trussed up like this. The handcuffs are supposed to fall off in a few minutes, that's what they said.' He moved his feet a little, to ease the stiffness in his legs.

'This is no game for elderly people,' Jane said. 'Whatever are they thinking of?'

'Can you shuffle sideways over to the sideboard? I just want to lean on something. I want to think.'

'I can't shuffle.'

'Do it. And let me think.' He walked forward to the sideboard, Jane staggering backwards behind him.

'They've left the phone and the dining room door key, so they must be coming back.'

'Well, that's a blessed relief,' she said. 'Yes, they must be coming back. They must be.'

Jane's nose began to run. She brought her hand up automatically to search for a napkin, but her hand would not reach around far enough. She found herself lift Victor's heavy arm on the thin handcuffs.

'Be careful, that cuts into me.'

'Oh God,' she said, 'my nose is running. I have to wipe it. And now I want a pee. They shouldn't play games on us like this. We're not up to it, Victor. I'm surprised at Reg, he should know better, being a cripple himself. And where is Peter in all this? He should know I would soon need the loo. I can't be doing with this. I don't think much of this silly game.'

Victor tried joking. 'That's not very PC of you, dear, calling Dr Reagent a cripple. You're always on at me for not honouring people for what they are or what they think they are or what they think they'd like to be.'

'What did I say? Oh, I don't know what I'm saying half the time. It's all this fuss and bother. I just want to get out of this game and make a start on the dishes. I don't want to play anymore.'

He let her rattle on, while he was thinking, there is the key and there is the phone. Has he left the key on the sideboard because he wants us to try the door? Or does he want us to understand that the door is wired, like Reg said, and there is no need for any key, because all we can do is look at the door and never attempt to get out of it?

And then this garish blue metallic phone on which he let Reg take the photograph. Is it Angove's phone? Or is Angove's phone under the carport? And if so, where is Angove? Under the carport too? He must have been joking. He must.

Paul was not joking. What did he once say? 'I never joke. I tell the truth.'

We're dead, Victor thought. We're two dead people walking. An old couple, just retired, waiting for death. Like anybody else, but not like anybody else. This is not happening. This is not happening to us. It wouldn't be right, it wouldn't be fair, not to her, not to Jane. Not fair to me, when I took them in and gave them the run of the place, out of charity, out of the goodness of my failing heart.

Stop it, he thought. Stop these thoughts that go round and round. Think.

If that phone works, I will ring 999. Even without a battery, don't these phones work for 999? I'm sure they do. If these handcuffs don't come off, what shall we do?

We shall wait. Everything comes to those who wait. That's your poor mother speaking, Victor. Wait. They will be back. They haven't finished with us yet. Besides, somebody will come to the house before long. Roy's young postman, he'll come. Then I can shout.

There's always a way. Always a way. We won't starve, so long as we can shuffle about. There's enough food and drink here to feed an army. And in a few days, the postman will come, Roy's blessed postman, in his shorts, with his tanned legs, with the little trolley he pulls around behind him. And we will shout, shout at the top of our lungs, hey run and tell Roy we are trapped, and we've been in here since Christmas Day.

Just as he lifted his head to look at the clock, he felt his handcuffs loosen and fall on to the chain connecting his to Jane's. As he turned and stood gazing, Jane's fell off onto the carpet.

'Victor?' Jane looked up at him. 'We're free, like they said we would be. Our hands are free.'

They both sat down at the table and stared at the door.

After a while, Jane said, 'Should we try the door? I mean, what they said can't be real, can it? Peter would never do that to me, never. They would never do what they said, not after we gave them everything. You were even willing to give them the house. Nobody could do better than that for a friend.' Her voice trailed off. Did she believe in her own little speech?

'No, I don't think Peter is capable of that.' He couldn't name that. 'But those other two are. Paul and Reg, I'd say they are capable of anything.'

They stared at the nondescript wooden dining room door again. Victor remembered a little grub screw falling from the round knob, oh some days ago now. Where was it? You wouldn't easily find another.

'No, I don't think it's booby trapped,' Victor said. 'But all the same, I think it's better to wait and see if they come back, or if the police can get us out.' The bomb disposal people, he thought, they would be able to get them out. They can do anything, and they are so brave. They have robots now.

Jane cleared a space at the table. She folded her arms and put her head down, as Victor had seen her do on a train, when she was tired and bored and waiting for a journey to be over. He put his head down as well, next to hers.

'Well, we're in a fine fix, aren't we?' he said. He took her two hands in his. 'At least those handcuffs are off. Shall I look at the phone? See whether it will ring out?'

'Yes, do that. Perhaps they are waiting for us to ring them, to say they are on their way to Bristol, and it was all, all a joke and they will see us in the New Year.' The last word ended in a sob.

'No, they're going to London. I heard them. Something to do with the Observatory and the Post Office Tower.'

Victor took a deep breath before trying the metallic blue phone. He said nothing to Jane, but he had heard of explosions being set off by ringing on a mobile phone.

'No Sim card. I knew it.'

'I don't want to know,' Jane said, her head still on her arms.' Just tell me when you've fixed it.'

I know it can be done, Victor thought. I know you can make an emergency call without a Sim card, because the Sim card only carries the account information, that's all. But you need a signal.

'Now it's dead. It hasn't enough power to make a call of any sort.'

Jane got up, out of her chair. 'Why did they do that? Why did they do that to us?'

Cruelty, he thought. Just torture.

'Where is our mobile?' Jane looked around the table, as though it might somehow be there.

'It was in the bedroom when I saw it last. No, they've gone, alright, leaving us a dud. Wait, though. Is there any kind of battery here in this room? If I could make a connection, any battery would do it. I only need a very small amount of power.'

He began to hunt through the drawers in the dresser, knowing that there was no battery there.

'Give it up,' Jane said. 'I want to sleep.' With that, she returned to her corner of the table and fell fast asleep.

She awoke with a start. Victor was still brooding over the metallic blue phone at his place at the table. They looked at each other for a while, a naked look that embraced all of the years that had been lived through before this moment, this agonising present.

In the silence, Jane said, 'Victor, are we insured?'

Victor stirred. 'Us?'

'The house.'

'Fire and flood, yes. Not a bloody demolition.'

'Well, I don't know, do I? Does that come under terrorism? Vandalism? It wouldn't be an accident or an act of God, would it.'

Victor stood up. His legs ached. 'I don't know. What would I blinking know? You want me to get the insurance documents out? They're under the bed with everything else we care about. We've been duped. You've been such a fool, Jane, taken in by them and their homeless immigrant status bollocks.'

'Swearing doesn't help, Victor.'

'Did you never think of checking on them? Of course not. That's your trouble. You've always been so trusting. You know what I think? They envy us our freedoms.'

Jane stood up. She put some pieces of perfectly cooked goose flesh between some slices of bread. 'Do you fancy a sandwich, while we're waiting?'

Victor sighed heavily. 'Waiting for what, Jane? To be blown to smithereens?'

Jane sat down in her place at the table. She took up her napkin. 'While we're waiting for the postman to come. We can call out to him, and we'll be saved.'

'Saved. Nothing is going to save us. You know that? As soon as somebody touches the door, the whole place will go up.'

'We don't know that. We still don't know that, Victor. It's only what Reg said. This may be a joke. It may still be a joke. A strange joke, a cruel joke on someone with your poor heath, but all the same...'

Victor moved his chair to the corner of the room. 'I'll have some pickle with that. And a drop of beer, since we're going to die. Might as well.'

After a few more minutes, the lights went out. Jane gasped and Victor stood up.

Nothing happened.

'That's it, then. Something's going to happen.' The second power supply, Plombe's supply. It was meant to switch over before this. The timer must be out.

Victor went and stood next to Jane.

'Is the light out in the hall and the porch?'

'Yes, they're out.'

'Something's up with the electric. A fuse has blown.'

Victor went to the dining room door and reached out to rattle the knob.

Jane caught his hand in time. 'Don't, Victor. If they were telling the truth, if it's not a prank, we'll never get into the hall. The whole place will go up. We need to be able to tell the first responders not to touch the doors. If we sit calmly and wait, someone will come.'

Jane's hand began to tremble with violence under Victor's hand. He remembered their wedding day, her hand resting on his, a flawless hand, pale in the light from the rose window in the Lady Chapel. He remembered the face of that priest, a bachelor looking faintly amused. She promised to obey. He was supposed to protect her. Down the years, the form of the ceremony became translated into a habit relentlessly acted out, or it was meant to.

Through a crack in the drawn curtains, an orange light fell in a line across the table.

'I made a vow to look after you,' he said. 'I would have done anything to save you from this.'

'And I too. I promised to love you, Victor, and I have done, and I'm sorry I haven't been good enough. I'm sorry I've fallen short.'

'And I'm sorry too, for all the wasted years of commuting and scrimping and saving and never doing anything that might have made life better for you. All the saving up and collecting, what was it worth?'

They stood together, gazing at the line of light that fell on the teak table, covered with the starched white linen that was stained with the partying and guzzling of what seemed like an age before.

'Do you regret marrying me, Jane?'

'No, never. I do not. We could draw the curtains, very carefully, though, to give us some light. We could at least do that. Then we could see anybody at the gate before they came down the path.'

Victor listened.

'The curtains stand out from the window, you see, Victor. We don't have to disturb the window. If we are careful. I'll do it. You stand back, in case.'

'No, I should be the one who does it.'

'No, Victor. I have a lighter touch.'

Gingerly, Jane pulled first one curtain, then the other, back to the wall, letting the orange light from the streetlamp shine bleakly in the room, casting long shadows. Nothing happened.

'That's it. It's a hoax. I knew it. It could still be a hoax. Ha-ha-ha, Jane, it could still be a hoax.' Victor hopped from one foot to another.

'I don't know. Look at those wires. If the bomb is wired to that window sensor, then they were right, our house will go up.'

They retreated to the other side of the room again.

'What time do you think it is?' Victor said.

'It will be some time before dawn. We ought to get some sleep, I suppose.'

They both lay down on their backs, on the carpet, their heads under the table, their feet facing the fireplace.

'What are you thinking?'

Jane said, 'I was thinking about something I read in the newspaper, oh, years ago now. About a Welsh couple. They sold their house, put their money in the bank and went to Spain to buy a place there.'

Victor sighed, a long, bored sigh.

'So, anyway, they met a pair of criminals posing as estate agents or owners. The men took them to a remote farmhouse and when they got there, they locked them up in the cellar.'

Victor turned on his side and tried to make out the pattern in the yellow wallpaper. It was a ghastly pattern. He meant to have it removed, but you never knew what the plaster was like underneath Anaglypta, so he'd hesitated. After the fish and chip throwing at the fireplace, the decorations in the dining room had stopped.

'Anyway, they locked them in a room in the cellar. Perhaps they told them it was for the wine. I never understood that. I often think about it. How could you end up locked in a room in a cellar? Well, the woman had a heart attack and died. Then, once that happened, they had to kill the man. So, they did, and they took all their money. They got the pin number out of the man, I suppose. They did get caught, though.'

'Good. I'm glad to hear that. And how does that help us?'

'Oh, Victor. Not everything is about us.'

Victor sat up. 'Do you realise what a fix we are in?'

Jane rolled over on the carpet on to her knees. 'Yes, I do. I do, Victor, but I can't do anything about it until the postman comes.'

There was one moment, he thought, one moment of possibility for an escape. It lay in the seconds between the delayed switchover in the power supplies. Before Plombe's supply kicked in, the house was safe. That was what the handcuffs were all about. A diversion designed to confuse him. In that long moment, he and Jane could have staggered outside together. He'd even been listening when Paul and Reg were discussing it, but he hadn't understood. Now, it was all too late.

Jane must never know.

He thought about it. It was strange to think of them no longer here. His mind wound forward to a time when the bomb went off. He heard the reporters on the national news: 'Victor Everley and his wife, Jane, a retired couple from Chingford, were thought to be careless with gas. Still, it is a mystery how such an explosion could ever have taken place.' Then they would fall out of the news. The joint fire brigades would be able to make little of it, and the inspectors from London already had too much on their hands to worry about a misfortune in a seaside village, three hundred miles away. There were occasional gas explosions all over Britain.

After the clear-up, the story would end six months later, with an enquiry. No insurance company was involved. No claim would be made. Victor and Jane had no known relatives. In due course, the land, the empty space would fall to the Crown, and it would be put up for auction. Portmarrow was a popular resort.

Considering the circumstances, the auctioneer would expect a good price, sold probably to a speculative builder from up-country, looking for planning permission to build a modest, two-storey house. Yes, that's how it would be.

Victor looked savage, unshaven, wisps of hair adrift from his scalp. He imagined something worse. 'Can you think,' he said, 'how it will look when I have to go to the post office and that man Roy knows that I have been fooled by a pair of clowns? Just like he told me. And how can I go on living in Portmarrow when it gets out that I was stuck in my own dining room all night with my wife, terrified to move in case the house went up? After they partied at my expense, with that legless, one-armed Reg. He's obviously a terrorist, if ever I saw one. I don't care who they are, Jane, I'm not having it. Not in my own house that I worked all my life to pay for, taking the smelly bus and the tube five days a week from Chingford to Walthamstow to the City and back again for well-nigh forty years. I don't care who they are or where they come from, I won't have it. Not in my own house.'

'We could just wait a while, until the postman comes. We've waited all night, after all.'

'Wait for what? Wait for him to deliver the junk mail? Then what?'

'Well, then we'll know it was a joke, and we'll get out somehow. The fire brigade can disable any wiring, make sure the dining room door is safe, and we can get out that way. Anyway, once Plombe's supply is disabled, this place is safe to move about in. Isn't the power supply coming from Plombe's place now, like Reg said? The changeover in supply happened when the lights went out. We don't have to touch the window until it's checked. Once we're out, we can have the window checked by a proper electrician and get rid of any wires that are not needed. We won't even have to explain. Victor, for pity's sake.'

Victor had opened the tap and was emptying the beer barrel into the carpet.

'Victor, find some jugs and things. There's the John Bull toby jug on the shelf up there. Don't spoil the new carpet. Don't make it wet. It will stink for months.'

The beer ran in rivulets and pooled by the fireplace. Jane looked on in despair. 'It will take months to dry out. Months. Peter will be back soon; I know he will.'

'Right. Will you shut up and take the other end?'

'What are you going to do?'

Victor had the now half-full barrel on his shoulder. 'I'm going to put it through the window, that's what I'm going to do. They want destruction, they can have it. No sneaking, crawling, homeless bastard migrant from central Europe is going to tell me what I can and cannot do in my own house, coming here, trying to sell me cheap Chinese paintings when I've got fine Japanese prints under the bed. Are you going to help me or not?'

'Don't be foolish, Victor. And don't speak about Peter and Paul like that.'

Victor pulled back a corner of the heavy table, sweeping plates and food on the floor.

Jane's fingers came up to her cheeks and pulled down at the flesh. 'Please, Victor.'

He ran at the window. The barrel touched the glass, sprang back and fell to the floor, toppling Victor with it.

Jane went forward to help her husband. 'Come on, Victor, stop it now.'

He stood up, his red-nosed reindeer jumper soaked in beer. Victory, Victor. Victory at all costs. Without Victor there will be no victory.

No explosion.

He heard Jane's small voice again. 'Victor, have you learned nothing? Nothing at all? You took them in because you wanted something for nothing. You held this superiority about everything and everybody. Instead of being thankful, you turned your privileged position at London Bridge into a nightmare, for yourself and everybody else. The yacht club was not good enough, Monica was not good enough; they were there to be exploited, the lowest of the low, the talented, the stateless, the homeless. You took from their talent and gave them nothing but contempt. At least I fed and watered them and loved them. What did you do but use them to feed your arrogance, your jingoism, your racism? It may be that we are not wired up, that we can turn the knob and walk out of that door. But I want us to learn from this. We exist, Victor, to bring out the best in people, not the worst.'

'You don't know what you're talking about, with your little vanity, you sentimental fool, carrying on with that boy at your age…'

Calmer than he had ever been, he looked around him. 'The gas fire,' he said. 'The stand-alone gas fire. The fire that we rarely light in case of gas leaks. Uncouple the bottle, Jane. Let's deal with this, once and for all. Let us see who is master in his own house here. Cover your eyes.'

Before she could stop him, he hefted the heavy blue bottle on to his shoulder. He paused a moment, then clutching the pronged neck, he backed into the central pane of the window, shouting to the stars, 'Rule Britannia!'

For half a second, nothing happened.

Then there came a dull yellow light.

Then a roar.

In the early morning air, a mushroom cloud of black smoke, concrete debris, shards of glass, plasterboard, cladding and stone rose over the village. Lighter particles floated eastwards across the land. Heavier particles fell, un-noticed over the allotment, over Harry's fields and the industrial estate beyond. A telephone keypad fell into Jenner's pond. A wedding ring with a third finger in it bounced on a campsite roof and nestled into a gutter filled with leaf debris. Later on in the afternoon, a little grub screw, separated from its doorknob would be prodded, swallowed in and ejected by a goldfish.

Where the small bungalow had been, there remained a blackened crater with tangled wires and an unexploded gas cylinder. It looked as though somebody had dumped a hot pile of scrap and rubble there. The old kinetic disassembly. Over-wired. Disappointing. What Reg would call the embarrassingly unnecessarily big bang. What the Cornish would disassemble with a spoonful of black powder and an iron bar.

Roy heard the roar and felt the blast. In a daze he got up from his bed, banged open a window and gazed down Beach Road, where a crowd was running.

Books by Myrna Combellack

The Playing Place: A Cornish Round

A Fine Place: The Cornish Estate

A Place to Stay: The Cornish By-Pass

The Permanent History of Penaluna's Van

Cuts in the Face: Stories from Cornwall

The Mistress of Grammar

Between the Shafts

The Camborne Play: a verse translation of *Beunans Meriasek*

Beunans Meriasek: a critical edition (forthcoming)